Made in England

Dominic Holland

Made in England

Made in England was written during lockdown on my Patreon to fill my empty diary and to keep my loyal followers sufficiently entertained. I am grateful to those supporters who followed the writing process and offered both their encouragement and notes as the story evolved. They are too numerous to name individually, but they know who they are, and I am grateful to them all. This book is for them. Onwards.

Foreword

Although, *Made in England* reads as a stand-alone novel, it is certainly stronger and more enjoyable if readers have already met Milly and Jonson in my debut novel, *Only in America*. This is not a sales pitch. *Only in America* is FREE to kindle readers and previous print editions are available for as little as £0.02 which is heartening and dispiriting in equal measure.

Those who have read *Only in America* and specifically the eagle eyed, might expect the heroes of this new adventure to be in their mid-50's. Why then, have I made them a decade younger? Ageism, I'm afraid. The younger, the sexier and the more commercial and at my age, I should know.

And finally and being mindful of spoilers, readers familiar with my novel, *The Fruit Bowl* are set to gain the most from *Made in England*. I know, this sounds like another vulgar sales ploy. But believe me, I only have my reader's best interests at heart.

In order then, and for maximum feel-good, read *Only in America* first, then *The Fruit Bowl* and finally, *Made in England*. All will become clear. You might even wish to thank me, although this is not necessary. Coming to my books is ample thanks enough.

Happy reading of *Made in England*... (eventually!)

Chapter One

'*ood morning, Los Angeles...*' The radio host chirped with far too much verve for a Tuesday morning.

'*Let me tell you people... that Tuesday, May Six has arrived safely, and it will be with us all-day-long. Yes, indeedy. AND, I can tell you thatttt... It's gonna be a hot one, people. Oh yes, a beautiful day is set for the good people of Los Angeles, Californ-'i'-'a'...*'

Milly changed lanes and turned off her car radio, finally pushed over the edge by the 'i-a', but also because she had lived in LA long enough to no longer need a heads up on the weather. It would be sunny as night follows day. Snow would be noteworthy for the city's residents, who were up and at it and hoping for a good one.

Los Angeles is a truly global city, accommodating people from across the United States and indeed the entire world who arrive in droves with dreams of a better life. Few of them will succeed like Juliet Millhouse, more affectionately known as Milly. She arrived from London twenty years ago as the finished article, armed with her movie script that Hollywood was already enamoured with. That script became the hit movie *Untitled*.

1

Pacific Studios produced it, and her life was never the same again. It was the LA success story that all wannabes dream of. Today and every 'sunny' day in LA, there is a continual arrival of actors, writers, models, body-builders... all keen to take their shot. Almost all will miss.

Milly needed to remind herself of this ratio and how well she had fared. It is so important to keep a decent perspective on life. Remain rooted. She tried to keep her remarkable good fortune in mind whenever she sensed a wave of anxiety stirring within. Like so many writers, Milly was in the midst of a fallow period, and she was drawing upon all positive resources on her way to a meeting with Bob Steward at Columbia Studios. She smiled as she reminisced about her LA arrival all those years ago, courtesy of her oldest friend, Jonson Clarke. Thoughts of Jonson always made her smile. Without his intervention, she might well be back in London and still taking instructions from her old boss, Mr Mahmood. That bleak morning as reception 'manager' at the Shelton Tower Hotel on London's Park Lane when Mr Mahmood charged her to be on the lookout for stubbornly buoyant toilet waste was a memory she often used for motivation.

A soft top, flame-red Porsche cut in front of Milly's car, forcing her to brake. Perhaps an executive worried about his numbers, or a model wanting to be an actress and late for an audition? Milly didn't care, and she didn't react.

Her writing record was perfectly respectable. 'Solid', as the Americans might say. She had followed up *Untitled* with two further movies, although they had both fared worse than her mighty debut. Three films produced, however, put her in rarefied company. She had two further scripts in 'development', and her latest screenplay, according to her agent, was getting good coverage and traction. But still, her doubts and anxieties remained. *Untitled* was always going to be a high bar to straddle.

That difficult second film. Everything had lined up for *Untitled*. It had been fated; plus, she was young and beautiful. Hollywood embraced her, and the cute story of how she was discovered was lapped up by the media giving her invaluable publicity. Milly and her errant script was a story even before filming began. The avalanche of favourable publicity on the movie's release was compounded when Milly married Mitch Carmichael, her real-life Hollywood hero. It was intoxicating and heady stuff, but things were more normal now. The Hollywood grind had arrived and settled in, and Milly worried that Bob Steward of Columbia was about to ruin her forty-fourth birthday. Earlier in the day, a birthday brunch with some girlfriends had been a useful distraction, but, ever punctual, Milly arrived at the Columbia lot with fifteen minutes to spare.

The assistant at the front desk adjusted her head set and casually glanced up as Milly arrived for her noon appointment. She was mid-to-late-twenties and very LA: strikingly attractive but with a confected tinge. Identikit beauty with everything worked on, teased and honed. The young woman did her best to smile, but so soon after her session with her beautician, she could only manage a grimace until her facial muscles eased a little.

'Bob's-outta'-town,' She drawled casually.

Milly adjusted herself as she absorbed the blow. 'Oh.'

'Yeah-he-apologizes-but-something-came-up...'

This was new territory for Milly. Her birthday definitely hung now in the balance, and she adjusted a little further.

'...but-Cynthia-will-see-you.'

Milly managed a faint smile. Cynthia Rosen was the young development exec with a big future. Everyone knew it, especially Cynthia. Being referred to by her Christian name only was a sure sign. Milly would much prefer to see Bob, but since 'something came up...'

Milly took a seat and picked up a copy of The Hollywood Reporter. Another cover for Leonardo Di Caprio, an actor sitting atop the Hollywood mountain without a care in the world. Not yet, anyway.

She had never imagined relocating to Los Angeles, and her parents were aghast. She loved England too much to ever leave until the craziest set of circumstances intervened and turned her life upside down. She went to the ball in true fairy-tale fashion, married the Prince and now lived in a palace. It had been a crazy five-year period, which could only really happen in America and why she affectionately refers to it as Only in America. The head of the studio, the infamous Albert T. Willenheim, led the charge for her living in LA and put it delicately after the opening weekend of Untitled.

'...staying in London? The fuck you are. I need your pretty little ass in LA where I can get to it.' Albert always had great timing, retiring just ahead of the 'Me Too' movement, which would surely have swept him from office anyway.

Her husband, Mitch, had tried to rekindle his own Hollywood career, but without too much energy and commitment. Movies had never been his thing, and seeing Milly's germinate so quickly and then the arrival of their first daughter, Mary (now thirteen), he was happy to live in Milly's shadow. Their family unit was completed by Isla, who arrived four years later. Mitch would smile easily whenever he was teased about his lacking a son. He enjoyed life too much to ever dwell on what he didn't have, and this carefree demeanour was his greatest blessing. He passed his sports genes on to his girls, though, who excelled at the inordinately expensive Beverly Hills Academy, where they rubbed shoulders with the offspring of the west coast elite: Hollywood executives, movie stars and sports heroes mainly. This gave Mr and Mrs Carmichael a useful insight into how extraordinary and dysfunctional lives could be and, in turn, how lucky they were.

Milly looked at the wall clock above the receptionist, who still couldn't smile. It would be a few days yet before she could. Almost 12.30: a half-hour late. Milly bristled.

'Juliet,' a voice called out, making Milly jolt. Cynthia half appeared through a double door. She had retained her name, Juliet Millhouse, for her writing, but everyone called her Milly. Cynthia grabbed a series of memo notes from the desk and flicked through them quickly. Nothing so important that couldn't wait. Just like Milly had done. They shook hands, and Milly followed Cynthia into the historic building.

Not historic by Egyptian standards or even English, but certainly for new-world America, the studio offices at Columbia were hallowed turf. They were a living and working movie museum. Classic film posters adorned the walls of the narrow corridors, letting on to cramped offices on either side, in which film luminaries had spun the magical movie webs that had captivated the world. Hitchcock, Capra and Chaplin would once have occupied these spaces and toiled over their craft. They were small, badly lit spaces, without the opulence one associates with the silver screen; functional but highly productive little spaces. Milly loved the place.

'Can I get you anything: coffee, water?' Cynthia asked, with a barely-concealed tone that she was busy and would rather they just got down to it. Busy, Busy. People working here. The mantra of LA. Fine with Milly, and she batted the offer back.

Cynthia nodded as she sucked on her paper straw, drawing up a bright green drink waiting for her on her desk. Pulped grass from the steppes of the Himalayas perhaps, with crushed ice from Norway.

'Okay, so, the thing is...' Cynthia began, and in this instant, Milly knew.

'...but I think I know what the problem is.'

Milly tensed a little more. Get straight to it, why don't you. Never mind easing me in with the bits that are working. If there are any, that is. It was a confident opening and typical of a young exec on the up. Cynthia's days of offering soft landings were behind her.

Writers cede their power the moment they submit their work. You click a mouse, and the waiting begins. Milly reminisced wistfully. There would be no chance nowadays of an errant paper script falling into the right hands at the right time and coming to her rescue again.

'This script. It feels way too safe.' Cynthia continued.

Milly nodded, and her eyes narrowed. Safe can be a great thing. Feeling safe and secure is integral to being happy. A safe flight is a bare minimum. But in the context of writing, safe is never good. Other more obvious words are available: bland, vanilla, routine, samey, been-done-already and Milly bristled accordingly.

'D'you know what I mean?' Cynthia asked, more as a statement than a question, which was fine by Milly.

'It's too samey. You know?'

Milly sighed.

'And you know what else...' Cynthia continued.

Milly could hardly wait.

'...people have moved on from this kinda stuff.'

Ouch.

'Oh, really?' is what Milly wanted to reply, but she didn't. Too polite, as always.

'You know how fast everything is these days? Every freaking day, it's something new. Something different. Right?'

'Er...'

'The movies you write. Erm, romantic comedies...' Cynthia stopped to leave it hanging.

'Yes.'

'I get it. They used to be massive. Pretty Woman, Working Girl... People loved those movies.'

Used to be? Past tense.

'But not anymore. And why'd you think that is?' Cynthia asked. Finally, she expected an answer. Milly sighed, not really knowing where to begin, but Cynthia quickly filled the gap.

'Romance, sure. I get it. People still love romance, I guess.'

Well, that's a relief, Milly thought to herself.

'I mean, I don't get it personally. You know, romance, but what do I know?'

Dunno, bugger-all.

Cynthia now took on a guilty look. 'But women still go for romance. Or some women, anyway. Don't quote me on that. But you know what I mean?'

Milly managed another strained smile.

'Date nights, stuff like that. Okay, sure, but it has to be romance that's right for now.'

Milly didn't have a clue what this meant as she stared at the squat, plain and highly powerful woman sitting opposite. The saying has it that there's someone for everyone, but whoever coined that probably hadn't met Cynthia Rosen.

'Little girls. They're not dreaming of getting married anymore. They don't want to be saved. It's sisters doing the rescuing right now. Our turn, huh?'

Milly would have loved a sister to grow up with, but she resented the use of the word in this context, as though all women must be bonded and think the same way.

'Happy ever after, sure. But on our terms. She gets the guy, and he does as he's told. That's the shit I need you to write.'

Milly nodded. Finally, a word she understood and could agree with.

'So you're passing then?' Milly asked, needing to actually hear it. Masochism or just a need for clarity.

'On this script. Yes. Definitely.'

Okay, thank you. That is clear, and a birthday in ruins.

'But we're not passing on you.'

Oh, what a relief.

'Not yet, at least!' Cynthia shrieked with laughter, not noticing that Milly didn't join her.

'Hollywood loves women writers right now. And women filmmakers. It's our turn, right?'

Milly managed a nod.

'But we gotta make the movies that women want.'

Somehow, Milly kept smiling. 'Right. You mean more empowering?' Milly asked.

'Sure, if you like. But whatever you call it. It's the same thing. Women saying get-the-fuck-outta-my-way.'

Milly needed the meeting to end now. She wanted to go home to her family.

'You're British, right?'

What a dumb question, Milly thought.

'Yes. I'm from London.' Milly replied in her best English accent. You've heard of London, right? It's the capital of England and the United Kingdom. Although not the capital of Wales or Scotland. And although Northern Ireland is included in the United Kingdom, London is not its capital. Belfast is...

'Okay. Great. London. I love London. London is super cool right now. So channel some of that cool.'

Milly sneered at something so vague. 'Channel some, what?' Milly asked, her polite cool slipping. 'Cynthia, I speak pretty good English, maybe even perfect, but what the fuck does that even mean?' Milly wouldn't normally swear in such a meeting, but since Cynthia had expressly requested more strident females and it was her birthday, she felt it was fitting.

Cynthia did not appear to be offended. On the contrary, she welcomed the attitude and vernacular and wracked her brain for an example. Then she clapped her hands loudly in an 'I got it' kinda way.

'Fuck, what am I thinking. I just had lunch with her. Jee-sus, how fuckin' stoopid am I?'

Milly wanted to answer but didn't.

'Okay, so what's coming outta Britain right now that everyone loves? And I mean freaking LOVES.'

'Er...'

'Come on. TV show. Genius.'

Milly immediately panicked. What were her parents watching?

'Er, Line of Duty?'

'What? No. What the fuck is that?'

Milly scrambled for something else. Not *The Crown*, surely?

'Come on. *Fleabag*.'

'Oh...'

'Okay, not so recent maybe, but that's the point. People are still talking about it.'

'Right, yes, *Fleabag*,' Milly clutched.

'Everyone loves *Fleabag*.' Cynthia stated firmly. 'And everyone loves Phoebe, right?'

Milly nodded.

'You've seen it, right?'

'Yes, of course. Love it,' Milly lied.

She knew of *Fleabag*, of course, but she hadn't watched it, apart from occasional clips from award shows and snippets online. And she knew of its star and creator too, pictured on various stages clutching her array of gongs. Good for her. Cynthia slapped her hand on her old desk, a desk that Frank Capra might have worked on. 'That's what you need to write.

Write movies like *Fleabag*.'

Duly noted and something to research at least, but Milly continued to flounder.

'Because what is *Fleabag*?' Cynthia asked.

Milly rolled her eyes. The questions were getting harder.

'A woman who doesn't give a fuck,' Cynthia answered for her.

Milly nodded. 'Sure, sassy. Strident. Er, funny...' Milly reached.

'Funny? She's as funny as fuck. She's fucking hilarious.'

'Right. Yes.'

'Look, how it opens. You gotta love that. Straight off the bat. Season One. Episode one. Right there. Bang. Now, that's an opening.'

Milly said nothing. Just continued to look at Cynthia and hoped she might stop with the questions.

'You've seen it, right?'

Milly fudged, and Cynthia carried on.

'We open on *Fleabag* getting fucked by a complete stranger. Boom. I love that.'

Milly blanched. Really?

'And you know where?'

'Er...'

Milly didn't have a clue. In her bedroom?

'In her ass.' Cynthia clapped one final time. 'How about that?'

Milly didn't know how to respond. Should she clap as well?

'That's what you need to write.'

The meeting was over. Thank God. Milly made a mental note to check out *Fleabag*, particularly its opening. But not today, perhaps; it was her birthday after all.

Chapter Two

The concourse at Tottenham Court Road tube station was its usual flurry of activity as London discharged its army of workers at the end of another day. People of all ages, shapes and sizes were scurrying home and hoping for the best. The customary bottle necks had formed at the ticket barriers before the rush for the escalators, almost empty on their way up but completely solid with people heading down. This evening, though, at least the fast-left lane of the down escalator was still moving. Stand on the right and walk on the left: the opposite to how we drive in the UK and so, with hindsight, probably a mistake. Jonson Clarke had never stood on an escalator in his life, up or down. Life is too short. Cool black guy with a life to lead and things to do, coming through. But halfway down, he reached a blockage, and his descent came to a standstill. Jonson sighed and tried to catch a glimpse of the culprit. Most usually a tourist who can't read, an elderly couple who wants to stand next to each other, or else a mum with a pram, which is the least egregious (although they could always use the lift).

Jonson scolded himself because he could so easily have walked the mile or so to the wine bar where his friend was celebrating his 50th birthday and where very little wine would be consumed. Keith was a pal he still played football with after all these years, and it was a party that was likely to get messy and be never-ending. Always just one more venue to attend and more drinks to consume. From bar to restaurant to club and on and on it goes, until suddenly the birds are chirping and explanations and excuses are being prepared. Anywhere to avoid going home for some people. Not Jonson, though. He was long past such antics, and he planned to cry off long before the messy later stages: in fact, as soon as his mates were drunk enough so that they wouldn't notice his absence. He even had the option of remaining out all night because he was home alone this evening, yet this prospect held little appeal for him. His wife, Anna and their youngest were taking the Harry Potter studio tour and staying at his in-laws in Harpenden, north of London. His two teenage boys would be home, but they didn't count.

The years had been kind to Jonson. His enormous fro had gone, of course. It did return after his notorious Christening incident, which Milly had immortalized in her first film *Untitled*, but his days of follicle-posturing were over, opting now to join the ranks with a close shave, which suited him. He would be forty-five next month, but he looked younger: black don't crack, as the saying goes. He kept the male paunch at bay, and with this, he preserved his youthful good looks.

Finally, he shuffled onto the crowded platform. A train door opened, and the first few rows waited for any people alighting before squeezing themselves aboard. The doors closed shut, and, after a beat, the train creaked away as the remaining passengers on the platform shunted forward. Grim- faced work-ers. Earphones in, heads down, eyes on their phones, no one talking. Just trying to make it home and thinking of stuff: what to eat, what to watch, the chances of sex tonight? Probably slim.

But Jonson wasn't going home, and he rebuked himself again. It was a pleasant July evening; he should have walked instead of being huddled underground with the masses. The great unwashed. He glanced at the screen.

Next train, Ealing Broadway - 2 minutes

Jonson half-smiled. Ealing Broadway was his stop for home, and how this train would suit him later on in the evening when he sloped off early from Keith's birthday.

Later, the wine bar was almost as claustrophobic as Jonson's train to Marble Arch station. It featured a large central area of tiled flooring and wood paneling with glass and chrome; the designers of the bar had given scant consideration to the acoustics of the room. The only fabric to absorb the deafening noise were the patrons' clothes, and with fashions as they are, skinny jeans and tight tops on the men and half the women practically naked - it was all hopelessly insufficient, and patrons had to scream at each other to be heard as volumes inexorably rose.

A heavy-set man in Keith's party who Jonson hadn't met before latched on to him for longer than was comfortable. A troubled man, he needed to unload and was probably drawn to Jonson's kind face and his easy manner. People liked Jonson and gravitated toward him, and he would soon discover that this could be a problem. Especially in a room as loud as this. Even cupping his ear, Jonson could only discern every third word or so.

'She... younger... me...'

Jonson nodded and smiled politely.

'...wife. Ten years. ...Fit... you get...?' The man gestured with his hands, drawing a womanly figure. Jonson thought he understood and nodded knowingly.

'...fitter... me. Anyway...' The man shouted as loudly as

possible, but still, Jonson could not hear. The man laughed heartily now, so Jonson joined him.

'...her tennis coach, ...believe that?'

Jonson nodded hopelessly.

'...cking cliché, huh.'

Jonson added a smile now. He thought he had the gist. Something about having a voluptuous young wife who played tennis. Jonson might have easily given him an approving thumbs up.

'Nice,' Jonson bellowed, 'Have you got kids?' Jonson asked this politely, although he was not interested. There is nothing quite as tedious as people talking about their kids.

'She'll get the.... And the house, of course... Nice...'

More nodding from Jonson. Something about having a nice house. What an odd guy, Jonson thought to himself. He needed to get away before he got on to how tall his kids were. Jonson gestured that he needed to pee, but, ever-polite, he assured him that he would return to resume their painful conversation.

Outside the bar, Jonson swayed a little in the cold air as he waited for his phone call to be connected. He was cross with himself for already drinking more than he had intended.

'Hey, Jonson. How's it going?' Anna asked.

'Yeah, good. How was Potter?'

'Yeah. You'd have hated it.'

'But Ella loved it, right?'

'Yeah, totally. Where are you?' Anna asked, perhaps hearing the noise and sensing that he was not home.

'I'm at a birthday do... Keith's... I told you... Oh, just some bar in Marble Arch.'

'Who's, Keith?'

Jonson tutted.

'Just one of the guys I play football with.'

'Wait. Not that Keith.'

Jonson sighed.

'Not the Keith you play football with?'

Jonson rolled his eyes.

'Yes, but this time...'

'You remember what happened last time?'

Jonson did, and he winced.

'You ended up at West Ruislip Station, and I had to...'

'Yeah, well, that's not going to happen again.'

'I found you in a bus depot.'

'Anna. I'm not even drinking tonight,' he lied and looked at his watch, wondering if he might even slope off now. Keith wouldn't notice, and the prospect of being accosted again by his boastful friend with the hot wife and nice house didn't appeal at all.

'What time are you back tomorrow?' Jonson asked.

'Not sure. But not so early. I'm going to walk the dogs with mum, and then I expect dad will do one of his breakfasts. You know, using every pan and utensil in the house.'

Jonson smiled. He loved Anna's folks. The odd couple, as he called them. Her mum had been a ballet dancer and had passed on her beauty and poise to her daughter. Her dad had been a copper, a proper flat-foot, complete with estuary accent and agricultural gait, but thankfully nature had intervened: Anna was a clone of her mum and the apple of her dad's eye, his beautiful only daughter who could do no wrong. When she met Jonson, Anna was appearing regularly in television dramas and had her pick of West End roles, not to mention London's most eligible young suitors. Even accounting for his good looks and charm, Jonson was an odd choice and in-between one of his many start-up projects; he must have worried Anna's parents, and yet they made him feel so welcome.

'Sometime after lunch, I'd say.'

Jonson made a mental note that he could enjoy a decent lie

in tomorrow before giving the house the all-important spruce up.

'Okay, cool. See you tomorrow. Drive carefully.'

'I will. And don't do anything stupid.'

Jonson smiled and didn't protest because his wife made a good point. It wasn't something he could explain or account for: he just happened to be accident-prone. Things happened to him, odd things not of his own making. Things like setting his head on fire at a christening, inspiring the 'grab-em' opening of his best friend's debut screenplay and changing her life to boot. Sometimes the outcome was good and sometimes less so. Milly referred to such occurrences as OTJ's (Only to Jonson). They were part of his charm and why a woman like Anna had fallen in love with him.

Regrettably, that phone call with Anna was the last thing that Jonson could clearly recall of Keith's party and against his better judgement, he did consume a lot more alcohol on his return to the bar. He recalled that the boring man with the tennis fetish wife had bought him another drink, an obscure orange concoction he hadn't asked for. After that, everything was a haze. He could only recall snatches of his train journey home with any confidence.

The next morning at 4.30 am, Jonson woke with a start, instantly relieved that he had been dreaming. But this was scant relief against a head pain which he thought might kill him.

The immense pain aside, it was good to be awake. At least he was alive. Overnight, as his liver had called upon all bodily water reserves to process the poison, his brain had shrivelled and caused him a most vivid and terrifying nightmare. He adjusted his eyes as he stared at his unfamiliar ceiling when a moment of terror stabbed at him. He was not in his bed. What the hell. It wasn't even a bed but a couch he was lying on. His eyes widened painfully. Jesus, where am I? Oh, no. What have I done? These were all pressing questions but not as pressing as the acute pain between his temples and his raging thirst. He needed water before his head exploded.

Jonson fumbled about the strange room, looking for a glass of water or, even better, a running tap. He was so thirsty that if he chanced upon a vase of pungent Stargazer Lilies, he would have drained the water and then started munching on the stalks. If he couldn't find a tap, then at the very least, a door out of this bloody room would suffice. Jesus, please help me. Where am I? Keith's spare room, perhaps? This would be bad but probably recoverable. Anna would be unimpressed but would forgive him, and they would laugh about it, eventually. Silly old Jonson. He didn't know how long he had been asleep, but he guessed it had been long enough, given the nightmare his mind had conjured for him. His dream put him at the Royal Albert Hall for a concert by the world-renowned London Philharmonic Orchestra. This might have been a happy experience if Jonson had been in the comfortable stalls listening to the music. But in true Jonson style, he was in the orchestra. Front and centre. The country's best musicians and Jonson Clarke with his grade 1 piano and basic three-chord guitar ability. He might have blended in okay if he had a triangle or possibly a single drum, but Jonson was the lead violinist with an impending solo. And it was so freaking vivid. Fellow musicians gave furtive looks to the sweatiest violinist they had never played with before. These musicians had dedicated their lives in order to occupy such hallowed seats, and next to them sat this chancer who had never even held a violin before. The conductor was a hefty chap with a balding curly mane of hair. Full of vim and bluster and complete with a white scarf, he stared daggers at his terrified soloist.

Jonson's moment was about to arrive. Like a train hurtling for the buffers, he faced a stark choice. He could feign death, or maybe he could pretend to play while an intuitive violinist nearby covered for him. But such sensible options were not in the Jonson Clarke playbook. *Only to Jonson,* as the saying goes, and so when the orchestra fell quiet, he rose to his feet and massacred Mozart's greatest work. Five thousand people resplendent in dinner suits and ball gowns stared at him in horror.

Jonson lay still now in the peculiar room, trying to make some sense of his circumstances and find a position where the pain was the least excruciating. Look for the upsides was one of Jonson's many life mantras. He was alive. For now, anyway. He pulled himself upright and clambered onto a nearby easy chair, and, in doing so, his backside activated a remote control. A large blue screen lit up on the wall opposite. The light pierced his bruised cranium, and he moved his head slowly. On the floor, he noticed his shoes that he must have kicked off but also a pair of his football boots. And in the corner of the room was a dartboard and a photo of Anna on the wall. Jonson smiled as best he could. He had been home all along. The realization and the sheer relief engulfed him. He almost laughed, and for a moment,; even his pain eased.

'Oh, thank God,' Jonson sobbed.

Somehow, he had slept in his garden room, his man cave, cinema room, over-spill repository; it didn't matter what it was called. He was home after all, and everything was fine. Thank God. Panic over. Everything was well. Onwards.

Chapter Three

Milly eased her natty electric Porsche through the automatic gates of her home and smiled at the scene that greeted her. Mary, her eldest daughter, was chipping golf balls into a large netted bucket under the careful tutelage of her dad. On seeing mum's car, she quickly teed up a ball and promptly clipped it home. Bullseye. Mitch held his hands aloft, and Mary doffed her imaginary cap to the galleries.

'Hey, birthday girl.' Mitch bounded over to greet Milly as she emerged from her car, and he kissed her fondly.

'How'd it go with Bob?' Mitch asked casually.

'Ah, you know...' Milly replied.

Mitch tutted knowingly and then smiled broadly.

'Oh well. It doesn't matter because Mary's gonna win the US Open.'

Milly chuckled. 'Good. She might need to.'

Mitch looked at her, a little bemused now.

'So, come on, what? What did Bob say?'

Milly pursed her lips and raised her perfectly manicured eyebrows.

'Bob was not in.'

Mitch exhaled. 'No, really?'

'Yep. Bob was a no show.'

'But you had a meeting.'

Milly smiled ruefully. 'I know. I had a meeting.'

Mitch hung his head to one side. 'Really, Bob ghosted you?'

'I know.' Milly was smiling now. 'Is that where I am now?'

Mitch knew Bob, and he also knew Milly's script, and now he was doubly confused.

'That's not like him.'

Milly tutted. 'But Cynthia was in, though.'

Mitch's face fell. 'Oh.'

Milly laughed. 'Yeah.'

'And how'd that go?' Mitch asked.

Milly didn't say anything. She didn't need to. She just sighed a little. It was her birthday, after all, and she wanted to have a lovely evening.

'Have you seen *Fleabag*?'

Milly was delighted at the prospect of dinner at home as her birthday treat. Their spectacular home was not long finished, and their view of the lake this late afternoon was particularly welcome and tranquil. Brenda, their maid, would preside over the important elements of the cooking, with Mitch granted dispensation to flash the tuna steaks on his ultra-modern outdoor range and grill, which he had yet to use, and his degree of excitement was borderline worrying. What is it with men and fire? Something carnal and deep in their marrow. Mitch couldn't wait for the great fireball in the sky to finally call it a day so that he could spark up his log fire in the centre of their new suite of terrace furniture.

Milly opened her presents and caught up on some messages from colleagues and friends. A card from her mum and dad was welcome but a little dispiriting for its bland birthday wishes and little more. A missed FaceTime call from Jonson was more exciting though, and she mentally scheduled another memo to return his call.

'Dinner in fifteen.' Mitch called out to no one in particular. Isla, their youngest, was on FaceTime with what looked like a boy, and Mitch craned his neck for a better view.

'Dad,' Isla called out indignantly.

'Is that a boy?' Mitch asked cheekily.

Isla ended the call abruptly and shook her head in disbelief on her way to her room, cursing why dads are always so embarrassing. Mitch revelled in being a 'doofus' and feigned hurt.

'Hey, dad, what's for dinner?' Mary asked.

'Grilled tuna steaks on my new range,' Mitch gushed, 'green salad and Brenda's done that thing with the cauliflower.'

Mary looked much less excited than her dad. 'Cauliflower, really?'

'You like this cauliflower. The spicy kind. It's delicious. And it's mom's birthday, so we've got a crumble.'

Finally, Mary smiled. Their daughters were all-American girls, but they loved their English heritage. They visited England regularly and could both score points at school by doing perfect English accents when called upon. Apple crumble is England's equivalent to American apple pie and was a firm family favourite. Mitch beamed at his beautiful daughter, his excitement infectious. He had remembered to turn on their outdoor jacuzzi also, just on the off chance that it might get some use once the girls had gone to bed. It was a special day after all. Mitch was deliriously happy. Who cared that Bob had bombed out of Milly's meeting?

Renovating their home had been an eighteen-month project. It was a 1930's period property that Burt Reynolds had briefly called home until another ruinous divorce had snatched it from him. Milly's old friend Georgina had advised on the interior design, without being asked, but her input had been helpful and welcome. Fortunately, the house was completed on time and on budget. It was spectacular, and the Carmichaels loved it.

'Milly!' Mitch called out with a cold beer in one hand and a large metal ice bucket in the other. Fire and ice seem to be the two things that most excite and inspire the modern man. Brenda smiled at her incorrigible boss as she checked his range for temperature, just to be on the safe side. Line-caught tuna was easily and expensively ruined.

Brenda had been with the family since their marriage and was now a permanent member. One of the so-called illegals, she had arrived from Mexico almost forty years ago, and, with two grown-up American kids, she was an integral part of Californian life and was never going to be returned. Brenda wasn't her real name, but it was what everyone called her. She was one of the best cooks on the west coast, and Mitch was happy to have her culinary supervision.

Mitch left the drinks to chill a little further and hopped up the three stairs of their covered terrace. He breezed into the open plan living room and kitchen, decked in muted greys and whites.

'Hey Mary. Where's mom?'

'Upstairs, I think.'

Mitch entered their large master suite to find Milly at her dresser, fiddling with a remote control.

'Hey sweetheart. I'm about to put the steaks on.'

'Oh, great, I'm starving. But can you just wait just one second?'

'Sure, what you watching?'

'Here. Sit down. You can watch it with me. I just need to see the beginning.'

Mitch did as he was told, intrigued now.

'What is it?'

'You've heard of *Fleabag*, right?'

'Sure. The British show. I haven't seen much of it. Phoebe, right?'

'Yeah, I just need to see the opening.' Milly lumbered with the sleek remote. In younger hands, she would be halfway through season one already.

'Okay, and why's that?'

'Oh, nothing, just something Cynthia said.'

Finally, the episode began, and it didn't take long. It was just as Cynthia had described. Milly and Mitch stared at the screen as a stranger arrived at a woman's house in the middle of the night. Then, cut to the bedroom. They are having sex. Phoebe is naked and, on all fours, talking to the camera about how much it hurts. It is definitely an opening to grab the attention. Milly stared agog. Mitch too, thought of the meal ahead and the possibility of using the hot tub later. Good planning on his part. And just on the off chance.

Chapter Four

Jonson rummaged through the usual places in their house on the hunt for medicine, still relieved by his narrow escape but also cross with his irresponsibility. Things could have been much worse. Yet another cupboard had nothing for his headache. He seethed as he emptied a second drawer bare and found further tubes of haemorrhoid cream, plasters and antacids but no pain relief.

'Jesus. Who has piles? Does Anna have piles?'

Finally, in the cupboard over the kettle, he found a packet of soluble painkillers. He ripped open the box and the blister pack and tipped two tablets into a glass of water, which he drank during the fizzing and before they had fully dissolved. And then he took on another couple of pints of water before crawling upstairs to his actual bed.

More than five hours later, Jonson was woken by his eldest son, Noah, plonking a mug of tea on his bedside table. Jonson moaned loudly.

'I thought you'd want to be woken...' Noah said knowingly.

More moaning from Jonson.

'...you know, what with mum coming back.'

Jonson's eyes opened at this, and slowly his mind began to compute and make assessments. Noah shook his head at his accident-prone dad. He had just turned nineteen and was Jonson's biggest fan and critic.

'What time did you get back?' Noah asked with a wicked grin. It took a moment for the question and its implications to register. Jonson re-focused his bruised mind and tried to sit up. He winced and groaned.

'Not that late. Why?'

Noah scoffed. 'After three, 'cos that's involved got home.'

Jonson closed his eyes and blew out heavily. 'Blimey, what a night.'

'What happened?' Noah asked.

'God knows. Nothing bad, though.' His evening had so quickly gone awry. 'Had this awful nightmare,' Jonson said softly.

'Yeah, what about?'

Jonson thought for a moment, and half chuckled. Silly, really. 'A violin.'

Noah looked bemused as Jonson pressed both of his eyes gently. Such a vivid dream that the bloody thing had resumed as soon as he had fallen asleep again. As though the scary conductor had been waiting for him. Most dreams can't even be recalled, let alone revisited like a blinking sequel.

'What time did you get in, then?' Noah repeated his question more knowingly.

'I dunno,' Jonson answered, 'but late. Too late. Don't tell your mum.'

Noah smiled. His dad was a hero, and he loved him. Everyone did. 'Blimey, dad. What are you like?'

Jonson shook his head. Don't ask such futile questions.

'Anyway, I'm off to see Wendy. Then I've got a match. What time is mum back?'

'Good question. After lunch, sometime. What time is it now?'

'Just before ten.'

Jonson nodded. Good. He still had time. Nice.

'Where's your brother?'

'Upstairs, asleep.'

Even better. He can help me with the all-important spruce.

'Hey Noah.'

'Yeah.'

'My mad dream.'

'Yeah, what about it.'

'I'm dead proud that you can play the piano, man.'

Noah looked at his dad, a little confused. 'Thanks, dad.'

'No, seriously. Being able to play. You must keep it up, man.'

'Did mum tell you...'

'No, I'm just saying. It's just a very cool thing. That's all.'

Jonson propped himself on his pillow and found a position where his head hurt the least, and he could sip his tea. It was a little off boiling, but he drank it anyway. Any liquid that wasn't alcohol was good. He gently massaged his temples and tried to recall his evening again. He had never had an evening completely erased by alcohol before, not even in his younger days. Until now, he thought such things were a myth. Just male posturing and bravado. He remembered getting on a train at Marble Arch station and snatches of a conversation with a guard on a platform. But at Ealing Broadway or Marble Arch? He couldn't recall, but the man had been rude and dismissive. But why would he speak to a member of staff? He could also recall various fragments outside Ealing Broadway station. The night was cold for July, and there had been a taxi queue, so he had decided to walk to clear his head and get his daily steps up. Two birds, right there. He rubbed his furry teeth with his tongue and wondered if he had stopped for a kebab. It tasted like he had, but he couldn't recall.

And then this dream recurred again. His musical humiliation on repeat. Wendy was Noah's piano teacher and had been since he was five years old, guiding him through the successive grades. Anna was in tears when he passed the vaunted eighth grade, which made him a proper pianist. Jonson was proud too. He took a few deep breaths and pressed his swollen eyes again. No real harm done, he decided. Some liver damage, no doubt, but, as all drinkers avow and desperately hope, this organ regenerates. He was due some more pain relief by now, and this time he would let the tablets fully dissolve.

He went downstairs and was pleasantly surprised by the state of the house. The kitchen was not looking too bad, and the lounge was presentable. It wouldn't take much of an effort for Anna to notice that a spruce had occurred and what a lucky woman she was. Every experienced husband knows that the key to a successful wife-being-away-spruce is to complete a noticeable chore. Jonson glugged down the fizzy water, and in that moment, he resolved to polish the silver: a job with a high coefficient of results-to-energy-required ratio and which, by its gleaming outcome, would also be highly noticeable. It also helped that they didn't have too much silver, just the odd picture frame and a few candle holders, wedding presents that had somehow survived. Jonson smiled at his guile. He didn't have an array of letters after his name, but he was street smart and knew what to do. There were only two silver-framed photographs on their mantelpiece: a wedding photograph with Anna looking stunning and a photo of Jonson with Noah, which he grabbed to look at now. It had featured heavily in local press and online when it had been taken on the pitch at Wembley Stadium. Noah was gripping a large trophy and grinning broadly. The zenith of his football life, when a career in the game was still a possibility for him. Genes had been kind and conspired well for young Noah, taking the best of what his parents had to offer. Jonson smiled at his good fortune. He would spruce the house, and he couldn't wait to see Anna and his daughter, Ella.

Things continued to improve throughout the rest of the morning. In the fridge was a brand-new bottle of cold milk. His phone buzzed with WhatsApp alerts and not a call from Anna. A series of messages in Keith's birthday group chat, the last one reading:

J *where you at? We r in gaff up road. Out of club. Left. First gaff on right. Across road. We r all wankered!*

Jonson congratulated himself on his early retirement from the debauchery. He scrolled through other notifications and saw that Milly had replied to his birthday greetings. It had been a year since her last visit home, and time she made the trip again. He thought to text her but decided against it because of the time difference.

In bed together, Milly and Mitch enjoyed a post-coital cuddle to round off what had been a lovely birthday. They hadn't used the jacuzzi as Mitch had hoped, but the range had worked well, and everyone agreed that the fire pit was a hit. Heat and something cool to look at: what's not to like? Mitch was particularly relieved that Milly's earlier non-meeting had not spoiled her evening. There are many luxuries of being successful, one of which is that setbacks, although painful, are affordable.

'That was a lovely day. Thank you, Mitch.'

'Hey, of course.'

'The girls were particularly gorgeous, weren't they?'

'Were they?' Mitch joked, and Milly punched his strong shoulder.

'Yeah, they were.' He agreed. 'But that's the advantage the young have.'

This fixed Milly for a moment, it being her birthday, and she was now nearer to fifty than forty. She thought of Cynthia. And poor old *Fleabag*, on all fours and taking one for the team. She was tired and needed some sleep. She would speak with Lyal, her agent, tomorrow. He was semi-retired now, but he remained available for his 'star' clients and emergencies. And this felt like the beginning of an emergency, at least. Lyal would reassure her. He would know what to say. Milly would call him in the morning.

Unable to sleep at 2 a.m., Milly crawled out of bed and snuck into her adjoining office to place a call to Lyal, a mistake, as it turned out.

'*Fleabag*. Love it. Who doesn't?' Lyal gushed.

'Hey. I've got it,' Lyal enthused, 'Why don't you sit down with Phoebe? Spend some time with the young charges. Her agent's a doll. She might even be in LA right now. Shall I set that up...'

'Lyal, that's not why I'm calling. It's just...'

'What is it?' Lyal asked, full of drama.

Milly sighed, regretting her call already.' I met Cynthia Rosen today at Columbia and...'

'Love Cynthia. How is she?'

'Er...'

'Give it five years, and she'll be running the place. So my advice, keep in with our Cynth.'

Milly grimaced.

'What did she have to say?' Lyal asked.

'Columbia are passing.'

'Oh...'

Milly waited.

'Well, that is a shame. Did they say why?' Lyal asked a little too coolly.

'They want something grittier.'

'Mmm...' Lyal murmured, a sort of tacit agreement, which aggrieved Milly even more.

'Something more like *Fleabag*, it seems.'

Lyal added another murmur.

'So, you agree then?'

'Milly, darling. It's shifting sand, and none of us can stand still. None of us. We all have to move.'

Milly rolled her eyes and didn't respond.

'All of us need to keep up with the flow, or else we vanish.' Lyal continued with his sand metaphor.

'Milly, I have one word for you. It's a new genre which doesn't bear repeating. I coined it myself.'

'Go on,' Milly beckoned, intrigued now.

'Vulver!' Lyal exclaimed triumphantly.

'What?' Milly asked, wondering if she'd misheard.

'Vulver!' he repeated, enjoying its shock value.

'What the hell does that mean?' Milly demanded.

'Vulgar but clever: vulver. It's what everyone wants now. It's modern and progressive. Women being strident and claiming their futures. And I think it could be great for you. I really do.'

Milly stared at her phone. She needed to ring off, but now she had even less chance of getting back to sleep. He hadn't even asked what she was doing up in the middle of the night nor mentioned her birthday either. She ended the call a little abruptly and pushed open the large bifold doors letting on to their roof terrace, overlooking their gardens and the lake beyond. The rolling hills of Santa Monica off in the distance were about to make their dawn entrance. Over the years, Milly had learned to live with her anxiety, which more often involved accommodating rather than trying to defeat it. But she recognized the signs to be mindful of, particularly the destructive feelings of self-pity. Milly knew how blessed she was and how ugly self-pity can be. Since her miserable marriage to Elliot and her stuttering writing career, she now had it all. She had a husband who looked like he appeared in her movies and two beautiful daughters. And yet Milly couldn't shake her sense of melancholy. The realization that she was expendable. And the notion of becoming 'vulver' didn't feel like much of a solution, even if she could achieve such a thing, which she doubted. She wondered if she was being too prudish. She thought of the infamous opening scene of Fleabag again and then the famous song, *Strangers in the Night*. A beautiful ditty about two strangers and their fleeting encounter. Wondering about their chances and how they'd be lovers before this very night was through. Okay, fine. But not up the arse, Milly thought to herself. That little dirty detail would have ruined the song, surely?

She assured herself that she remained relevant and that her despondence was as likely symptomatic of her middle age. Quite normal and nothing to be ashamed of, she decided. And there was nothing wrong either with needing to be cheered up, so she placed another phone call. Jonson answered immediately. 'Hey, Mills. What are you doing up so early?'

Milly smiled, instantly feeling better. 'Oh, you know, couldn't sleep.'

'How come? Everything okay?'

She felt embarrassed now about her very lofty problems.

'How was your birthday? I did call.'

'Yeah, I saw that. Thanks. I meant to return...'

'Bloody hell, *return*. Listen to you. You need to get back to England girl, before we lose you. And it's not too late for the girls. We can make them English. There's still time.'

Milly chuckled. Jonson always made her laugh.

'Anyway, how are you? What you up to?' Milly asked.

'Right now, I'm polishing the silver.'

Milly laughed. 'Why? What have you done this time?'

'Nothing. Anna's been at her folks. She took Ella with her. So, you know, I thought I'd get some points in the bank.'

'Very wise.' Milly chuckled as she imagined the scene. 'The old-husband spruce up, you mean?'

Jonson cackled. 'Yep, you got it. That's it, exactly. I love that. "The husband spruce-up". You should write that down. That's funny.'

Milly had already made a mental note but quickly 'vulver' barged it out of the way as a reminder that her whimsical musings were old hat.

'But also...' Jonson began, his tone more conciliatory now, 'Last night, I was out with some of the lads, and it all went very wrong.'

'Oh dear.'

'Yeah. I'm in a lot of pain, actually.'

'Oh, poor you. Make sure you tell Anna, so she can give you a cuddle.'

Jonson tutted. 'And do you know what? I can't even remember what happened.'

Milly stopped at this. 'That's not like you.'

'I know. Seriously, I think I might have been drugged. You know these date rape drugs you hear about.'

Milly snorted her derision, which only encouraged Jonson to continue.

'...no listen. It could have happened. The place was packed with young totty. And you know me, I'm there giving off my 'unavailable' vibes, but, looking like I do, I'm like a challenge.'

Milly hooted with laughter and, at the same time, tutted her disapproval.

'My advice, Jonson?'

'Yep, go on. I'm all ears.'

'That theory of yours. About being drugged. I wouldn't share that with Anna.'

Jonson laughed now. 'No, of course not. But she'll know I was out late and that I was drunk. Wife's intuition. That's why I'm sprucing.'

'Good. Then polish hard.'

Jonson jolted now as an image occurred to him. A flashback from his nightmare. 'Bloody hell...' Jonson began.

'What?'

'Last night, I had this crazy dream. And I've just realised you were in it!'

'Really?'

Jonson's mind fixed now on his new image. He was standing on stage with his violin, staring out at the audience. Before him was a sea of disgruntled scowls, except for one single approving face: his oldest friend, Milly. Jonson related this to Milly and her part therein.

'Well, that sounds mad and very you,' Milly offered.

'Yeah, it was. So if any of your freaky LA mates know anything about dreams, then perhaps I'll share it with them.'

Milly smiled again.

'Hey, Milly, I gotta go. The girls could be back any moment, and I still haven't sanded the floors.

'Jonson, you're such a dick.'

'I know, but a loveable one, eh?'

'I'd say incorrigible.'

'Right, which is why you write for a living, and I don't. Speaking of which, it's about time you paid us a visit.'

Milly ended the call, her spirits duly lifted and her mind on a possible trip to London. Not a bad idea. The kids always loved it, and Mitch never took much persuading either.

Chapter Five

Just after 1pm, Jonson was in his lounge when Anna's Audi pulled into their drive. His head still hurt, and recollections remained vague. In their tiled hallway, he picked up an errant piece of fluff his hoover had missed and opened the solid front door, with its attractive stained-glass paneling, before the two women in his life had reached the threshold of their home. He smiled broadly as they approached. Anna looked a little frazzled. Traffic was the most likely culprit, but clearing up after her dad's breakfast probably hadn't helped.

'How was breakfast?'

'Don't ask. Who uses a wok?'

Jonson took her bag and kissed her affectionately. 'Welcome home. You could have stayed longer.' Anna smiled as she shook her head. One night was enough, and she was delighted to be home again in their attractive Edwardian house in the queen of London's suburbs. It appreciated in value each year by more than its occupants made in salary.

'Hey Ella. How was Harry Potter?' Jonson asked as he picked her up for his hug. The young lady looked a little disappointed, and Ella quickly explained.

'Daniel wasn't there.'

'Oh...'

'She wanted to see Daniel,' Anna added.

'They had models of him though,' Ella explained, 'but daddy, they weren't his actual real-life size.'

Anna made a look.

Ella smiled as she whipped her hand from around her back. 'And look, mummy bought me a wand.'

'Wow. A wand. Does it work?'

'Yes, of course it works. It's magic.'

'Cup of tea?' Jonson asked Anna, which she answered with a smile.

'Where are the boys?'

'Both out. Noah was at Wendy's; then he had a match. Luke's just out.'

Anna now took in the house, sensing the spruce and that Jonson was waiting expectantly. But first, she needed to see more to determine how many points to award. And to tease him. She moved from the lounge into the dining room, idly dragging a finger along a sideboard on her way. And then she stopped.

'Jonson...'

'Yeah, what's up?' he said as casually as possible.

'You've done the silver.'

'Yeah, so.' He added casually. Anna's demeanour altered a little now.

'Why?' she asked.

'What?'

'Why have you done the silver?'

Jonson tutted at her implication. Er, because it needed doing, perhaps. Or just that I'm a hero. Anna half-smiled. Her female intuition still whirring. It was difficult to discern with her husband, but something was awry and knowing him as she did, most likely he didn't have a clue either. She looked at the end of her finger. Clean as a whistle. This had been a major spruce.

'Jonson, the house looks lovely. Thank you so much.'

Jonson plonked her tea down in her favourite china mug and shrugged his modest hero gesture, which he'd honed over the years.

'It's like I told your dad all those years ago...'

'Yeah, yeah.' Anna stopped him. 'How was your evening?'

Jonson sighed heavily as Noah burst into the room, his face dirty with mud and disappointment, but Jonson decided to ask him anyway.

'How'd you get on?'

'The referee was a complete arsehole...'

Jonson smiled.

'Okay, dad, one question. Just answer me this. 'Is a ricochet a back pass?'

Jonson chuckled and held his hands aloft at this hackneyed debate. After watching so many of his boy's matches down the years, he had come to feel most sorry for the referees. They were abused by the players themselves, but even more so by the touchline parents, hurling invective at the men in black. Jonson was a silent spectator and attended fewer games these days since the boys were older now, and having dad along might be awkward and is certainly not cool.

'Hey mum, you look great.'

'Oh, thanks love.'

Noah kissed his mum before turning his attention to his little sister.

'Hey, Ella, what you got there?'

'It's my wand.'

'Cool, is it magic?'

'It's a wand, Noah. Of course, it's magic.'

'Okay, great. Then can you cast a spell for me on this referee?'

Ella laughed hard. 'Yes, but how bad was he? Because with this, I can actually have him killed.'

'Ella.' Anna rebuked her daughter.

'Well, maybe not kill him.' Noah replied. 'But maybe break his legs.'

'Noah.' Jonson stepped in now, and Noah chuckled. 'Or maybe, it could help dad to remember how he got home last night?'

Anna's ears pricked up at this. She looked to Jonson, who was now recalibrating down his due brownie points. Jonson scowled at his treacherous firstborn and then smiled easily at his wife.

'Don't worry: I can explain.'

'Oh, really?' Noah smirked, enjoying himself now, his match forgotten. Jonson took a beat. 'Actually, no, I can't.' And with this, he burst out laughing.

'Jonson!' Anna called loudly, smiling too.

'What can I say? I think I was drugged.'

Their afternoon evaporated quickly, and soon Jonson was hauling two bags of Indian takeaway home from Moksha, his favourite local curry house. Anna would have preferred anything else, but Jonson deserved his monthly curry for his silver polishing alone.

A single police car, without blue lights or fanfare, pulled to a stop outside Ealing Broadway Underground Station in West London. A sleek black Audi the size of a boat was already parked up, its engine idling, but you would never know it. German engineering for you. A bored-looking police officer exited his squad car, and a man emerged from the Audi shortly thereafter. Audi man was Asian, late twenties and immaculately dressed in a navy suit and bespoke white shirt with no tie. He had a serious air. He was purposeful but was clearly a man under considerable strain; in contrast, the police officer was scruffy and bored looking. His uniform was ill-fitting, as though he had borrowed it from lost property.

Observing the scene was Barry Shenfield, a freelance journalist with the nose of a Labrador and the guile of an alley cat. Barry was there on a tip-off, and, as ever, he was hopeful of a story. Audi-man and Police-Man shook hands tentatively, with Barry looking on, making mental notes on everything before him. He was tall for an Indian, and Barry considered him carefully. He looked the part all right, but Barry was sure he didn't own the Audi. More likely, he worked for the owner of such an expensive ride. He noted the number plates but only out of habit. Owners of such cars don't like to be identifiable, so they register their cars to a company.

Audi-man looked handsome, with his thick dark hair swept back and his thin, pinched nose and dark eyes; the police officer was balding, squat and with one chin too many. A career in the police would not have been an option for him back in the day.

Barry had been a long-time employee of London Underground, now the more pompously titled Transport for London. Since taking his generous redundancy, Barry had been careful to maintain a solid and reliable contact list within the enormous organization. After all, it was the world's oldest and largest underground train network, used each and every day by millions of people. A fertile ground of human interest and woe, and woe is where the money is. Woe is what people want to read about: anything that makes them feel better about their own lives, especially on their way home from jobs they hate.

Nigel Bethell had spent his entire working life at Transport for London and, more recently had made a nice supplementary income collaborating with his ex-colleague Barry. Every year, with its all-seeing cameras, the underground network watches everything that life has to offer. It bears witness frequently to the moment of conception, sometimes to the miracle of birth, and all-too-often to the tragedy of death. Some are pushed by a patient not taking their meds, but most are people deciding that they've had enough as they wander into the tunnels. And despite the constant announcements imploring passengers to take their personal belongings with them, the amount of clobber that people leave behind is utterly bewildering: hundreds of thousands of umbrellas, phones, wallets, medication, flowers, jewellery and, occasionally, a priceless musical instrument. Nigel knew what exactly to look and listen for, and he always called Barry before anyone else.

A 'valuable violin' immediately caught Nigel's attention. It first came to his attention in a phone call from an unidentified man on Saturday afternoon, which Barry assumed had been Audi-Man. The man sounded strained and evasive, and he gave what Barry felt was not his real name. He couldn't explain this. Just a feeling he had.

Nigel listened to the call a few times, and quickly he associated it with another call received earlier in the day. This call had been from a young woman, clearly very upset about a missing violin. He checked the online register of found items. No violin had shown up as yet, which was interesting and possibly good news. The man's phone call had mentioned the Central Line and Ealing Broadway station, enough for Nigel to begin a search of the CCTV footage. It didn't take him long to find what he was looking for. He smiled and called Barry immediately.

Barry got to work with what he had, and quickly his interest was piqued. But to create a story of any interest and value, he would need a decent photograph of either of the unidentified callers. To do this, Barry needed to set a trap. Posing as a member of staff, Barry called the number that the male caller had left to give him the good news that his violin had been recovered and was waiting for him at Ealing Broadway station. Naturally, Barry was also present, and he was intrigued that a police officer should be in attendance.

The stallion and the donkey made their way into the underground station. They made an odd couple and drew curious looks from passers-by. Barry cautiously followed them, gesturing furiously at his colleague who was exiting a café with two coffees and a paper bag of pastries.

In the foyer, the two men were greeted by a station manager, and quickly all three disappeared through a door, which closed firmly after them. Barry whipped out his phone to make a record of the policeman's ID number, which he had spied on his shoulder. His scruffy colleague had caught up to him by now.

'They didn't have a Danish, Barry, so I got you a doughnut.'

Barry fidgeted with his earpiece. No photo, no story is the rule for newspapers, and there would be no payday without a story being placed. Barry's colleague appeared more interested in his doughnut, probably about to finally hit the jam.

'Jees man, never mind your doughnut. There's no violin so they won't be long. Get your bloody camera ready. I need a shot of this bloke.'

'Which one, Barry?'

Barry glared at this colleague. 'Who do you think? The tall one. The Indian bloke.'

Chapter Six

'And what about a career? Have you thought about what you might like to do?' Jonson asked the young man sitting opposite. Jordon was a final year student about to make his entrance into the big wide world. He stared at Mr Clarke and just shrugged.

Jonson worked as a mentor at a technical college in Holborn for kids who were technically failing to get their shit together. His job was basically an old-fashioned careers adviser, but like so many professions these days, it had been up-skilled and rebranded by the social scientists: his official job title was currently *Youth Training and Development Consultant*. His role was to inspire his charges to become the very best adults within their capability. Jonson took his role seriously, but, unfortunately, too many of his charges did not.

Mondays were always hard-going for Jonson, with his students still recovering after their weekends of clubbing. Fridays weren't much better because his students had their eyes on the new weekend. Their ambitions were not broad, ranking in order from rapper, singer or DJ to something now known as an 'influencer' and finally and more generally, just to be famous. Jonson's mission was a painful one, but one he had chosen to accept: namely, to suggest more pedestrian, less lucrative, but ultimately more realistic and fulfilling careers. Jordan's 'dunno' shrug was the most typical response that Jonson encountered. Milly had spoken to his class a few years ago about the wonders and perils of being a writer. But all it seemed they could agree on, however, was that she was hot. It was a thankless task, and on this Monday, Jonson was relieved to set out for home at bang on 5pm.

London was busy as millions of people surged home from work. Jonson didn't normally take a copy of the free evening newspaper, but he did so this evening. He tucked the newspaper under his arm, headed into the throng and finally made it onto a train bound for Ealing Broadway. During this journey, he briefly reflected on the last journey he had taken on this very train the previous Friday night. Standing and crushed against the doors of the packed train, he still hadn't opened his newspaper. A few stops later, he had eased further into the train and now had a glass pane to lean on. He peered at the smug people with seats, flicking through their apps, attending to their make-up or reading their free-sheets. A lady had her newspaper open to page 3, and something caught Jonson's eye. His eyes narrowed at a photograph: a picture of a suave looking Indian man standing outside what looked like Ealing Broadway Station. Jonson craned his head, but the lady turned the page as though she knew it would annoy him. Jonson couldn't consult his own copy of the newspaper without upsetting those around him, so it would have to wait. Something to look forward to. It wasn't until Shepherds Bush that a heavy man in a suit hauled himself to his feet, and Jonson finally got to sit down. This was a relief until he felt the damp warmth of the seat. Finally, Jonson unfurled his newspaper and placed it on his lap. His eyes widened immediately.

"Priceless violin lost on London's underground."

The mere mention of the word violin was unnerving for Jonson; especially one lost on the tube, not to mention the word, "priceless". Barry Shenfield, the journalist of this piece, didn't know it was priceless, of course, but he was happy to call it so. When was the last time you saw a lost violin that wasn't 'priceless', right?

Jonson skimmed the short amount of copy on the front page then turned to page three for more information. Immediately, the colour drained from his face. His fatigue was instantly wiped out by a dollop of adrenalin that was dumped into his bloodstream. Suddenly, his brain fired as synapses snapped and sprang to life, making connections and trying to decipher odd fragments of data, like an old jigsaw puzzle with pieces missing. An image of a violin gripped him, and immediately he thought of his unusual dream. His eye scoured the copy.

"...believed to be lost on Friday evening and thought to have been on the Central Line."

Jonson's mouth dried, and he drew a deep breath as his train headed for Ealing Broadway, which was also featured in the newspaper. A tall Indian man was pictured outside the station. The caption below read: "A man believed to be Nihal Khan, a personal envoy of a wealthy family living in London". Using the Audi's registration, Barry had called in considerable favours to establish the identity of the man and who he worked for. He withheld this information from his editor because they would never publish it, but anyway, Barry had other ideas of how such information might be useful to him.

Finally emerging from the train tunnel, Jonson's phone reconnected itself with the world, and he thought about calling home to speak with Anna. Quickly, he scotched such an idea.

What would he ask her, and how would he explain himself? His best chance would be to get home before anyone else so that he could check the house for any stray violins. Jonson admonished himself for being so ridiculous. Did Anna have a late class this evening? He wasn't sure, but he hoped so. Or else he might need to wait to check out their garden room.

As Jonson's train eased out of East Acton station, Wormwood Scrubs loomed into view, one of London's most infamous prisons. Every time it held Jonson's gaze, he imagined the drama and sadness played out daily within its foreboding walls. It was the sort of place that a thief of a priceless violin might get to see. Jonson's ability to catastrophize was highly developed. People sitting on the train could have no idea of the conflicts going on within the mind of the pleasant-looking man sitting amongst them.

If he did have the bloody violin, which he didn't, then his crime was failing to hand the thing in and nothing more. So, no biggie. Is that even a crime, he wondered? But it was all immaterial anyway because he didn't have it. And yet, something nagged at him. It was all Keith's fault and his boring mate who had spiked his drink. Jonson closed his eyes and tried to think calm thoughts. He stretched his jaw and rubbed his eyes. He turned to the back page as a useful distraction. A Tottenham player featured prominently: their Korean star, Heung Min Son, whom Jonson immediately connected with his conundrum. Weren't most violinists Chinese these days, and Koreans look a lot like Chinese people, right? Terrible stereotyping and logic but such was his panic that he couldn't help it.

As he turned into his street, his house looked quiet. He hoped it might be empty of people and, for that matter, violins. He turned the key and pushed open his front door.

'Hiya,' Anna called immediately. Normally, Jonson would be delighted by such a greeting but not this evening.

'Hi, love. You okay?' He called back, keen to get to his garden room and put his insane theory to rest. Anna came into the hall with a loving smile and embraced him warmly. She was wearing gloves and had her hair tied up.

'Guess what?' She asked.

'What?' Jonson asked, although he wasn't interested. Not until he knew that he wasn't in trouble. And why is she wearing gloves? Jesus Christ, are they gardening gloves?

'I've got an audition for a new TV drama. The director asked for me personally.'

Jonson nodded. 'Wow, that's great, love.'

'What's wrong?' Anna asked quickly, knowing her husband too well.

'What? Nothing. Nothing's wrong. Hey, that's great news.'

'I haven't got it yet.'

'Yet!' Jonson smiled, his eyes still wandering and distracted. 'Why are you wearing gloves?'

'Jonson...' Anna said in a parental manner before a naughty child.

'What? Nothing's wrong!' Despite all his practice, Jonson remained a very poor liar.

'What's with the gloves?' he asked with a forced smile.

'I'm doing the garden.'

Jonson looked to the ceiling. What the hell. Anna never did the garden, apart from the only day of the year that Jonson needed her not to be in the bloody garden. His eyes took in their French doors. The safe play now was to say nothing. Just play it cool. Plenty of time to check it out later once Anna had finished her weeding. Only there wasn't plenty of time. If he did have the wretched thing, with every passing minute, his crime would be compounded.

'Jonson, what's going on?' Anna asked firmly now.

'No, nothing. Not really...'

Anna shook her head. 'Jonson, your nothing is never nothing. So, come on, what is it?'

Jonson sighed heavily, almost relieved to share his burden. 'Have you seen The Standard tonight?'

'No, why?'

'Oh, nothing. It's just there's a violin that's gone missing, that's all.'

Anna stared at Jonson, a man who was impossible to fully understand.

'What are you talking about?' she asked incredulously.

'Just that a violin has gone missing. That's all.'

'Right, and why do you care?'

'I don't.'

'Then why are you telling me?'

'No reason, really.'

Anna's eyes narrowed. 'So, why are you panicking then?'

'I'm not panicking. Who's panicking? Not me. I just think everyone should check, that's all,' Jonson uttered feebly, his voice faltering now, 'you know, just in case... they happen to have it.'

Anna said nothing. Just continued to stare.

'The violin,' he whimpered.

'And have you got it?'

'Me? No. No, I do not. Well, I don't think I have, anyway. Although to be fair, I haven't checked yet. Not everywhere anyway. Like the garden room?'

'Our garden room?' Anna asked incredulously. 'Why would it be in the garden room?'

'It isn't. But it's best to check. You know, just to be sure.'

'Right. Well then, let's check together.'

Jonson gulped.

Jonson opened the door to their garden room with a sense of

trepidation with Anna right behind him. He pushed open the door and instantly let out a yelp.

'What? What is it?' Anna asked.

Jonson stared at the desk in the corner of the room, where his guitar was strewn casually. Next to it was a violin case.

'Oh shit.'

Chapter Seven

'Yes, I can see that. But what the hell is it doing here?' Anna shouted. A logical question, but not one that Jonson could answer, so he shrugged. Gingerly, they approached the desk. Anna clutched Jonson's arm, and Jonson clutched at straws; his best hope was that he had the wrong violin. His reckoning was that the case appeared to be new, and valuable violins are old, right?

'You'd better open it,' Jonson suggested.

Anna looked at him oddly. 'What, why me?'

'Because you've got gloves on.'

'So what?'

Jonson tutted. 'Well, we don't want our fingerprints on it, do we?'

Anna grimaced. 'Jonson, you're such an idiot. You brought the bloody thing home, remember?'

'No. Actually, I don't remember. I was drugged, if you recall?'

'Oh, shut up. You were drugged, all right, by lager.'

'I did not have...'

'Oh, shut up and just open the bloody thing.'

A chastened Jonson picked up the case. It felt too light. He slid the two brass oblong buttons in opposite directions from each other, and the catches snapped open with an expensive sound. This was another good sign because surely a valuable instrument comes in a case that is locked. Anna held her breath as Jonson eased it open until they could peer inside. At nothing. The case was empty.

Jonson didn't know how to react. Unsure whether this was good news or bad, but, ever the optimist, he erred firmly on the side of good. It certainly diminished whatever crime he had inadvertently committed. Failure to hand in a case that had once housed a valuable violin is much less of an indiscretion than failure to hand in said violin. Anna, too, was searching for meaning and pointlessly looking to her husband to provide it.

'It's empty.' Anna stated.

'Yeah, I can see that.'

'Bloody hell, Jonson. What is it with you?'

This, too, was not an unreasonable question because such events did tend to find her husband. Jonson sighed and tried to think. 'I tell you what this is.'

Anna said nothing.

'Bad luck. I'm telling you. Bad luck. I've had it all my life.'

'Oh, thanks a lot,' Anna huffed.

'No, but you know what I mean. Because this is typical me. Of all the people on a tube train, I'm the one who ends up with it.'

'Well, that's the question we're going to be asked, so you'd better start remembering.'

'Yeah, okay, I'm trying,' Jonson moaned.

'Yeah, tell me about it.'

That 'trying' could also mean exasperating was a familiar joke in the Clarke household, but it had long lost any potency and was unlikely to raise a chuckle now. Not in these circumstances anyway.

'You'll need to hand it in,' Anna said curtly.

'Yeah, I know that. Of course I'll hand it in. I'm not going to keep it, am I? Result: I got myself a violin case!'

Anna didn't laugh. 'When?' she asked, taking Jonson by surprise.

'I dunno. I'll do it tomorrow.'

Anna shook her head. 'No, Jonson, you need to do it now.'

He glanced at his wife with a deliberate tinge of vulnerability. A look he had specifically perfected to defuse anger.

'Why?' Jonson added.

'Why? Because this violin is worth more than our bloody house, and it's missing.'

'No. You don't know that.'

'Er, yes I do. It says so in the newspaper.'

'Yes, but...'

The door opened, and Noah appeared, looking smart in his suit and cool with his Air Pods. He liberated one ear and looked inquiringly at his parents.

'What's up?'

They both exhaled hard.

Noah spotted the violin and frowned. 'What's with the case?'

Jonson closed his eyes.

'Ask your dad. It's his.'

'No, it's not.'

'Well, you brought it home.'

Noah's mind was firing now. One theory occurred, but it was pretty unlikely. Although with his dad, anything was possible. 'That's a violin case, right?'

'It's just a case,' Jonson scoffed in a casual no-biggie manner.

Noah stared at his dad, his mind still processing. 'Where d'you get it?'

'He doesn't remember,' Anna explained.

'Oh shit, not the violin?'

Anna whimpered.

'What do you mean, the violin?' Jonson asked pointlessly, placing his neck in the noose.

'The violin they're talking about on the news?'

'Oh, bloody hell.' Anna looked to the ceiling.

Jonson needed to step up now and establish some authority. Not to mention some blinking sense. 'Honestly, you two, panicking. Just because I've found a violin case...'

'Where from? Where'd you find it?' Noah asked, ignoring his dad's faux calm.

'Don't interrupt me.' Jonson rebuked him to buy himself some time. 'It's just a case. No priceless violin here, your honour.'

Noah and Anna looked at each other.

'But honey, you found it on the tube?'

'I don't know where I found it. I was drugged.'

'Have you spoken with Keith?' Anna demanded.

'Yes, of course I have. And the lads don't remember anything either.'

Noah continued to ponder. 'Bit of a coincidence, though, dad?'

'No. Not really.' Jonson parried. 'Violins are small. People leave shit on the tube all the time. Do you know how many umbrellas-'

'Yeah, but Dad, umbrellas don't cost ten million quid.'

Anna fixed on the new value.

'Bollocks. Ten million? It said five million in the paper,' Jonson reasoned.

'Oh. Well, that's all right then.' Anna threw her hands aloft. 'If it's only worth five million quid, then no problem.'

'Said ten million on the radio,' Noah countered.

'Shut up, Noah, you're not helping, mate. That's just clickbait. How can a violin be worth ten million quid? What the fuck is wrong with people? And anyway, whatever the value is, I don't care, because I haven't got it. All I've got is a bloody case.'

Case closed then, using Jonson's logic. But they could all see a gaping hole in his defence.

'Right then, sir...' Noah continued in his best police officer voice. 'And what have you done with the instrument, then?'

This stopped Jonson dead. 'Oh, shit.'

Sidhu Sharma was just as frantic as Jonson Clarke but for very different reasons. She squeezed her eyes shut and scolded herself quietly. 'Sidhu, what were you thinking?'.

What had at first seemed like a good idea had quickly unraveled. She ran through her possible options, all of them threadbare and none of them very appealing. At least her father was away on one of his many business trips. But for how long? Nihal would inform him, of course, and he seemed to enjoy explaining that Mr Sharma might even cut short his trip to Saudi Arabia. Sidhu shuddered at this prospect, and yet she held firm her story. That her violin was missing and quite possibly stolen. Nihal eyed her carefully. Sidhu had answered none of his questions adequately, and his doubts were obvious.

Sitting alone in her bedroom suite, Sidhu rubbed an expensive moisturizer into her delicate hands and breathed in its fragrant cedar and bergamot perfume. The bottle stated 'soothing', but in this instance it failed miserably. Not that her hands needed moisturizing. Nor did her face either, which glowed naturally and didn't require any help from the cosmetics industry. Her delicate beauty had long been another thing for people to resent her for. She wanted for nothing in life. She had youth, beauty and talent, and she hailed from a family of great wealth and power; empathy was, therefore, one of the few things in short supply for her, especially from her father, Sanjeev.

Sanjeev Sharma was one of India's foremost industrialists and businessmen, the founder and CEO of Sharma Chemical. His wife Prikash had been a model and flirted with Bollywood until she secured her prized husband and promptly retired. Sidhu was their eldest child at nineteen. Then came two boys and finally another daughter. The family home and business base were Mumbai, but the family were luxury itinerants. Mr Sharma had homes across the globe, which his family chased to and fro as his business empire demanded. London had been home for the last two years and where Sidhu had been happiest. Part of their reason for staying so long was to allow Sidhu to attend the world-renowned Royal College of Music (RCM) to pursue her father's dream of her becoming an elite violinist. And of particular appeal was RCM's recent announcement of the residency of Eleanor Heinzog, one of the world's most distinguished violinists.

Ahead of arriving in the United Kingdom, Sanjeev purchased and fully renovated a beautiful Georgian mansion bordering Regents Park. A white stucco double-fronted property, it now had a basement swimming pool complex, cinema and a garage for a dozen cars. It was undoubtedly one of the capital's most desirable residences, but it's grand and exquisite exterior belied the anguish that lay within.

Sidhu had been banished to her room while Nihal Khan took charge of bringing this embarrassing incident to a rapid close, including retrieving her valuable violin.

Initially, Nihal had spied an opportunity in Sidhu's latest drama and held off from informing his boss or the family's army of PR 'professionals' in the hope of resolving this situation himself. Perhaps his last throw of the dice to demonstrate to Mr Sharma what an excellent son-in-law he would make?

London life suited the Sharma family, but its one emerging drawback was Sidhu's distance from her culture and traditions. This is something he and his wife had clashed over frequently as Sidhu became ever more strident and determined. She suspected Nihal's intentions immediately and gave him short shrift, telling her father that he should never think of dictating her life for her. Sidhu loved her father, but she loathed his power and his control.

As Sanjeev's personal private secretary, Nihal was officially charged with the safety and welfare of the Sharma family and unofficially to be on-hand to take whatever blame was necessary to protect any family members.

Nihal thumbed his phone, waiting for various calls to be returned, calls he hoped might resolve matters and get his life back on track. But time was against him. It was a distinct possibility he would be fired and which might suit Sidhu. He even wondered if that was her intention with what he believed was just a cry for help of a spoiled little rich girl. Nihal had been with the family since moving to London, and this made him a long-term employee. Staff turnover was high in the Sharma household. Like all self-respecting self-made billionaires, Sanjeev was exacting and set impossible standards.

None of Sidhu's story added up. Nihal played her version of events in his mind. All bullshit, he decided; there was something he wasn't seeing. What the hell had she been doing on the underground? This alone was a sackable offence for the family chaperone. His career would depend on Sanjeev's mood and what resolution Nihal could present him with. His violin, at the very least! For those interested, it was known as The Carrodos Guarneri, made by Guarneri Del Gesu a year before his death in 1743 and named after its famous former owner John Tiplady Carrodos. It had passed through many owners but was most recently sold to an anonymous buyer at auction in New York in 2012, and it had been in the hands of one Sidhu Sharma ever since. Until now that is.

Nihal had badly miscalculated. His photo in the newspaper had changed everything and compounded his decision to delay informing Mr Sharma. In his mind, Nihal began to prepare his CV in case he could not present quick resolutions. Calling his daughter, Sidhu, a liar was tempting but not an option. But really: taking the London Underground for the very first time in her charmed life, and she just so happens to leave behind her priceless Guarneri. Nihal brimmed with anger and impotence. The sole consolation was that the Sharma name had not been mentioned in the newspaper. This offered him some reprieve, for now at least.

Chapter Eight

Milly assessed the size of the hole and thought about expanding it a little more. She wiped her forehead gently. Yet another beautiful day was in store, and, even at this early hour, the sun was already asserting itself. Milly was cross that she hadn't put a cap on. What would have really suited her today would have been a torrential downpour, that great tradition of the English summer, with planned BBQs being relocated to garages with the doors open. Milly had plenty of fresh water available from her newly installed irrigation system, but water from below is never as satisfying as water from above.

She backfilled the new shrub with soil, her hose ready when called upon. She sat back on her haunches to get a first look at her handsome hibiscus in-situ. It would make her wait a full year for its bountiful red flowers, but like a patient writer nurturing a script, the prospect filled Milly with hopeful joy.

Milly had long used distractions in her war against anxiety, and she called regularly on gardening. She always found an hour outside in the flowerbeds just as effective as anything big Pharma had to offer. When she and Elliot had squeezed into their one bedroom first floor flat in South Ealing, she had steadily filled the tiny space with anything green as a distraction from her failing marriage. Something about the hope of renewal and being able to depend on them. To see her Easter cactus bloom each year was always a fillip as Elliot sought his pleasures elsewhere. They were a passion and a powerful therapy, but plants' healing powers are not exponential. The inordinately expensive mature olive tree Milly planted last week provided no more succour than the Peace lily in her London flat every time it pushed out a new flange, and a beautiful white flower would unfurl.

Mitch also loved the outdoors but mainly confined himself to golf and BBQs. He knew not to interfere with Milly and her plants.

'You should wear gloves.' He smiled as Milly drenched her hands in soap under the running water in their boot room.

'Morning, you.' Milly smiled as Mitch cuddled her from behind, still in his boxers and tee shirt.

'You're up early.' He said.

'Yeah. Didn't sleep so well.'

He breathed heavily into the nape of her neck.

'Everything okay?' he asked kindly.

'Yeah, I'm fine...'

Mitch released her. He didn't believe her, but he didn't push because he knew what was upsetting her, and there was nothing he could do about it. Show business has a way of exposing the insecurities of all its participants, no matter where they find themselves on its ladder.

'I've made juice.' Mitch chirped. Juice was another of Mitch's things which gave Brenda one less thing to do each morning and was very welcome. Milly dried her hands and went on through to their breakfast room which had been laid out by Brenda. An array of fresh fruits, homemade granola and cold fresh yoghurt. A pot of coffee and Mitch's juice. Milly was living the dream, and she smiled.

'What are you up to today?' Mitch asked as he poured them both a glass. It was a deep purple this morning, so beetroot had been included.

Milly took a mouthful as her goofy husband still waited for her approval after so many years and so much squeezed fruit and veg. They were always delicious, but the surprises with secret ingredients were rare now. Milly swilled her mouth and licked her lips like a sommelier. 'Did you buy too much ginger?'

Mitch laughed as he shook his head in faux disappointment. 'I have a meeting today. A lunch, actually.'

'Oh, okay. Wait. Not with Cynthia?'

'No. But maybe because of Cynthia.'

'Okay, good. Who with?'

They'd had a few conversations since her unhappy meeting with Cynthia, and she had done some thinking of her own, of course. She called her old friend, Georgina. She was a firm *Fleabag* advocate and encouraged her to set a few days aside for a proper binge and to definitely seek a meeting with Phoebe if it was available. She had also read over some of her current work through Cynthia's prism, but her confusion remained, so she organized today's meeting: lunch with Hollywood's infamous Mr Albert T. Willenheim.

Late into the evening, Jonson walked the block one more time, hoping for something to occur: if not inspiration, then at least some further recollections of his fateful journey. Anna and Noah were at home conferring and no doubt besmirching his good name. As best he could recall, he was certain that he had not encountered anyone on the train. He did recall an exchange with a member of staff and that it had been at Ealing, not

Marble Arch, but he couldn't remember why. Perhaps when he was trying to hand in the violin case? But why wouldn't the guard accept it?

'So why then would he refuse?' Jonson asked himself aloud, hoping for an answer.

Because it was late, and I was drunk, he imagined. And a violin is not your everyday item that is handed in. It can't just be thrown into a drawer like a phone, and it might require paperwork that needs to be completed. Plus, it was late, Jonson reminded himself. The member of staff wanted to go home, and Jonson was trying to give him a chore. A violin is a suspicious item, especially one worth five million quid. Jonson was sticking to the earlier valuation in the newspaper.

"...if you see anything suspicious..."

Jonson grimaced at the incessant security announcements that grate and torment Londoners.

"See it, say it, sorted."

Jonson seethed at this glib phrase and the clowns who signed off on it.

"Sorted!"

So street and hip. So down wiv da kids. But Jonson reserved most of his ire for himself for being so stupid. Indeed, he should have heeded the advice of the announcement because 'seeing it' and 'saying it' are very different from picking the fucking thing up and taking the fucking thing home.

Jonson clung to his theory that a violin case was indeed a suspicious package. It could be concealing anything. A bomb, cash, drugs. Wild animals even, like snakes or eagle's eggs. A suspicious package all day long, and he had tried to do the right thing. He had tried to hand it in, and because of an uppity member of station staff refusing to do his job, he had then taken it home with him as any responsible adult would.

Back at home, Anna supped at yet another cup of tea.

'The chances of your dad coming through that door with a solution?'

Noah chuckled until he realised that his mum meant this as a question and not a statement.

'You still think that's the best thing?' she asked.

'No, mum: the only thing to do. He'd be mad to hand it in now.'

She understood his logic, but it still felt wrong.

'Mum, it's just a case. An empty case. I've been online; you can get 'em for buttons...'

'But it still belongs to someone.'

'Oh, so what?'

'Noah...'

'No, mum, listen, please. Even if this is THE case. You know, the case of the missing violin?'

'Right?'

'Whoever owns it, they're not going to thank you for finding it.'

Anna nodded at this logic.

'Er, where is our violin? Is what they'll ask. And guess who'll be suspect number one?'

Anna played out different scenarios. All of them troubling. But Noah's advice was sound. The case needed to be binned. To hell with ethics. Ethics would not come to Jonson's rescue, especially when his explanation hinged on being drugged or drunk.

'But not here,' Anna suggested as an after-thought.

'No, of course not. I'll take a drive. Somewhere quiet and away from here.'

Anna still didn't like it, but it was the only way.

'Who do you think has it?' she asked.

'I dunno, but not dad. And whoever the owners are, they're

stinking rich, so they can afford another one. Plus it'll be insured.'

'Yeah, I guess.'

'Bound to be. Especially if the owner is stupid enough to leave it on a train.'

Just then, the front door opened and closed, and a few moments later, a sheepish Jonson appeared in the living room. He had an air about him.

'Hey guys. Guess what?'

Anna and Noah waited.

'I've got it.' Jonson smiled.

'What, the violin?' Noah joked.

'No, don't be so stupid, Noah; why would you say that?'

'I'm joking.'

'Well, don't. Now is not the time for jokes. Not when your mum is so stressed already,' Jonson reasoned. He added a confident smile to demonstrate his calm and that he was back in control. Nothing to see here. Move along, thank you. But never mind gestures; Anna and Noah needed to hear solutions and appealed to him.

'I've figured out what we should do with the case.'

'Yes, go on,' Anna said.

'I just need to hand it in.'

Chapter Nine

B arry Shenfield could sense that his usual pathways were being obstructed, probably by some expensive PR outfits. But this is to be expected with something so valuable and only whetted his appetite. Blocked by whom and, more importantly, why? Barry sensed a bigger story beyond simple absentmindedness and so many possibilities which might be lucrative for him. To undervalue the violin by as much as half might have embarrassed other journalists, but not Barry. On the contrary, Barry was thrilled by his error.

Ten million quid is a big number: the preserve of the super-rich. Such people will pay handsomely for the recovery of their goods and to keep their names out of newspapers. Barry felt a jolt of excitement. But he needed to move quickly because other hacks would be on to it now, like scavengers to steal his kill. His man Nigel at Transport for London assured him that the CCTV footage had been stored, but he refused Barry a chance to get his hands on it. This implied many things. It could be a sign the police were involved, and this was now being treated as a crime. Or more likely that Nigel, the bastard, had a handle on what his information might be really worth. But no matter. He had out-witted Nigel before and would do so again. All just grist to his mill.

He skipped down the stairs of the entrance to Ealing Broadway Station. Barry pinned his success on many things, but chiefly he thrived by being ahead of the game and also by being direct. Every man has his price: let's just get to the number. Quickly, Barry spotted the member of staff, a middle-aged man who was probably younger than he looked.

'Hello. Barry Shenfield. I'm a private detective,' Barry lied, 'might I have a word?'

The man's face registered surprise and then a faint degree of excitement. Anything to pep up a job which depended on a ticket barrier malfunctioning.

'What sort of detective are you?' the man asked, which struck Barry as an odd question.

'The generous kind, if you know what I mean.' Barry smiled and might as well have winked and offered him a nudge too. The man understood, and his face eased now. Like a Fruit Machine with two lemons and the final wheel still spinning. Another lemon, hopefully.

'Friday night. The late trains coming in on the Central Line.' Barry got straight to it.

'How much?' the man asked bluntly, stopping Barry. A man after his own heart. Barry liked him immediately.

'Well, that depends on what you've got for me.'

The man gestured: plenty.

'Who was on duty...'

'I was,' he answered immediately.

'You were?'

'Yep. Saw every train come in... and every person off.'

Barry eyed him carefully. He had a sense of knowing about him, and Barry needed to assess what he knew and, more importantly, its value. In his pocket, Barry had five small brown envelopes, each containing one hundred pounds cash.

'It's about the violin, right?'

Barry didn't answer, determined to give nothing away. Everyone knows the first rule of negotiation is to start low, especially when dealing with people who are not very bright. Barry took a little breath to indicate a sort of reset.

'If you can tell me anything about a violin, I've got a hundred for you.'

The man looked at Barry quizzically.

'Sorry, one hundred pounds?'

'Yep. In cash.'

The man shifted a little and looked about furtively to ensure he wasn't being watched. He was tall and needed to stoop down a little to beckon for his payment. Barry grinned at the sucker and did something against his best instincts. He handed over a single envelope which disappeared quickly into the man's jacket. Barry beckoned for his information in return. The man took another glance about the concourse, and then he leaned in and spoke quietly.

'A violin looks like a guitar. Only it's smaller.'

Barry glared at the man, struggling to take in what had just occurred.

'I've got more info if you want,' the man suggested, but with a smirk now and obviously enjoying himself. Barry managed to maintain his cool and nodded his head to concede. Round One lost. Seconds out, Round Two, for which Barry would adjust accordingly.

'Well, that's fascinating,' Barry began, 'thank you very much for that.'

'No problem at all, and, as I said, I've got more. They're usually brown.'

'Is that right? Because I've got more also,' Barry hissed,

which stopped him, 'but only if you stop pissing about and give me what I need.' Barry was tired already of this shyster in uniform. The man pursed his lips as he considered his options. 'Violin like that, though. Ten million quid's worth of violin...'

'Five million,' Barry corrected him.

'Same rules I'm afraid...'

Barry liked him much less now.

The man pulled at his beard; so fashionable these days.

'How do I know what you've got is worth anything?' Barry asked angrily.

'You don't,' he answered confidently, 'you'll need to trust me.'

'Well, you see, that's a problem because you've just stolen a hundred quid off me.'

The man leant in again. 'I saw the man with the violin. I even spoke to him.'

Barry quickly fingered two envelopes from his breast pocket and handed them over. He stared at Barry coolly. This time he quickly checked the contents and then buried them in his jacket.

'A passenger found the violin on the train. He tried to hand it in, but I wouldn't take it.'

'Why not?'

'Doesn't matter. Lots of reasons.'

'Such as?'

'He was pissed. It'd been a busy night. Lots of drunks. Two women had a fight. One of 'em threw up on me. It was late. I was cold and ready to go home. I didn't want to deal with it.'

Barry drew up a mental picture in his mind. 'What did he look like?'

The man chewed his lip but said nothing. Just made a sound.

'What does that mean?' Barry asked.

'I'm just wondering something...'

'Yeah, what's that?' Barry snapped.

'If you're working for the owner...'

'I'm not.'

'Because the owner is likely to have more envelopes than just-'

'Listen, pal, do I look like I'm working for someone who owns a fucking violin?' Barry spat.

'What was it you said, 'the generous kind'?'

Barry hated this guy now. A clever son-of-a-bitch. What the hell was he doing checking tickets for a living?

'Listen, pal; I need something I can use.'

'Late thirties. Tall. Handsome. Cool looking guy. The kind that women like. Little bit of facial hair. Dark hair. Brown eyes. Athletic build. Smart casual, I'd say.'

'No name?'

Now the man smiled broadly.

'I can do better than that. Question is, can you?'

Barry scowled. This fucking guy.

'What have you got?' Barry asked, his concession implicit, damn it.

'How about his photo?'

Barry's eyes widened.

'But you're going to need to get some more envelopes.'

'For fuck sake.'

'And I'll need a little time to run it off. Give me half an hour,' the man lied. He had a copy of the image already. It was the first thing he did at work yesterday when he fielded the first frantic telephone call from central control. He looked at his watch but more as a gesture to chivvy Barry along.

'Come back in an hour, and I'll have a photo for you.'

Barry nodded, conscious that they hadn't agreed on a price, but he had a feeling that it was coming.

'Oh, and you're gonna need ten more envelopes.'

In the palatial home of Crown Prince Murquin Bin Sulaman on the outskirts of Riyadh, Sanjeev and his team were meeting some senior figures from the Ministry of the Interior about a new gas plant that Sharma Chemical was building when Nihal called with his rather awkward news about Sidhu. Nihal had gone through the correct chains of command and explained to his private business adviser that he really needed to speak with Mr Sharma.

'This is not a very good-'

'It's about Sidhu,' Nihal interrupted.

Sitting at an oval board table with almost forty people, Sanjeev excused himself and took the phone from his assistant. He listened intently while Nihal did his best to explain.

'Would you mind if we reconvene in fifteen minutes? There is something I need to attend to.'

His assistant led Mr Sharma from the meeting room, across a landing area to a quiet anteroom. Mr Sharma held the phone by his waist, the call still active, and waited for his assistant to leave him alone. As soon as the door clicked shut, Mr Sharma exploded in rage.

Nihal held the phone from his ear. He imagined Mr Sharma in-situ, his staff running for cover and hastily rescheduling his diary for an impromptu return to London.

'No, sir, I have not issued any reward. Absolutely not,' Nihal stated firmly, 'not without your authorization,' he added for good measure, able and loyal servant that he was.

'I am on my way home,' Sanjeev seethed.

'Yes sir, very good.' Nihal lied expertly at this, the worst outcome for him. His jet would be refuelling now, and his two pilots were plotting a trip, not to Moscow as they had expected, but to Northolt, the military airfield in West London that Mr Sharma liked to use.

Nihal's career now hung in the balance. It would pivot on keeping the Sharma name private, and for this to have any chance at all, normal family life must resume. Sidhu must attend college in the usual way, with or without the violin. Sidhu had missed college on Monday with a stomach bug, but Nihal was firm today that she must attend with or without her cramps.

'I don't care. You are going, and that is it.'

'But I-'

'But nothing. I have spoken with your father. He is so furious; I cannot tell you.'

'Good. Then don't. Because I do not need you to tell me.'

Nihal waved his hand in the air dismissively. 'You are going to college in the normal way. You must...'

'"Must". What is must?' Sidhu protested.

'Do you want people talking? Do you want to be in the newspapers?'

'No. Of course not.'

'So things must remain normal. You have a masterclass today, remember?'

This silenced Sidhu. With all the anxiety about her father's impromptu return, she had forgotten her private class with Ms Heinzog. Sidhu faltered. She felt faint as she considered options that were no longer available to her. Now that her father was wheels up, she felt trapped, first by her stupidity and then by her obstinacy.

'You will be driven to college; do you hear me?'

'No,' Sidhu protested.

'Yes, damn it. Or you can explain why to Mr Sharma. And you will be driven home again,' Nihal added stonily.

'I am not a bloody child.'

'Then stop acting like one,' Nihal spat venomously, 'because I am tired of your theatrics.'

Sidhu glared at him. *Theatrics* was a well-chosen word because it wounded so easily. Nihal had a look about him, too, as though he knew something. He was cunning and clever. He should have stuck to the law.

Nihal had spent much of yesterday securing a suitable replacement violin for her, as much to demonstrate his initiative to Mr Sharma as to protect his daughter. It was desperate stuff, but Nihal needed to demonstrate willingness at least. He had used various brokers and specialists to rent an appropriate instrument. It came with exorbitant guarantees and insurances, including that the instrument is transported in a private vehicle at all times.

Sidhu noted that her father had not tried to call her. He was likely saving his fury for his arrival home. Equally, she had not tried to call him to assure him and allay his fears. Perhaps she needed a showdown with one of India's most powerful men, who just so happened to be her father. She didn't dare to imagine his anger, though. Bringing shame on his good name would be high on his charge sheet. As yet, no one had dared to blame Sidhu, but her father certainly would, and she shuddered at the prospect.

'And so what?' Sidhu tried to assure herself. Of course, it was her fault, but what could he do? What could he really do? Wasn't the more pertinent question, why she should have behaved in such a way? And what part did her father play in her reasoning and thinking? But Sidhu's bravado felt hollow. His inevitable screaming and shouting, she could endure. And his sulking too. But he could indeed inflict great hardships on her, as her mother had warned, like repatriating the family back to Mumbai.

Nihal presented her with her new instrument.

'What's this?'

'What do you think it is? You'll need a violin, no?'

'But I have other-'

Nihal snarled, 'you will take this violin.'

Sidhu opened it and peered inside.

'I went to a lot of trouble-'

'Then you've wasted your time.'

Nihal glared at Sidhu.

'Five thousand pounds a day. Plus the insurance alone. Just for your information.'

'I don't care what it costs.'

'No, and why would you?'

Sidhu went to slap him, but he caught her swinging hand mid-air and applied just enough pressure to show his anger and strength before he released her. Her nostrils flared, and she hung her hand in faux pain before tearing from the room, with Nihal watching after her.

Nihal knew little about musicianship, even less than he knew about courtship and winning the heart of a billionaire's daughter. But his idea to hire a violin had been foolish and only compounded Sidhu's problem. He had secured an instrument by Emanuel Hoyer dating from 1867. It was an exquisite piece, but it could never be confused for a Guarneri: if not to the eye, then certainly to the ear of people who knew their violins. Today, Sidhu would have a private recital with the world-renowned Eleanor Heinzog, and, brilliant though Sidhu was, she could not make her instrument sound like a Guarneri. Nobody could, not even her famous tutor, who presumably would want to know the whereabouts of her Guarneri.

The Royal College of Music is located almost directly opposite the Royal Albert Hall. Opened in 1871, it is a regal and treasured building, and no doubt it both inspires and intimidates the young charges across the road, hoping that in the future, they might play in the famous venue. The RCM stages an annual concert at the Hall, a tradition which began just after the second world war and continues to this day on the third Monday of July each year. Former students, staff and anyone associated with the college are invited. Every year the event is sold out, particularly this year when Ms Eleanor Heinzog was confirmed as a soloist.

At college, Sidhu exchanged some pleasantries with her fellow students after her previous day's absence. She looked tired and distracted, which some friends noticed and enquired about, but Sidhu deflected easily enough. Just the usual pressures that come with attempting to become a world-class musician. Her year group was a collection of the best young musicians from across the world, all from families with very high expectations. The talk amongst the students was the usual frivolous fare, but they enjoyed the intrigue of the lost violin over the weekend. Sidhu fielded some awkward questions about her own Guarneri, and she smiled easily and held up her case. Not mine, thank God.

Her two-hour lesson with Eleanor Heinzog was a master class, not a lesson. Not all students qualified for such a privilege, and such access had to be used wisely because Ms Heinzog's patronage carried as much weight in the music world as the sound that Sidhu could coax from her instrument.

Ms Heinzog, too had been keeping up with the news, and, knowing that her student was the owner of such a fine and rare violin, she was looking forward to their encounter. A worldly woman, she could recognize a young person who was lost just as easily as a mistimed note. One of them was due today, a brilliant young violinist from India called Sidhu Sharma, a girl who seemingly had it all. Ms Heinzog suspected there was more to her story. Over her career, encountering so many such young students, she had come to recognize the signs of loneliness.

Sidhu entered the beautiful music room at the Royal College, with its high ceilings and central ceiling rose, bordered by the original and bold coving. An enormous marble fireplace dominated the far end of the room, but it only served decorative purposes now in our modern age. Net curtains were drawn across the full height French doors letting onto the expansive and pristine grounds, allowing a sheen of brilliant natural light to fill the room. Ms Heinzog watched her young student keenly. Immediately she registered some tension. Students are always nervous ahead of a masterclass, but there was some evidence of earlier tears. Her student's newly applied make-up was immaculate on her delicate face and framed by her magnificent thick dark hair. Sidhu's striking looks would serve her well, not that anyone from the rarefied world of classical music would ever admit to such a thing.

'How has your practice been?'

'Fine, thank you. I have been working hard.'

'Good. And the Chopin?'

Sidhu nodded. She opened her case, and Ms Heinzog strained a little to get a peek at what instrument might emerge. She was even a little disappointed to see that her Guarneri was present and accounted for.

Last Friday evening, Sidhu had started a predictable row with her mother over anything and everything: practice, boys, food, music, her proposed tattoo, friends and her life ahead more generally. Her mother's anger was really her father's bidding, and when she threatened to remove her from the 'bad influences' in London, Sidhu fled to her room. She wanted to smash her violin to pieces as a way to hurt him. The high arts suited Sanjeev Sharma perfectly, and he particularly loved classical music: its aura and elitism, the majesty of its sound, but also its history and the cache of the violin, the most revered instrument of all. She hadn't smashed it, of course. She was too frightened to do such a thing and too responsible. Her violin was a work of art and an important piece of history. Her father would never forgive her. Instead, she conceived another petulant and ill-considered plan. To pretend it was lost or stolen, to punish him and to demonstrate what is really important in life. It all seemed so logical in that moment, but it embarrassed her now, and she hadn't ever imagined the trouble it might cause.

Chapter Ten

'Some view, huh.'

Milly turned from the large window and smiled as the big man entered the room, only he was not so big these days. Perhaps his retirement had diminished him, or maybe Milly had just overestimated his size when she had first encountered him in the reception of the Shelton Tower Park Lane. Funny to think of that fateful time and how they would become work colleagues and quasi-friends. Close enough anyway for Albert to cancel their lunch reservation and invite her to his home. It was quiet and private, and he had his own chef in residence and a wine cellar to rival any eatery downtown. He shuffled into the room with his default irate expression and always-busy cloak still heavy on his shoulders. He still had so much to do and people to shout at. They kissed politely, and he gestured that it was good to see her.

'I thought we'd eat outside. It should be set up. I told them to set it up. It better be set up.'

He pushed the patio doors open onto his magnificent grounds. They were by far the most beautiful gardens Milly had ever seen. Pristine turf and beautiful borders competed for attention with sculptures and artwork.

'Er, wow.'

'Yeah, I guess. I didn't have too much to do with it. Just the bill, you know.' Albert breathed out heavily and seemed relieved.

'That's good. They've set up for lunch.'

A stunning dining table waited for them. Albert poured them both a glass of water.

'You want shade?' he barked, 'you're English: you can't be in the sun, right?'

Albert grabbed a remote from the table and flicked a button. A mottled grey fabric screen emerged from the marble patio until their table was shielded but without ruining their view. If Milly felt any guilt about her luxurious home, Albert's sprawling residence was a reassuring reminder that she had nothing to be embarrassed about. The place was bigger than Milly's primary school in London, which had afforded views of a municipal recycling centre and not the views of the Pacific Ocean that Albert enjoyed on his clifftop.

Milly finished her salad and freshly-seared Kingfish before Albert prompted her to move on from life and generalities to the reason for her visit. Entertainment or show business had dominated his entire working life and had been very kind to him. He listened to Milly carefully and without interruption, without realizing that he was still intimidating. Milly made a decent fist of explaining her plight without, she hoped, erring into self-indulgence. When she had finished, Albert considered her for a moment. He popped another giant olive into his heavy mouth, munched for a moment and then retrieved the stone. He scratched his waxy head with his bulbous index finger and fished out some errant olive flesh from his teeth with his tongue. Then he breathed out heavily, as though troubled.

'I'm surprised you're coming to me with this. Because I hate writers. You know that, right?'

Milly smiled.

'I'm serious. Writers are like, the biggest pains in the ass. All of them.'

Milly looked at him sternly now.

'Okay, most of them. The problem with writers?' He continued, and Milly sat back and settled in. Albert was a man who was unaccustomed to being corrected.

'They take themselves way too seriously. And they're needy. Even more needy than movie stars but way less valuable. You hearing this?'

'Loud and clear. But movie stars need great stories-'

'Oh, come on, really. Not this again. Who's Bart Howard?'

'He wrote 'Fly Me to the Moon'.'

'Okay, very good. Because when people say *Fly Me to the Moon*, everyone else says Frank Sinatra. Everyone.'

Milly chuckled at this logic. 'The old star system,' she suggested.

'That's it. The only game in town. Movie stars, number one. They're why people watch movies. Because Washington, Hanks or Cruise are in it.' Albert held up his thumb for extra clarity.

'Or Streep and Roberts,' Milly added.

'Yeah, yeah, fine. Then, number two. Directors. The filmmakers.' His index finger joined his thumb for company. 'Then producers. Even DOP's. They all come ahead of writers.'

Milly shook her head. 'No. I don't buy that. The cameraman? Really? That's not fair.'

Albert popped another olive.

'You see. Right there. That! "It's not fair!"' Albert mimicked her with a whiny voice and accent for good measure.

'Oh, come on. Because it isn't. Great stories are-'

'Sure. But they're not because of great writers. Stories just exist. They're just out there, and there are only so many. Come on; you know this shit already.'

'Sure, the seven basic stories.'

'Right. Just different ways of showing the same thing – over and over.'

Milly mused on this and her incorrigible host.

'Fine, so then why bother with writers at all?'

'Now that is a great question,' Albert shrieked, 'the money I've wasted.'

Milly laughed and snarled at the man who had changed her life. 'So then, I wasted my time coming to see you then.'

Albert sighed. 'But you still want my take, right?'

Milly nodded.

'William Goldman was right. No one knows shit. Not even me. That's it. All of us, we're all just hoping and praying.'

Milly took in the vast ocean before her. Albert chuckled as his staff cleared their plates and offered more drinks, which Milly declined, and he accepted.

'Movies are like fashion. Things come and go. I see these LA guys now with their tight pants, jackets and no socks, and, you know what, it takes all my energy not to slap 'em.'

Milly laughed.

'Seriously. People want me to take them seriously, and they're wearing their kids' clothes. But whatever. Somehow, it's a thing. Movies are the same. Tootsie and Mrs Doubtfire. Great movies. Great business. But good luck getting them made now.'

Milly nodded. Certainly a can of worms.

'And this new dirty stuff. Gross-out, right? What d'you call it, vulver? What you're really asking me is, should I be writing this stuff?'

Milly nodded again.

'Well, that depends,'

'On what?'

'Whether you want to get produced or not.'

Milly took a beat and sighed, 'and what if I can't write it?'

'What do you mean you can't write it. Why not? You're a writer, no?'

'Or I don't want to write it?'

'Ah, now that's different. You have options, right?'

'Er...' Milly looked a little confused. 'You mean choices?'

'No. You have projects that have been optioned?'

'Oh, I see. Yes, I'm sorry. Yes. I have stuff optioned, sure,' Milly said dismissively.

'Hey, don't knock that. That's free money, right there.'

Milly nodded but looked unconvinced. 'It's never been about the money for me.'

Albert shuddered and held his two hands apart. 'Ah, man. Please, not the craft.'

Milly chuckled. 'Albert, I am so glad that I sought you out.'

He shrieked with laughter, and Milly chuckled too.

'No, really, you have been a rock.'

'You're welcome,' he boomed. 'And if you don't move with the fashion. What then?'

'I don't know. Maybe, wait.'

'Okay, fine. But for how long?' Albert demanded.

'I don't know...'

'One year, two years?'

'I don't know.'

'No. You never wait. Waiting is dying in this town. And the longer you wait, the quicker you die. That's it.'

'That's a good line; I like that. You could have been a writer,' Milly suggested. Albert shrieked with more laughter at this absurd notion. 'Hey, I don't say things to make people feel good. You know that, right?'

'I do now,' Milly chuckled.

Albert waved his hand at her.

'Hey, your first movie, *Untitled*. You remember when I was setting that up?'

'Er...' Milly pondered this for comic effect. 'Do I remember that? Now, let me think...'

'Right. It was exciting. I was excited. Fuck, I was about to get fired myself, if you recall.'

'You're welcome.'

'Yes, thank you. And you remember our thing with the title?'

Milly smiled. 'Of course. You told me to change it.'

'Right.'

'In fact, I remember your exact words.'

'Oh no...'

'Dumb fuckin' title. Doesn't work, change it.'

Willenheim roared again.

'And what did you do?' he asked.

'I ignored you.'

'Exactly. And look now. I was wrong. So, Goldman was right. No one knows nothing.'

'But you knew the script had legs.'

'No. I thought it did, and I was desperate.'

'Oh, thanks.'

'But I didn't really know. Not really. I hated the title. I still do. It's stupid. But what happens? It becomes a thing. People want to talk about the stupid title. Who knew? Not me. It adds to the whole missing script thing with Carmichael chasing his tail. The whole Cinderella thing, yada, yada...'

It was not the first reference that had ever been made to the Disney all-time classic, but it still made her smile. She recalled their trip to Japan on the press tour where Mitch had proposed. The whole thing had been surreal, like a movie itself. How she hankered for a story now as compelling.

'How is Carmichael? Is he still golfing?'

Milly breathed out heavily. 'He's still playing golf. And he's still scratch.'

Willenheim shook his head. 'Jesus, I'd love to hit a ball like that. He's got the game, the girl and the kids. Cat got the cream, huh? Which is great because he was a fuckin' hopeless executive. No offence.'

'None taken. He has you down as his worst ever boss.'

Albert laughed. 'Yeah, well, that's a pretty crowded room, right there. So what, then? What are you going to do?'

'I don't know. But I doubt I'm going to go the vulver route. And you said-'

'Then you weren't listening. Pygmalion to Pretty Woman. Same story. Different storyteller. That's it. That's where you live. How do you tell the story?'

Milly smiled. Their two hours had flown by.

'You keep in touch with your buddies in London.'

'Of course. They keep me sane.'

'What was the name of the guy at your hotel?'

'Lucas?'

'Tiny, little guy. Middle-'

'Oh, Mr Mahmood.'

Albert snapped his fingers. 'That's him. Mr Mahmood. That guy was intense.'

Milly laughed.

'And what about the guy with all the hair?'

'Jonson?'

'That's him, the Christening guy? How's he doing?' Albert asked. 'Still got the hair?'

'No. He got old. Wears it short now.'

'Yeah, well, that happens, I'm afraid.'

'I'll send him your regards.'

'Yeah, do that. I liked him. Made me laugh, but without meaning to, if you know what I mean.'

'Yep, that's him. My first and best friend.'

'Good for you. We could all use friends like that.'

His eye line was drawn over Milly's shoulder. She heard a car pull up and park. Mrs Willenheim had arrived home. Milly turned to catch the latest Mrs W waving briefly as she made for the house with an armful of expensive- looking shopping bags. She was about Milly's age or thereabouts; it's difficult to pinpoint after the surgeons get to work.

Chapter Eleven

Sidhu spent the day fretting. She checked her watch continuously, wondering where in his journey home her father was. A journey she had forced on him and one she could have so easily avoided. He would be furious. Yet Sidhu wondered if the whole thing might yet bear fruit. She looked at her watch again. How long was the flight, and what was the time difference? Sidhu shuddered at the prospect of what could only be described as a showdown, but one that was necessary. They might not listen to her, but they would certainly hear her, Sidhu assured herself bravely. But such bravery felt hollow. She felt lost and alone. She felt terrified when she entered the music room for her masterclass.

Everything about Eleanor Heinzog was enigmatic. A world-renowned musician, she was a woman admired and feared in equal measure. A private woman, unrestrained by social conventions. She enjoyed the quiet. A maverick, eccentric genius. Ms Heinzog was precisely what people want and expect of a great artist. An affectation, perhaps? Observers could decide for themselves, but Ms Heinzog did not care a jot for anyone's conclusion. She had no children and had never married. She lived her life in the public gaze, and yet so much of her life remained a mystery, including how she came to be so wealthy with a fine home on London's fashionable Eaton Square. Her ancestry was colourful and complex: an only child to a Jewish Lithuanian mother and an orthodox Christian Hungarian father. Born in Budapest but raised in Berlin and then New York. In addition to her masterly musicianship, she was fluent in five languages and had a fierce intellect. Rail thin, with brilliant grey hair tied back neatly, her age was impossible to determine, and even Wikipedia conceded her a range. A severe woman of few words and economy in everything she did. Even her exquisite playing was a study in energy conservation. All her energy was targeted at her instrument and nothing else. With her piercing blue eyes and defined cheekbones, she intimidated naturally and easily, something she understood early in her life and fully embraced.

The only solid footing when discussing Eleanor Heinzog was her musical brilliance and remarkable career. It was all dutifully recorded and easily accounted for. Where she studied, her residencies and her recitals across the globe and for the world's elite. Kings and Queens, Popes, presidents, CEOs and luminaries from the arts and sciences had all been beguiled by Eleanor Heinzog. Her impending appearance at the Royal Albert Hall would attract music lovers from all over the world.

But everything else was opaque and mere speculation, particularly where her personal life was concerned. Her array of alleged suitors, many of them supposedly rich and famous, were offered as an explanation for her magnificent residence.

Less known about her though, was that her keen mind was matched by her insatiable sense of adventure. And so too, her empathy and emotional tuning. For all her accomplishments, on balance, Eleanor herself would reason that her life had not been a success. That her gains in life had not been commensurate with her losses and sacrifices. This reality made her melancholic and attuned to recognize similar foibles in her young charges. It was ironic then that her students so coveted her life and career. A musical career that would very probably elude them all, a reality that troubled her. They weren't yet aware that so much disappointment lay ahead. And if not their own disappointment, then their parents which in many ways is even more difficult for a young person to bear.

Sidhu Sharma fitted neatly into this category. The moment she arrived today for her masterclass, Ms Heinzog's interest was piqued. Her sense of mischief was rather deflated that it wasn't Sidhu's violin that was missing after all. Something, though, was wrong beyond the normal master-class nerves. Sidhu was evasive and avoided eye contact. She mumbled her greeting and fussed with her things. Usually, Sidhu was contained and measured, but today she appeared overwhelmed. Ms Heinzog, however, was more intrigued than concerned. She hoped that she might even share. There was a chance that it might be a better use of a masterclass than actually playing her violin, brilliant musician though she undoubtedly was.

The master waited patiently. As a rule, Ms Heinzog rationed her smiles: all part of the uniform of the creative master, as used by certain arty types who want to be taken seriously. In public, Ms Heinzog limited herself to a few smiles per decade and never on stage. And so this morning, smiling so warmly at Sidhu was all that it took to unlock her student before her. Like a lifebuoy to a flagging swimmer, Sidhu stared at the woman she admired so much, and then in a moment everything seemed to alter. Sidhu wept uncontrollably, making her skin glisten and shine even more brightly. Ms Heinzog was patient and understanding. A little ashamedly, she also felt excited and almost exhilarated because she could sense that the tearful young woman was about to confide in her.

Between sniffles, tissues and Ms Heinzog's assurances for her to continue, Sidhu explained everything that had happened over the weekend. That she had claimed to have lost her violin on the underground when in fact, it had never even left her house. 'Whoever found it. They only have a violin case.'

This was not as salacious as Ms Heinzog might have hoped for, but it was an intriguing explanation, and she was rapt. Their session was more like a confession than a masterclass. Ms Heinzog's one abiding question was why she hadn't just come clean and explain all of this to her charges and thus avoided what now waited for her at home. But her instincts were to stay silent and ask nothing, to just allow Sidhu to empty out all her hurt and woe.

'Even going on the underground... it felt daring and dangerous to me,' Sidhu exclaimed, 'it felt thrilling to be down there. And with people I didn't know. Just regular people on their way to places. Does that sound ridiculous?' Sidhu asked. Ms Heinzog shook her head.

Sidhu had left her home carrying her violin case and walked into the West End, finally boarding the Central line train at Tottenham Court Road. She chose a carriage that was not so busy and took a seat. A handsome man opposite caught her eye. It all felt thrilling. She wondered if this was how people met each other. She almost wanted to speak to him, but she didn't, of course. A bunch of exuberant teenagers dominated the space by the doors, all of them in continuing fits of hysterics. What could possibly be so funny, Sidhu wondered? Other passengers were visibly irked by their noise and general intrusion, but not Sidhu. She enjoyed their exuberance.

She felt envious of them, how carefree they were compared with her cosseted life. She was always monitored by her parents and largely confined to her home. And she was wedded to her music of course, playing every day without fail. She fingered her empty case and resented what it represented, the practice and the time it consumed in the hope of her joining Ms Heinzog's ranks. Sidhu nestled the case between the end of the carriage and her thigh, and she faltered. Her grand plan seemed much more of a folly now. The handsome man and the noisy kids had already alighted, and she wondered what the evening held for them all. Maybe something that would surprise them. They might go someplace and meet someone? Perhaps that special someone? The only surprises in her life were confined to generous birthday presents. Another beautiful watch or a piece of jewellery, which would quickly lose its allure.

And then, in a moment of clarity, completing her plan felt like the right thing to do. It felt daring and wrong, and it thrilled her. Sidhu stood up, leaving her case on the seat. Just having both hands free felt invigorating, and she walked effortlessly towards the doors as the train slowed into Bond Street Station. She half expected someone to alert her, to call her back, only no one did. Too engrossed by their phones, perhaps? She took this to be another sign of approval. The train doors closed, and she experienced a peculiar emotion for the first time in her life. She stood and watched the train as it disappeared into the tunnel, the tracks crackling and sparking with electrical current, and she felt a surge of energy course through her. It was as though she had given up her crutch, and yet she did not limp as people had warned her. This was just the beginning. All that was missing was a case, but it would become so much more if she completed her plan and reported her violin missing. Her unlikely way to make her father listen.

Had her resolution waned, then she would not have made the teary phone call and set in motion the chain of events she had never accounted for. Few people would ever understand Sidhu's reasoning. Billionaires' daughters can expect a scant supply of sympathy, particularly ones who happen to look like her. Nihal was rightly furious seeing his picture in the newspaper, and things quickly unraveled. All little girls growing up want to be princesses, and yet when she overheard Nihal refer to her as such, it cut to her bone.

Ms Heinzog listened intently, and it appeared that her stern face was softening. As was her way, she said little but watched carefully. Sidhu was certainly a stricken young woman. Her tears continued, but now with less intrusive and awkward sobs. As her story tumbled forth, the similarities between their two lives were immediately apparent. Ms Heinzog had never enjoyed a masterclass quite as much.

'I wanted to scare my dad, that's all. To show him, you know?'

Ms Heinzog breathed quietly. Naïve would be the kindest way to explain her actions, but few people would be so understanding. There would be only one interpretation, and it terrified Sidhu even more than her father's wrath. Sidhu faltered at the prospect of her identity being so cruelly exposed in the newspaper and how they would frame the story.

Spoilt Princess's cry for help. An exclusive by Barry Shenfield.

Indeed, Barry was busy putting this very story together before any of his competitors beat him to it. On the face of it, it was a non-story. A missing violin: so what? But the story of the owner and the beautiful heiress was where the clicks and the value were. There is always an unhealthy fascination and interest in the super-rich, how much they have and what they spend their money on. Who lives in a house like this or who potters about the Med on a yacht like this? Even if the violin did turn up, Barry was not worried. The story would just alter its course towards the poor little heiress mired in sadness. Chances were, he could expect a large payment from the family to kill the story. Every which way, Barry Shenfield would come out on top.

Ms Heinzog could imagine various outcomes from Sidhu's actions, and few of them were very palatable. She had not met Mr and Mrs Sharma, but she could take an educated guess at what they were like. People of a type. Qualified by their wealth. But riches did not impress Ms Heinzog. In her experience, billionaires tended to be ghastly people. Either the ones born into it or those who had conjured it for themselves. Too much money is almost always corrosive and corrupting. It can throw everything off and out of kilter and even for the most vigilant, by just enough to affect the soul. The person is alive, but it can render them somehow inhuman: paranoid and distrusting.

Mr Sharma would take any humiliation of his daughter personally. They were a family, and they shared a surname. Ms Heinzog mused on how this could be something in Sidhu's favour. Her mind continued to wander and consider until something dragged her back into the present. Something that Sidhu had said.

'What did you just say?' Ms Heinzog asked, taking Sidhu by surprise.

'Er...'

'Just then. Your parents approval?' Ms Heinzog prompted her. Sidhu immediately looked a little bashful.

'That I do not need my parents to approve of my friends.'

Ms Heinzog nodded. 'And when you say, friends. You mean boys. Men.'

Sidhu blushed again.

'Well, yes. My parent's marriage was not arranged, but there are ways. And maybe I don't want to marry at all. You didn't.'

Ms Heinzog nodded.

'I might be gay,' Sidhu offered, but not very convincingly.

'And are you?'

'No. But he doesn't know this. My father just assumes he knows everything about me and that he knows best. And so I should always do as I am told.' Sidhu's voice faltered a little now. Never before had she ever been so candid with anyone and disloyal, let alone to a person as esteemed as Ms Heinzog. Her listening companion reflected on this sentiment. She regretted that she hadn't married. Or that she hadn't married successfully. There had been no shortage of proposals. Illustrious men too, some promising to leave their wives and children for her. She should have married her school teacher in Prague with whom she had a fleeting affair, but her lifestyle frightened him off. Something she had regretted ever since.

'I don't even want to be a musician,' Sidhu sobbed.

And so the circle completes; Ms Heinzog nodded. It was all so predictable.

'And what do you want to be? If not a musician.'

'I don't know,' Sidhu sobbed again now, 'I'm sorry...'

Ms Heinzog shook her head, perversely enjoying herself enormously.

'It's just that you smiled at me when I sat down.'

Sidhu breathed out wearily. Ms Heinzog smiled again now to show her patience and that she needn't rush.

'I don't think I've ever seen you smile before.'

Ms Heinzog chuckled at this. 'I could smile more often.'

'Or at all?' Sidhu ventured. It was a risky joke and out of character, but the older lady laughed, much to Sidhu's relief.

'You asked me what I wanted to be?'

Ms Heinzog gestured.

Sidhu took a deep breath; the sort of deep breath people take when standing on the top diving board. The one before we jump.

'I don't know what I want to be.'

Ms Heinzog waited, sensing that she hadn't finished.

'But I know who I want to be.'

This chimed with Ms Heinzog. She liked this sentiment.

'Good, because this is a good place to be. And do you wish to tell me?'

Sidhu nodded. 'I want to be happy.'

Ms Heinzog pursed her lips. It was bland and generic, yet she understood it precisely. She also recognized Sidhu's dilemma. She knew how this particular ambition of hers would be received and misconstrued. To have so much and yet to be unhappy is, for many people, the ultimate sin. But Ms Heinzog understood it, and she admired her honesty and her maturity. She also envied her because her life was ahead of her, and she might have the verve to actually go after such happiness: the Holy Grail that we all crave.

With so many parallels with her young self, Ms Heinzog was determined to assist her. Self-made billionaires tend to be formidable people. They like to prevail, and, in this instance, Ms Heinzog relished such a prospect. Everything about it appealed to her. It felt clandestine and daring. There was also an unavoidable element of comedy to the manic hunt for a musical instrument that was not even lost. It presented itself like the plot of a bad airport novel. She saw the opportunity to play a leading role in helping a child in need and giving a billionaire a bloody nose.

'I will help you, Sidhu,' Ms Heinzog offered calmly.

Sidhu heard what she said and stared at her mentor.

'But how?'

It was a good question and one that Ms Heinzog could not answer. Not just yet, anyway. But a solution would come; they always did.

'You will come with me today,' Ms Heinzog announced.

'To where?'

'To my home, in London. It is quiet there, and we can talk. I can play you my Shostakovich.'

Sidhu spluttered at such a foolhardy yet enticing proposition, and, for the second time in her masterclass, she entirely changed her plans. But this time, her decision had much graver implications. Her father was on board his jet, flying home for a showdown with his errant daughter, and she would be absent. Yet her fears evaporated, extinguished so easily by one of the world's most famous and eccentric musicians. No doubt, her anxieties would return. They might even be exacerbated, and yet it felt like the right thing to do. Sidhu wiped her eyes, and finally, she was able to smile.

Karl Hibbert looked at the CCTV image on his screen: a man alighting from a train and carrying a violin case. An image that might be very lucrative for Barry, who was waiting patiently in the editors' office.

'Well?' Barry asked, his patience finally running out, but Karl would not be rushed. Not by a chancer like Shenfield. Karl was a veteran newspaper man approaching his retirement. As a journalist with a sense of pride in his profession, he didn't really care for Barry and his new breed. Barry was more opportunist than journalist, but he did have an undeniably useful knack for sniffing out stories. He had spent over thirty years in newsrooms, and many of his colleagues had departed already, many fired for saying the wrong thing or not saying the right thing, and the rest just burnt out. Karl had needed all his wits to survive for so long.

Barry's violin story was frivolous, fun, and welcome in a slow news week. More than anything, it was safe because it was unlikely to upset the thought police. This insight into the bizarre lives of the super-rich would allow everyone to share some mirth and glee in their loss. But this CCTV image was not a development that Karl welcomed.

'I don't like it.'

'What?' Barry held his hands. But Karl just shrugged, not keen to explain himself.

'Why?' Barry pushed in his customary way.

'I just don't like it. No crime has been committed.'

'We don't know that,' Barry countered.

'It's just a lost violin by some silly girl.'

Barry noted the assumption of the owner being female. This was surely a guess on Karl's part and a sexist one at that. But maybe Karl had some intel?

'And this is a man holding a violin,' Barry argued, enjoying himself a little too much.

'Right, so what? I imagine there is more than one violin in London. So I don't see the value in printing anyone's photo just yet.'

'Apart from the public service angle,' Barry suggested.

Karl scratched at his nose and looked directly at Barry.

'What the fuck are you talking about?'

'Well, where to start? Let's start with facilitating the safe return of such an important piece of musical culture.'

Karl grimaced. 'Fuck off Barry. And this helps the public, how?'

Barry ignored him and pressed on.

'Plus, there's interest in who might have it. It's like an unclaimed lottery ticket.'

'Well, not from me. I'm not interested. I couldn't give a toss,' Karl snapped, and Barry backed off a little. Let the man have some space. But quickly, a feeling of mischief caught him again.

'It's not because he's-'

'Fuck off with that shit, Barry.' Karl glared at him. 'Don't you dare come in here with any of that bollocks, you hear me?'

'What bollocks?' Barry asked.

'You know damn well what bollocks!' Karl screeched with his eyes on stalks, looking for anyone who might be within earshot. Barry chuckled and raised his hands in surrender.

'What if this bloke has got nothing to do with it?' Karl snarled.

'Karl. He's carrying a violin.'

'Yes, and last time I checked, that's not illegal.'

'Unless it's not yours.'

'And maybe it is his, huh? Have you considered that?'

Barry said nothing. Really?

'What?' Karl asked, pointing at the image of Jonson. 'That men like him don't tend to play the violin? Is that it?'

'Woah, slow down, Karl. You need to calm down, my friend.'

'I'm not your friend.'

Barry smiled as he retrieved something from his case and presented another image to Karl. An image of a man boarding a train, complete with date, time and caption – "Marble Arch station". Then he produced a picture of the same man in the previous image but now with 'his' violin. Karl studied the new image and shuffled awkwardly.

'You still think it's his violin?'

Karl ignored this, sick of being outmanoeuvred by him.

'Unless, of course, you believe in finders keepers.'

'Shut up, Barry, and let me think.'

Barry was grating, but he had his uses. And the story was better with the extra flesh on the bone. Barry would have no problems placing it elsewhere, and yet Karl's instincts still nagged at him.

'This still doesn't mean he's done anything wrong,' Karl contested.

'Yep, fine. We don't need to say anything. Just present the facts and let people draw their own conclusions.'

Karl bit his bottom lip. 'We don't state, suggest or infer anything?'

Barry opened his hands again. Absolutely.

'We don't name him,' Karl continued carefully, as though he were picking his way through a muddy field. Barry smiled.

'You bastard. You've got his name, haven't you?'

Barry beamed now.

'Jesus, Barry, you're like a bloodhound.'

'Thank you.'

'That isn't a compliment.'

Barry disagreed.

'Page seven, quarter page.'

'Today's issue?'

'Get out Barry.'

Another victory for Shenfield. A man on a roll. He looked at his watch and smiled at his digital timing. Plenty of time to get across to Holborn, where Mr Clarke worked. Barry was very much looking forward to meeting him.

Chapter Twelve

Jonson left his college early after a pretty satisfactory day. He'd had a productive meeting with a particularly troubled young student and his mum, and then a mid-afternoon fire alarm had called an early end to everyone's working day. Most likely, it had been activated by a bored student. Jonson called Anna to let her know his good news and to suggest that they might have a curry this evening. She hadn't agreed, but she didn't rule it out either, and he was hopeful.

'Excuse me, sir....' Jonson heard from his left, startling him. He turned to see before him a scruffy little man, and instinctively he protested that he didn't have any spare change. This reaction somewhat surprised Barry. He really ought to smarten himself up.

'Mr. Clarke, is it? Jonson Clarke?'

Jonson looked surprised now, and he did his best to adjust. 'Who are you?'

'Ah, excellent. Hello, my name is Barry Shenfield. I'm a journalist. Freelance.'

Jonson's eyes registered his creeping alarm. 'Yeah, and?' he asked cautiously.

'Yeah, sorry to bother you, but-'

'Have you been waiting for me?' Jonson asked curiously, becoming more anxious.

'Er... well, yes, I guess I have been. Which is lucky since you're out early. Fire alarm, eh? Was it a member of staff?' Barry joked. Jonson didn't laugh.

'False alarm, I take it?' Barry looked to the building that was very much not alight. Jonson nodded as exuberant students streamed this way and that, some of them watching Mr Clarke.

'So what do you want?' Jonson asked impatiently.

'I wanted to ask you about this violin...'

Barry carried on speaking, but Jonson couldn't hear him anymore as panic seized him. Had his body language been captured on film, psychology students would refer to it as a study in guilt. Unfortunately, Barry's colleague was doing just this, standing a short distance away and recording every moment of their exchange. Barry was tired of hearing about 'YouTubers' and their gargantuan incomes and made it a high priority to join their ranks.

'What violin?' Jonson floundered pointlessly, 'dunno what you're talking about.'

However, he wasn't fooling anyone, especially Barry, who just shrugged.

'Oh, really. The violin you found on the tube?'

Jonson shook his head vigorously. How did this little man know all this shit?

'I don't know what you're talking about,' Jonson repeated but more acerbically now and with a flash of teeth, but Barry didn't budge. Jonson considered making a run for it, confident that he could lose this guy. But scarpering would only imply guilt, and he felt his body language had been okay so far. With his good looks, in another life, he might have been an actor. He might even have starred in Milly's movies instead of just inspiring them, but now he needed to remain calm and deny everything.

'You've got the wrong bloke, mate. I ain't got no violin, man.' A statement which happened to be the truth, the whole truth and nothing but the truth, so help me, God. The same God his mum, Mrs C, prayed to every Sunday on his behalf.

'Is that right?' Barry asked calmly. Jonson didn't care for his tone or his swagger.

'Yeah, I'm more of a sax man, myself,' Jonson joked, but Barry didn't laugh.

'Only it's a very valuable violin.'

'Listen, man, are you deaf? I've just told you. I ain't got no violin.'

Earlier in the day, Jonson had counselled a student to be less aggressive in confrontations. Now he wanted nothing more than to punch Barry's lights out. Barry understood which videos would garner the most clicks, and he knew precisely which buttons to press. Indeed, getting whacked could be very lucrative and particularly attractive if the assailant is rich and likely to settle. Barry purchased a studio flat in Margate from the proceeds of an Emirati kid's embarrassment when he drove his supercar into him. Barry had obtained photos of him with a male escort and ambushed him with them outside Harrods as he over-revved his Ferrari. But he did not wish to get hit by Jonson. For one, he was too athletic, and, more importantly, he wasn't rich and worth going after.

'Fuck you, man,' Jonson spat venomously. 'Stop with your questions and get the fuck out of my way.'

Barry demurred a little now. He glanced at his colleague; he had what he needed. Jonson misinterpreted this and concluded that aggression really did have its uses. No one messes with Jonson Clarke, especially not a little fat man who looked homeless. But as Jonson started to move off, Barry was ready in true

Columbo style. Just one more thing. Barry whipped out a photograph for Jonson to consider. His eyes widened, and his whole body exhaled. Barry said nothing. Jonson was in no state to discuss it anyway; he needed to get home. Anna would know what to do. She would make things right. One thing was certain, though: his chances of a curry were now nil.

Jonson ran fast for the tube without stopping, something he should have done immediately. Barry didn't give chase. Not even in his heyday could he have kept up with Mr Clarke. He had calls to make anyway.

Jonson breathed heavily on the platform at Holborn Station, glancing backwards occasionally. Still ahead of rush hour, the platform was not so busy. He spied the board and nodded. The next train was his and due in two minutes. He thought of the photo and then peered at the domed ceiling of the station with cameras clinging to every vantage point. Jonson shut his eyes and wanted to scream. Once again, through no fault of his own, he found himself screwed. And this time over the small matter of ten million quid. 'Why me,' he whimpered. He looked along the platform. Cameras everywhere. Recording everything. Every nose pick and groin rummage. But also the thief taking a purse. Or the deranged madman who pushes a passenger onto the tracks. And, let us not forget, the civic-minded commuter who finds a violin and tries to do the right thing. Jonson clenched his fists and wondered over and over, why me?

Every week, diaries permitting, Mr and Mrs Carmichael attempted to play golf, with Milly only playing certain holes. This speeded things up and suited them both. Milly had just taken up the game and had only done so because the girls had recently caught the golf bug. But it was a devilishly hard game, and Milly needed to play on her terms. Having a target was key, so for now, she only played the par-three holes. They always teed off first in the day, and they raced around in little over two hours, leaving a full day still ahead. They headed for the final hole.

'Because that's what you've done in the past, right?' Mitch said cheerily. Milly's continuing writing trouble and apparent career block had featured heavily throughout their round.

'Yeah, I guess.'

'Right. And how'd that go for you?' Mitch gestured to their surroundings and the view of the ocean. The backdrop made his point better than any words he could muster. Milly felt ashamed. 'What about that other movie you wrote?'

'Which one?' Milly asked as Mitch teed up his ball for the final drive of the day.

'The car film? The movie about the Bentley?'

'*Metallic Paint?*'

'That's it. Great title. *Metallic Paint*. I love that title.'

But Milly was less enthused. A great title, but despite her many attempts, not a great script.

'It was a Rolls Royce,' Milly corrected him. Mitch huffed at her pedantry as he waggled his driver.

'Doesn't matter. A car that's worth more than the house. I love that. It's funny. And quirky. You should give that another pass. I don't know how, maybe update it. Make it more modern,' Mitch suggested, careful to avoid the 'V' word. Milly smiled as best she could. It was a quirky idea, but what she really craved was something new. Something to fire her imagination.

'And if not *Metallic Paint*, then something else will come along. Bound to.' Mitch now appealed for quiet as he thwacked his ball, and he smiled broadly while he watched after it. There was much to love about Mitch Carmichael, but his easy demeanour ranked highest on the list. He was, above all, a glass half full man, and whatever came to him was to be savoured and never squandered. The elevated tee box gave them a view of the ocean to their left and the beautifully manicured fairway ahead of them, sweeping away towards the white stucco clubhouse in the distance, where they would enjoy a coffee and a pastry together. Milly decided to reach for her driver as well. Occasionally she did hit on the eighteenth, a long par 4, and, infected by her husband's faith in her, today felt like that occasion. She followed her usual pre-shot routine. Mitch usually advised her to swing it easy. But today, he sensed the moment, and he knew just what to say.

'Rip the shit out of it, sweetheart.'

And she did. Her ball flew high and sailed over the bunker that usually gobbled it up. It was a thrilling feeling. Mitch's hoots of approval and their eventual hug was just what she needed.

Jonson stood for the first part of his train journey home. It would have been easier to stand and fidget, but by Holland Park station, he took a seat and grabbed the newspaper that someone had discarded with a dull sense of déjà vu. Just as the train trundled into Shepherds Bush station, he saw his photo, and his world fell apart.

Chapter Thirteen

Sanjeev Sharma had been scheduled to fly on to Moscow from Saudi to conclude the purchase of a gas plant, but this would now be delayed by his impromptu trip to London. His wife Prikash had tried to encourage him to stay at work and deal with things on his return, but with Sidhu not appearing home from college and being uncontactable on her phone, his decision now seemed prudent. The missing violin was irksome, but Sidhu's absence was another matter entirely. Unlike the violin, Sidhu was not insured.

Nihal waited patiently for when he could begin to properly explain what had happened and how he thought they should proceed. Prikash greeted her husband as their army of nannies fussed to have the children ready for a trip to Regents Park. Two security guards would join them at a distance, an initiative at Nihal's behest in the light of the circumstances. They would talk at length later, but for now, Prikash understood he needed to be alone. Better if the house were empty. Sanjeev had never been defied in such a way, and he wanted the privacy to vent and scream as loudly and as much as he liked. Sanjeev waited for the front door to close and then stared coldly at his private secretary. Nihal shuddered.

'A driver was waiting for her?'

'Yes sir.'

'And she never appeared?' Sanjeev seethed.

Nihal nodded, waiting for an appropriate time to begin a productive conversation. Sanjeev made much of his personal concerns for his daughter and her safety, but what worried him also was his family name and his honour. Billionaires tend to have more enemies than friends; how his would relish his good name being mocked.

Anna stared at her hapless husband. It was difficult to know where to begin.

'What am I going to do?' he asked the most obvious and pressing question. Retrieving the violin case was a possibility, not that it would prove very much. Noah closed the front door and immediately sensed something awry.

'What's up?'

Anna sighed heavily. 'Your dad's in the newspaper again.'

Jonson tutted. 'Anna, don't say it like that. Why would you say it like that?'

Noah grabbed the newspaper.

'Page 7,' Anna added for speed.

Jonson watched his capable son, hoping for some assurances or inspiration, a flicker of brilliance from the young man. His time to step up.

'Bloody hell, dad. Really?'

Not what Jonson was hoping for.

'Where's the case?' Noah asked.

'At the dump. I took it to the dump,' Jonson replied as a

thought occurred. 'Hey, d'you think they've got cameras at the dump? Because if they do...'

'Oh, so what? What use is it? It's empty, remember,' Anna reasoned.

'Yes, I remember that, thank you.'

'I'm just saying-'

'Well don't. It's not helpful. It's empty because it was always empty.'

'Hey, hey, you two, stop shouting at each other,' Noah admonished his parents. Jonson huffed impatiently while Noah mulled on possible options.

'There's only one thing for it...'

Jonson prompted him to continue.

'You gotta go to the police.'

'What?'

'Yeah, man. Be pre-emptive. Cos they're gonna come asking.'

'But they'll never believe me,' Jonson fretted, 'no one's gonna believe me. They'll think I've just stashed it somewhere. Or I've sold it.'

'Sold it? Who to?' Noah asked.

'Exactly. Like, I know someone who wants a violin.'

'Precisely,' Noah shot back, 'that's why you gotta go to them.'

'I think Noah is right.' Anna chipped in, and Jonson scowled.

'I tell you what, though, if that tosser at the station had done his job properly, then none of this would have happened.'

Anna's eyes narrowed at this, and Noah, too had an idea.

'Dad...' Isla called out from their TV snug. It was called a snug but was closer to the size of a lounge in a decent-sized London townhouse.

'Yep, honey,' Mitch answered as he made a smoothie in the kitchen.

'What's a Gownerey?'

Mitch finished typing his text, his mind not really focused on what Isla had asked.

'A what, honey?'

'A Gownerey,' Isla repeated, but this time slower and with more annunciation, neither of which was much help.

'Honey, I have no idea. You need to ask mom. She does words.'

'Mom!' Isla called out immediately.

'Hey Isla, come on, Mom's not here, obviously. She's taking a swim. So, google it.'

Isla stared at the television. Two shiny news anchors, a male and female, were smiling at the frivolous final story that bulletins like to end with. The cat that crosses an ocean in search of an owner who has to pretend to look pleased for the cameras. That kind of story.

"...and let me tell you, this is no ordinary violin. No Sir'ee. Unless you consider ten million bucks as ordinary.... No? Me neither. And guess what? It was left on the subway in London: how about that?"

"No way, are you serious?" his female colleague guffawed.

"Who does that?"

"I know. That's the question all of London is now asking."

A photograph of a violin filled the screen, although probably just a stock image and not an actual Guarneri. Isla left her TV show and walked into the kitchen just as Milly appeared in a robe with a towel wrapped around her head.

'It's a violin,' Isla said flatly.

'Hi, honey, what is?' Milly asked.

'A Gownerey. It's a type of violin.'

'Right,' Milly said, looking to Mitch for a little context, but he shook his head.

'That's what the guy said on the TV, anyway.' Isla grabbed a remote, and the small monitor above their kitchen island sprang into life. She quickly found the channel just as the item was being concluded.

"...so it's like a lost lottery ticket worth a cool ten million bucks that Londoners will be searching for right now?"

Milly's ears pricked up at the mention of London.

"But anyone finding it would hand it in, right? They can't just keep it." More laughter from both anchors.

"Yeah, but a violin like this. There's gotta be a reward, right?"

"You'd hope."

Huge laughter now. The laugh to finally sign off the bulletin. A perfect final story.

Isla turned the TV off and looked to Milly for answers.

'Mom, why are violins so expensive?'

'They're not, sweetheart. Just that one is. The Gownerey,' Mitch answered as Milly ruffled her hair with a towel.

'How come?' Isla asked, 'does it make a prettier sound?'

'Er, maybe,' Mitch began, 'I guess it might. But the sound won't be the reason, not really.'

'Why then?'

'Sweetie, that violin will be very old and very rare,' Milly chipped in, 'that's why it's so valuable.'

'Well, they're even more rare now,' Isla suggested.

'How come?' Milly asked.

'Because they've just lost one on the subway.'

Wanting Milly to share her joke, Mitch quickly brought her up to speed. Milly listened with great interest.

'It's worth ten million bucks, maybe more,' Isla stated proudly, as though breaking the story herself.

'Wow. That's a lot of money.'

'Why would someone spend that on a violin if it doesn't sound any better?'

A reasonable question, and one with so many answers. The prestige of such a thing. The bragging rights. An investment...

'Lots of reasons, but mostly because they can. Some people have so much money; they don't know what to do with it.'

Isla pondered this for a moment. 'Well, that doesn't make much sense. Not to me, anyway.'

Milly smiled. 'Good girl. Because that is the correct answer.'

'Maybe the owner has so much money they don't care about it being lost?' Isla suggested.

Milly chuckled. 'Oh, no, they'd care, all right.'

'Then why leave it on the subway?'

Another good question.

'I don't know, sweetie. Maybe by accident?' Milly suggested.

'Or they were just dog-tired?' Mitch weighed in.

'Yeah, that could be it,' Isla agreed, 'rich people must be tired because they have to work so hard, right?'

Mitch and Milly looked at each other and chuckled.

'Something like that,' Mitch conceded, hoping her questions might abate.

'Seems to be a thing, though, right?' Milly suggested.

'What do you mean?'

'That someone leaves a Stradivarius someplace dumb, like on a train or a park bench,' Milly suggested. Mitch pondered this. 'Yeah, maybe.'

'What's a Stradivarius?' Isla asked, and so their conversation began its second lap.

'That's another brand of violin,' Mitch piped up. This much

he did know. Milly tutted. 'They're not brands. They're not like Nike. They're makers. Violin makers.'

'Yeah, well, same thing, actually. If you think about it,' Mitch batted back playfully. Milly shook her head in faux disapproval and turned her attention to Isla.

'Honey, Stradivarius was an Italian violin maker. He wouldn't thank anyone for calling him a brand.'

'Yeah, well, he's not here anymore, so don't worry about it.'

Isla got her iPad out. Her inquiring mind required more clarity than her parents could provide.

Chapter Fourteen

The concourse supervisor at Ealing Broadway Station saw Jonson approaching with an attractive woman, possibly his wife. He recognized Jonson immediately and was curious and defensive.

'Hello,' Jonson began politely, half expecting the man to recognize him.

'Hello sir, how can I help?' he asked formally and with a tone that implied he was busy: stuff to do, so hurry it along. Jonson adjusted accordingly.

'Well, you might remember me?'

The man's eyes narrowed. Nope.

'I use this station a lot. Every day actually.'

The man breathed out heavily now. Busy station, pal. Anna nudged Jonson to get on with it.

'Right, but specifically last Friday night. Late. I came through very late, and I tried to hand in a violin.'

'Right,' The man replied blankly, 'who to?'

Jonson looked at the man curiously.

'To you.'

The man smiled ruefully. 'I don't think so.'

'Yeah, we spoke. It was late. Maybe 2am.'

The man just shrugged as if to say, 'I wish I could help.'

'You must remember,' Jonson implored, 'I was drunk.'

'Ah-' The man exclaimed.

'No. Not that drunk.'

The man shook his head again. He had work to do. Tickets to check.

'It was you. It was definitely you. We had a row, actually.'

'Did we?' the man asked somewhat indignantly, 'perhaps I should ask my colleague?'

Jonson shook his head. 'We rowed. I had a violin. You don't remember?'

'Like you said, you were drunk.'

Anna looked to the skies.

'I might forget phones handed in but not a violin. Maybe it was my colleague. Shall I go and ask?'

There wasn't any point, but Anna agreed, and the man left.

Jonson scowled. 'That fucking guy. I tell you, it was him.'

Within moments, the man returned with a colleague in tow. Jonson looked at them in disbelief. His colleague was female, barely five feet tall and Asian. From the Philippines or Malaysia. Jonson threw his hands in the air as he stomped off.

Sidhu had never imagined being in the home of Ms Eleanor Heinzog. How she wished it could be in different circumstances. Sitting in her exquisite drawing room, it was impossible to reconcile her recent actions with her current circumstances. She sipped her tea and took in the calm and soothing room. It was immaculately presented, with not a hair out of place. Towering ceilings above a solid and highly polished floor. Delicate antique furniture was illuminated by an enormous display of gleaming silver in the bay window, which was framed by heavy silk curtains. Ms Heinzog continued a grave sounding telephone conversation with a man called Gerald. Sidhu's phone remained firmly off, but in her hand, it still felt like a bomb, primed and ready to explode the moment she dared turn it on.

Ms Heinzog's conversation was unsettling, especially when she put the receiver down and looked at Sidhu mournfully. Certainly, she was less frivolous and playful than before. More like the old Ms Heinzog, who everyone was terrified of.

She chose her words carefully. 'That was my lawyer.'

'Why do you have a lawyer? Sidhu asked quickly.

'Well, he's a friend who happens to be a lawyer. But he's also my lawyer. It doesn't matter. But he's bright and wise. And he gives good advice.'

Sidhu nodded. 'Will he charge you for that phone call?'

Ms Heinzog chuckled. 'He could try.'

Sidhu was relieved to hear this. Her father was always complaining about his lawyers and how stringently they applied their fees. She was already in enough trouble without Ms Heinzog's legal bill adding to her woes.

'And what did he say? You said he gives good advice,' Sidhu asked, steeling herself.

'Well, a Guarneri is not an easy violin to lose quietly.'

'What does that mean?'

'An instrument like yours is very rare. They have provenance. The ownership of such instruments is always well-known, as is the case here. He's checking. But your father is already a well-known London resident, and he has a daughter at the Royal College.'

Sidhu felt nauseous.

'So, they know it's me?'

'No. But an educated guess and the connection will be made.'

Sidhu rebuked herself. What was she thinking coming here and not going home? Just prolonging the inevitable and making things worse. And it was all Ms Heinzog's fault. If she hadn't bloody well smiled. Sidhu grappled with her phone to turn it on.

'I need to call home.'

'Well, that depends on what you want,' Ms Heinzog said a little mischievously.

'What do you mean?' Sidhu snapped, tiring of her opacity and riddles.

'Well, firstly, I suggest that you calm down, young lady,' Ms Heinzog said sternly and dragged Sidhu's attention away from her phone.

'I'm sorry,' Sidhu demurred.

'In my experience, no good decisions are ever made in haste.'

Sidhu nodded, although time was against her. Her father would be home already and climbing the walls. Her phone connected to the network and began beeping incessantly.

'Some perspective here I feel is useful.'

'Yes, fine,' Sidhu accepted, 'but I am in a lot of trouble.'

Ms Heinzog shook her head. 'Yes and no, I would suggest.'

Sidhu's phone continued to buzz and demand attention.

'You have been impetuous and perhaps a little deceitful. Neither of which are crimes. And no one is dying. Not any quicker anyway than all of us are dying every day.'

Sidhu imagined this particular line of defense to her father.

'In fact, no one is even coming to any harm.'

Sidhu shrugged. Unless her father's spleen was accounted for.

'Well?' Ms Heinzog prompted.

'Yes, I suppose.'

'Right then. So there is no need to be impetuous.'

Sidhu imagined the pandemonium at home. And what example was she setting for her siblings?

'And easily resolved, of course.'

'What do you mean?' Sidhu asked.

'Well, you still have your violin?'

Sidhu nodded.

'Good. So then I suggest that you still have some time.'

Sidhu's phone continued on. Missed calls, texts, Whats-Apps and emails. Each vibration added to her anxiety. Sidhu glanced at the device. Like a stick of dynamite. Any moment, it could ring.

'Really, Ms Heinzog, you think I have time?'

Ms Heinzog smiled easily.

'Not silk or gold. Frankincense or myrrh. But time. Time is life's ultimate luxury. And yet it is what we all squander without even realizing.'

'Really?' Sidhu repeated.

'Yes, especially the young. We can alter a great deal of things in life. Our weight. How we appear. How we play the violin. But not time. No one has this power. Not the Pharaohs. Kings, Queens or Presidents. Time is a constant, and it is against us all. And anyone who understands this and embraces it has a great advantage.'

'How so?' Sidhu asked. Ms Heinzog thought carefully now.

'Well, consider when we play the violin: it is not just the notes that resonate, but also the space in-between. This space has no sound, and yet it is crucial. Without it, the music cannot be as exquisite as Mozart or Brahms envisioned.'

Stirring stuff, but Sidhu was out of time entirely. 'Yes, that's very beautiful, but how does it help me?'

'Ah...' Ms Heinzog's eyes widened. 'This is a situation with your father, yes. But more importantly, it is a situation about you and your life.'

'My happiness?'

'Quite. And I believe, with your actions, that you have accrued some more time.'

But Sidhu couldn't agree. Her urgent phone was a reminder of such.

'But the longer I leave things, surely the worse they will become?'

'Yes, perhaps. But only to a point. Certainly, you've been bold.' Ms Heinzog gestured to their location, and Sidhu blanched.

'But this was your idea.'

'Yes. And you can thank me later.'

Sidhu half-smiled. Ms Heinzog's self-confidence was admirable.

'Young lady, you must not lose sight of your advantage.'

'Oh, really, Ms Heinzog, but what advantage?' Sidhu implored.

'Well, when he calms down, I imagine that you will have your father's ear for once.'

Sidhu pondered this. Certainly, unprecedented territory.

'And there might well be other advantages and opportunities.'

'Like what?' Sidhu asked. She needed something tangible.

'I don't know. Unintended consequences. Things crop up. One never knows what might happen.'

'So, leave things to chance?' Sidhu scoffed.

'No: you are doing the very opposite.'

'What do you mean?'

'By being here now and not where you should be. You are forcing things. You are making things happen.'

Sidhu tried to interrupt, but Ms Heinzog wouldn't allow her.

'No, don't ask me what because I don't know. Which is why this is all so exciting.'

Sidhu's eyes widened. 'Really? You think this is exciting.'

'Absolutely, don't you?'

'No, I'm terrified.'

'But why? We have all the solutions. We are just delaying their application, that's all.'

Sidhu enjoyed the pronoun 'we'. It made her feel protected. And she even made it sound desirable.

'You have all the answers, and at present, you have the control of time. This is your power,' Ms Heinzog enthused, 'and you must use it to try and force whatever changes are needed in your life.'

Sidhu narrowed her eyes at such a prospect. Finally, Ms Heinzog was beginning to make some sense.

'Time might be infinite, but our time isn't. It is precious, and particularly so when you realize that none of us knows how much time we have. How much we have left of our one and only life.'

Sidhu stared at Ms Heinzog. The peerless musician and now the wise owl. Sidhu dearly wanted to share in her wisdom, but her father's crimson face kept nudging at her.

'And I suggest you turn that blasted thing off.' Ms Heinzog finally shrieked at Sidhu's phone. A small lapse of control and at odds with her spiritual healer incarnation. Ms Heinzog hated the blasted contraptions. The all-conquering ascendancy of technology. Creeping domination: first they were phones, then cameras, and now they have become an inter-connected life support system that people cannot survive without. She once stopped a concert in Vienna for a person who happened to be on his phone. She refused to play another note until the person removed himself from the auditorium. He happened to be an esteemed critic; it made international headlines, and his career was over. Sidhu turned her iPhone off, and with it, she immediately felt a sense of calm and relief. Her beautiful eyes now wet with tears. Ms Heinzog reached forward and took hold of her hands.

'It is appropriate to cry. Because what is this, what have you done, if not a cry for help?'

This pained Sidhu. This was an expression that had frequently been levelled at her. What has Sidhu Sharma, the beautiful heiress to cry about? And yet, put so by her spiritual/musical Goddess, for the first time, it did offer some comfort.

'And so we must make sure that you are helped.'

That pronoun again.

'And that you do not waste it.'

'Yes, fine, but you never say how?' Sidhu countered.

'Please, call me Eleanor. Where we are, I think we are equals and on first name terms.'

Sidhu blushed, deeply touched and grateful. Even the principal of her college referred to her as Ms Heinzog.

'Well,' Eleanor began, playing for time, 'no real harm done. Your father's ego notwithstanding.'

Her intelligent eyes suddenly sparkled as though something had occurred to her.

'Maybe this is a problem that only your mighty father can solve? And wouldn't this appeal to his sense of power?'

Sidhu stared. Her mind raced.

'He does like to solve problems.'

'Right, and this gives you power.'

'Does it?'

'Yes, of course. It gives you both power. It will make him think.'

But Sidhu fretted, thinking of how he always prevailed.

'Yes, he will be angry. But he will also be sad. What has

happened to his daughter? His beautiful daughter. The girl he has provided everything to, even a Guarneri?'

Sidhu winced.

'I didn't ask to be a rich girl,' Sidhu said sadly, 'and it doesn't follow that I have to always like it.'

'No. And I understand that.'

'Do you. How?' Sidhu asked.

'Well, I take it you wouldn't like to be poor?'

Sidhu nodded gently.

'And you said yourself that you aren't happy.'

Sidhu did not correct her.

'And if your father loves you, then you both want the same thing. To be happy.'

Ms Heinzog went quiet for a moment to allow the sentiment to hang before continuing.

'And for this to happen, he must listen to you.'

'And if he doesn't? If he won't?'

But Ms Heinzog dismissed this.

'And do what, instead? Sure, he can lock you up, like Rapunzel. Or take you back to India, even force you to marry. But at what cost, Sidhu? No man is so wealthy that he can afford such a loss.' Ms Heinzog wagged her finger for emphasis. Sidhu continued to soften.

'Will he do such a thing? If he knows he is making you unhappy?'

Sidhu shook her head, unsure.

'But my father does love me...'

Ms Heinzog seized on this. 'Good. And you say you have no power. You are mighty indeed. And nothing is missing.'

'But something is missing. Me. I am missing.'

'But are you in danger? Not from me.'

'But he doesn't know that. He will be worried.'

Ms Heinzog pondered this. 'And so you can contact him.'

'When, now?'

'Whenever you like, but maybe not just yet.'

'When, then?'

'Soon. When the time feels right. You can decide.

Sidhu nodded.

'Maybe not until you see him tomorrow, perhaps?'

Sidhu looked confused at this.

'Tomorrow? What are you suggesting...'

'That you stay here this evening. Yes. Why not? You keep doing the opposite of normal. Because the stakes are very high; this is your life.'

Her confidence was infectious. She made everything seem so logical and simple. She was a woman who had conquered the world and achieved so much. A woman who had had men even more powerful than Sidhu's father beholden to her. It was logical that such a woman should be so strident and why Sidhu should take refuge in her orbit. Sidhu smiled. No one was dying, and everyone could wait, her dad included. For the time being, at least.

Chapter Fifteen

Jonson and Anna rang the bell and waited. More vigilant now and wily, Jonson spied the cameras above recording his every move in their local police station. It was an awkward and confusing wait. He wasn't exactly handing himself in, just flagging his potential involvement in a multi-million-pound crime. Little wonder he was anxious. Bloody Noah and his bright ideas. After a few minutes, a tiny lady emerged through a scruffy door and approached the scratched Perspex screen, her eyes assessing what stood before her. She looked tired and conserved some energy by gesturing for Jonson to explain his presence.

'Yeah, hi. Er... I'm not entirely sure what the protocol is here,' Jonson began, in contrast to the confident and innocent man he wished to portray. The officer looked at him curiously. He was nice looking and with a kind face, but this didn't distract her. He was cagey and definitely had something to hide.

'You're either in trouble, or you need help. Which is it?' the officer prompted him.

'Okay, maybe both.' Jonson smiled broadly, but it was not returned.

'I'm here to report a crime. Well, not really-'

'It's not a crime,' Anna interrupted, and Jonson tutted. The officer looked at Anna now.

'This is my husband. He was on a train last week on the Central Line, and he found a violin. The violin-'

'No, not the violin. I found a-'

Anna glared at her husband and then waited for a flicker of recognition from the officer, but none came.

'What are your names?'

'Why do you-' Jonson began again, but Anna nudged him to be quiet. She just wanted to get this done.

'Jonson and Anna Clarke.'

The lady began tapping on her keyboard.

'With an 'e'. The Clarke,' Jonson added.

'Address...'

'We'd rather not say,' Jonson said firmly, trying to assert himself. The last thing he wanted was a baying mob of press outside his door. The lady looked hard at Jonson now, her brain finally processing the information and putting things in place.

'You said you found a violin.'

Anna nodded.

'On the Central Line. You mean *the* violin?'

Finally, a penny drops.

'Yeah. Afraid so. I'm the guy in the newspaper.'

The officer really perked up now.

'So what, you're handing it in?'

'No. That's what I was trying to say. I haven't got it.'

The officer looked pensive now and pressed a button on her console, which Jonson registered. Back up, perhaps? It felt like an alarm, the type you see in movies with bank robberies. Jonson half expected metal grills to suddenly drop down behind him and impede his exit.

'Well, where is it?'

'No. There never was a violin. I just found a case,' Jonson explained.

The officer let this ruminate and glanced briefly at Anna.

'You never had it?'

'Yes, that's right.'

'Mmm...'

A likely story confirming Jonson's fears. No one was going to believe him. A moment later, from the same scruffy door, a man appeared in plain clothes but with a look of copper about him. Jonson took him in and immediately started to make assessments. There was just something about him. He had an unusual look and air about him. His eyebrows perhaps? They looked interfered with and shaped, and his brow looked too smooth against the more generous allocation of skin around his neck. And he looked far too happy for a copper. This guy looked thrilled. Like he'd been chosen from the studio audience of one of those cheesy old TV shows.

'Mr and Mrs Clarke,' he gushed.

Jonson returned the smile as best he could.

'Hello, I'm Officer Dibble.'

Beware of a wounded animal is a well-known expression and equally applies to billionaires. Sanjeev Sharma was one such injured animal. He was in agony, made worse because this was unchartered territory for him. His lost violin was now forgotten. His insurance broker had called and joined the lengthening list of people seeking his attention. They would all have to wait. Sanjeev had lost money before but never a member of his family.

A housemaid laid down a silver tray with a pot of fresh mint tea and quickly made haste. Normally it was a drink known for its soothing properties, but today it was failing to have its desired effect. Sanjeev had already passed through the frenzied shouting phase with no desirable results or progress. He was really shouting at his daughter, but Nihal had borne the brunt of it. This was a stern test for Nihal: potentially a chance to demonstrate his credentials as a future son-in-law. But more than anything, he was fighting to keep his job; high stakes then.

Sanjeev was quiet now and pensive. He had worried that something untoward might have happened to Sidhu, but Nihal was quick to allay such concerns and that the police need not be informed. No one at the college had reported anything untoward, and the Sharma security detail concurred.

But still, Sanjeev fretted and seethed. He was accustomed to being in control. Nihal assured him that this was a teenage tantrum and nothing more. He was mindful of his words, careful not to offend or to suggest that Sidhu was unhappy.

'She was on the underground. What was my daughter doing on a fucking train?'

Nihal sighed. This was ground they had covered already.

'Mr Sharma, she is at a friend's house,' Nihal intoned as confidently as possible, but Sanjeev sneered. He looked forward to meeting this friend and, more importantly, her parents.

'And she doesn't call?' Sanjeev bellowed. He looked at his watch and made a quick calculation. His right eyelid twitched with fatigue and adrenaline, and not just at Sidhu's impromptu play-date. His new itinerary had him boarding a flight to Moscow already to complete this deal, but he could hardly leave now. Matters were out of his control, and he grimaced. Nihal took a call on the internal domestic phone line, listening carefully. Sanjeev eyed him and sensed a development. The family security consultants were at the park with his wife and children; he could intuit that this was someone unexpected. Nihal ended the call, and Sanjeev beckoned for information.

'There is a man here to see you.'

'Who is it?'

Nihal shook his head. 'He says he has information about your violin.'

'And Sidhu?'

Nihal shook his head. Maybe.

'Who is he?' Sanjeev snapped.

'His name is Barry Shenfield. That's all he said.'

The name meant nothing to either of them. Sanjeev hissed with anger. 'Bring him here, now.'

'Sir, really? Shouldn't we-'

'Do as you're told.'

Nihal hesitated. 'But sir, he could be anyone. Shouldn't we wait-'

Sanjeev jabbed his finger at Nihal's chest.

'My daughter is missing. Bring him in here.'

Officer Dibble could hardly believe his good fortune as Jonson Clarke came into his life: this was precisely the sort of case that he needed. He had recently spent a month off work with stress-related chronic fatigue, so it was particularly fortuitous that he happened to be at work in this police station at this very time. It felt fated and meant to be. Officer Dibble put great stock in things happening for a reason. In fact, his horoscope this morning had warned him to be on the lookout for a handsome stranger bearing gifts.

Mr Clarke was certainly handsome, and, having followed the story, he listened excitedly to his confession. He took a brief moment to play things over in his limited mind. They were sitting in a spartan interview room, just a box with pale walls, a table and only enough chairs for the three people present. Officer Dibble didn't believe Jonson's story. Jonson suspected this, but he didn't care. This guy was called Officer Dibble, for fuck sake. He might be too young to have seen the cartoon *Top Cat,* but surely his parents had seen it and might have suggested another profession for their son.

'So you never had the violin?' Dibble asked.

Jonson didn't bother to answer, tired of going over old ground.

'You just found a case?'

'Yes, that's correct.'

'Which you didn't hand in?' Dibble delivered with a sort of 'gotcha' tone; both Jonson and Anna rolled their eyes. You got me Sherlock. Perhaps his parents were Top Cat fans, and they wanted their son to be like the real Officer Dibble, who was run ragged by cats.

'I tried to.' Jonson began wearily. 'I've got the guy's name at the station if you want it. Nigel Fitzgerald.'

Dibble wrote this down and most likely misspelt it. He mulled a moment. He didn't know what offence had been committed if any, but he didn't care. The only important fact was that the missing violin was valuable and therefore gave Dibble a chance to get himself a bit of reflected glory. He couldn't wait to call Yvonne. Yvonne was the social media expert in charge of his platforms. Or his socials as some people now refer to them. He smiled broadly, and now Jonson noticed his teeth. They didn't look real: they were too bright and regular. They were all part of Officer Dibble's big career plans.

'Well, thank you for coming in today. We are still looking for the violin, of course.'

The officer seemed urgent now. Work to do.

'Good. I hope it turns up.'

'So do I. I have your contact details. And you have mine. I or one of my colleagues will be in touch.'

Jonson wondered who. Some other sleuth from 1970s Americana. Starsky and Hutch, perhaps? Given a choice,

Jonson would hope for one of Charlie's Angels. Ideally, Farah Fawcett Majors.

In truth, the police investigation Officer Dibble had referred to was non-existent. No crime had even been reported. But solving crime was no longer of much interest to Office Gareth Dibble. Soon into his career with the Metropolitan Police, he had realised that it was never going to be enough. He took no issue with the drudgery, but he couldn't stand the anonymity of it all. Simply put, Gareth Dibble wanted to be famous and by any means necessary.

In the last few years, Gareth had appeared on four television shows, mainly quizzes, in which he had not fared so well. But it was all exposure. Rather than exercise his brain to improve his quizzing skills, Gareth started to exercise and modify his body in the hope of securing a berth on the TV show of his dreams: Love Paradise: The Oldies on ITV5. The first series was currently filming at a holiday camp in Benidorm, which Gareth had narrowly missed out on. It was enormously disappointing; he had needed two weeks off work to recover. The producers didn't give a specific reason as to why he hadn't made the cut, but Gareth could make an uneducated guess, and he resolved to reapply for the next series. He would be leaner, sexier and crucially somewhat famous. Gareth would do anything to stand out from the slush pile of wannabes. He would be forty next year (although on dating apps, he successfully presented himself as thirty-two and with no complaints so far). He would stand naked and stare at his reflection. Work to do, for sure. Fat concealing pants might work for hook-ups but not for Love Paradise. He slapped his paunch. His moobs remained an issue also. Or two issues. Hanging low, they had stubbornly not responded to his regimen of press-ups. He had already seen a surgeon; maybe it was time. But his enhanced appearance would pale in comparison to him being better known, and this was where Yvonne came in. To boost his follow-ers. To take him into 'influencer' territory. And being the police "dish" from the story about that missing violin would be a great start.

Barry was quiet as he waited in the ante-room of the Sharma mansion. It was listed as one of the capital's most expensive homes, and yet here was Barry Shenfield, in-situ, about to lob a few grenades about the place. Barry loved his job. He almost pinched himself. He could scarcely believe he had been allowed in by door-stepping such an impregnable gaff. Barry smiled, peering at a wall mirror and wondering if there wasn't an ex-SAS killer staring at him. Billionaires have much to protect. They're bound to become paranoid. The room was plush but nondescript, with thick carpet, expensive wallpaper, a comfort-able sofa and a coffee table with an array of magazines, none of which interested Barry. He hadn't been offered a drink, but he didn't care. He hadn't come for coffee. An intriguing story was brewing with lots of unanswered questions, and Barry wanted to be the person to tell it.

Ever thorough, he had done his research and at some consid-erable cost. Nigel had been adamant that no further CCTV footage could be made available. It was unethical, he said. Contrary to data protection laws, an invasion of privacy and a violation of his employment contract. But all of this went away when Barry coughed up five grand. Every man has his price. Barry watched the relevant footage with glee as it displayed young Sidhu Sharma boarding the train with her violin. He noted her striking looks, always valuable currency in any story. She alighted the train at Bond Street, leaving her violin behind, but her furtive glance backwards piqued Barry's interest. The plot thickened. With Barry's cunning and the assistance of the world wide web, it had not taken him long to establish her identity, where she studied and where she lived, and his excitement grew with each revelation. Sanjeev Sharma was well-known in the highest circles of London society and was an enormous fish to hook. The challenge was landing him. He had at least managed to get into his home. A reward for the violin was an obvious angle, but Barry's nous sensed a bigger prize elsewhere. He just didn't know what yet.

The Sharma family would want their name kept from the press, and this process might be more valuable than a reward. Barry smiled. He held all the cards. It felt that the Sharma family was in some kind of crisis, and in moments of crisis, people make mistakes. Their PR team had already dropped the ball by allowing his stories to run, and Barry sensed further errors ahead.

Chapter Sixteen

Milly stared at her computer screen in disbelief. At Isla's insistence, her initial online searches gave up very little other than the most salient facts. But finally, the ubiquitous Mail Online put a little more flesh on the bones and crucially carried a photograph, not just of the violin, but of a man seen carrying it.

'Mom, is that Uncle Jonson.'

Milly's eyes bore into her screen. She pushed her head closer just to be sure. She clicked her touchpad to make the image larger, only for it to blur.

'Honey. Get me my phone, will you?'

Milly scrolled down her recent calls and quickly located JC. Her eyes turned back to the screen again as she hit the green button. A few moments elapsed for technology to do its thing. Jonson picked up immediately.

'Hey Milly, how you doing?' He sounded defeated.

'Yeah, I'm online. And I'm confused because-'

'I'm glad you called, actually,' Jonson sighed.

'Why, what's up?' Milly asked, hoping for a plausible explanation, but with Jonson, this was unlikely. She could hear his anguish from thousands of miles away.

'Okay, you're not going to believe this, but...' Milly's hopes plummeted. 'I'm in a bit of a bind. But it's not my fault, I swear...'

'Hey, Milly,' Anna chipped in.

'Hey, Anna. What's he done now?' Milly asked kindly.

'Yeah, Anna's here,' Jonson added needlessly, 'hang on, I'll put you on speaker.'

'Hey, Milly. He's in trouble again.' Anna, too, sounded tired.

'Hi, Auntie Anna,' Isla chimed, but Milly appealed to her now for some adult time.

'You can speak with Anna in a moment. But honey, let me speak to them first.'

Isla nodded. Something was afoot, and now might be a good time to grab another choc-ice.

'Jonson, tell me, what's happened?'

'Right. Not my fault. But I'm coming home the other night, and I'm a bit pissed-'

'You mean, like, drunk?' Milly clarified.

'Yes, pissed. English pissed,' Jonson answered with some irritation at his allegedly English pal, but now I'm American pissed too. Because I found this poxy violin on the train-'

'Not a violin,' Anna interrupted, 'Stop saying you found a violin.'

'Okay,' Jonson tutted at Anna, 'if you'd let me finish-'

'Well, hurry up because our phone might be tapped,' Anna said, immediately wishing that she hadn't. Jonson glared at her.

'No one is tapping our phone,' Jonson stated firmly.

'How do you know? They tapped Hugh Grant's phone,' Anna answered defensively.

'What? Hugh Grant, the movie star? You mean, the million-aire famous bloke?'

Anna could see his point, but she wouldn't concede.

'Well, this violin makes us multi-millionaires-'

'No, it doesn't. I haven't got it, remember.'

Milly's patience was straining now.

'Er, guys... hello. Milly here, without a clue...'

Half an hour later, Milly ended her phone call with more questions than answers; but this was often the way with Jonson.

'Isla, where's daddy?' Milly called out. Her daughter entered the room, careful that no evidence from the choc-ice would give her up.

'Where's dad?'

'He's on his lawnmower again. It doesn't even need cutting. He just likes driving something with blades.'

Milly chuckled at this.

'Okay, but he'll need to do it when we all get home again,' Milly said with a cryptic smirk.

'I was thinking that we might go and see Uncle Jonson in London.'

Isla squealed with delight, and Milly's spirit soared to feel Isla's exhilaration, and all because of her oldest and most incorrigible friend. Were it not for Jonson, most likely, her breakthrough script would have remained in a slush pile somewhere. Her writing career, meeting Mitch and having a family could all be laid at the door of Jonson Clarke. And now he was in some kind of trouble again, so Milly and her cohort were in-bound. It felt like the right thing to do, if only to cheer him up and offer her support.

'Go and tell your dad to get off his mower.'

Isla ran for the door as fast as she could until Milly called her back. The young girl turned and appealed for her mom to be quick. Whatever it was, it had to be important.

'I know you had another choc-ice, by the way.'

Isla's face fell. Her mom was a witch. There could be no other explanation.

As Barry was led through the billionaire's home, his eyes were on stalks at the Artworks, some of which he thought he recognized. The lady leading the way was quiet and efficient. Finally, she came to a large set of double doors, and she paused. She turned briefly as though to see if Barry was ready. Barry smiled easily. Let's do it, baby. She pushed the doors open and stood aside for Barry to enter. Barry charged through confidently. Sure enough, Audi Man, Mr Smooth, was present but so too was the man himself. Barry's jaw slackened. Fuck me.

'Who are you?' Sanjeev shouted aggressively.

What, no pleasantries. And still no drink? 'Hello, Mr Sharma. An honour to meet you, sir. Barry Shenfield, sir.'

Barry held out his hand, but it might as well have been his dick.

'Who are you?' Nihal demanded.

'I'm a private detective,' Barry lied, deciding it would be a much better option than journalist. Barry reached into his right-hand pocket where he kept his 'detective' business cards and handed one to both gentlemen present.

'Where is my daughter?' Sanjeev hissed, casting Barry's cheap card aside. Nihal bristled at his boss's indiscretion, but he didn't say anything.

'I am afraid I have no idea,' Barry answered truthfully, adding this juicy new morsel of information to his story.

'Then why are you here in my fucking house?' Sanjeev spat.

Barry nodded. He was not entirely surprised by his venom or vernacular. The poor man: first his priceless violin and now his daughter. But his anger suited Barry. Angry people are easier to manipulate.

'Because I would like to offer my assistance to you in this difficult and sensitive time.'

Barry had rehearsed this line and deliberately chosen the word sensitive.

Nihal felt threatened, and he scoffed. 'Don't waste our time with your faux sincerity,' he spat. Barry looked at Audi Man coldly.

'Sorry, you are?' Barry asked, 'I know who Mr Sharma is, but I didn't catch your name.'

'My name is Nihal. I am Mr Sharma's assistant.'

'Well... Nihal. I can see how busy you both are, and I will not insult you by wasting your valuable time. Whilst your insinuation is rude, it is not entirely without substance-'

'What do you want?' Nihal shouted.

'The same as you. To help Mr Sharma. To make all of this go away.' Barry deliberately left his daughter's name out of it. Too sensitive.

'How dare you come here,' Nihal spat.

'Sir, if I could finish?' Barry appealed directly to Mr Sharma, whose snarl remained, but he had a look of curiosity as well. To Nihal's dismay, he gestured for him to continue.

'Thank you, sir. With respect to you both, I am a difficult professional to categorize. I know people. I know how things work. And I can get things done, quietly.'

By now, Nihal had heard enough. 'Get out. How dare you. You think you can come in to this house-'

But Sanjeev stopped him again with a cold stare, which he now trained on Barry. He was desperate, and his patience was thinning.

'Let me help you. I'm assuming that your family's privacy is paramount,' Barry continued, which hit a nerve. Sanjeev stared hard at him, his eyes narrowing.

'And what exactly can you do about it?' Sanjeev barked.

Barry smiled and added a little shrug. The way a magician might when asked for his secrets.

'Mr Sharma-' Nihal protested.

'Shut up.'

'But sir-'

Mr Sharma now reverted to his own language and fired some acidic speech at his employee. Nihal stood down, and Sanjeev turned his gaze towards Barry once again. Sharma's mind was a flurry with Sidhu's absence, his deal in Moscow and not forgetting his ten million quid fiddle. His expensive PR team had been less than useless, and here was this scruffy bloke inside his house. But it occurred to him that such a man might have his uses.

'I know people. I can get-'

'For what?' Sanjeev asked curtly.

Nihal could scarcely believe his ears. Barry adjusted his footing. Even in his wildest dreams, he hadn't imagined negotiating with Sharma. But Barry lived for moments like this, and he remained calm. He had done his research. For men like Sharma, kidnapping is their worst fear. Such a thing would be out of Barry's league, but he suspected that this was just a petulant strop by a confused young girl. But just like a kidnapper, however, Barry was happy to take this rich dude for some cash. And to think this whole angle of his had just been speculative. But Barry needed to strike now, and he was about to, but for an almighty row that erupted between the two men and in their own language.

Barry waited patiently and could barely contain his excitement. Although he could not understand a word between them, he sensed a connection with the big man. At one point Sanjeev crashed his fists onto his desk and then swiped right and left in true Hollywood style, sending the contents flying, including a glass statue, which Nihal leapt and acrobatically clutched out of the air. Brilliantly caught in the slips and an indication that this was no ordinary paperweight. What fun, Barry thought. Nihal placed the item down gingerly as their exchange resumed. Sanjeev aggressive. Nihal conciliatory and respectful but no less forceful. Amazing the universality of body language, Barry marveled. Finally, after a few minutes, Sanjeev raised his hand for silence. He looked shaken as he turned his attention to their visitor. Barry smiled. People always underestimate the power and the value of a smile.

'You will report to Nihal and no one else,' Sanjeev seethed.

Barry demurred a little. He was excited but also a little wary at the absence of any due payment being mentioned.

'We will see how you can get things done,' Sanjeev spat dismissively.

Barry baulked now.

'You want paying, I assume?' Sanjeev sneered as Nihal continued to shift.

'Well, you know, a man's gotta eat.'

Sanjeev nodded, his mind calculating.

'What I will need is-'

'You do not negotiate with me. How fucking dare you!' Sanjeev bellowed and slammed his desk once more.

'Give him your details,' he instructed with a wave of his jeweled hand. Barry flapped for another card, and this time, a plastic one.

'How much-'

'Shut up,' Nihal spat. Sanjeev eyed the man carefully.

'Judging by the look of you, this will be enough. You work for me now. And no one else. Now get out.'

They exchanged details, and Barry exited the building in a blur. Along from the property, he noticed the large Audi with two men in the front. Behind it was a smart, sleek people carrier decanting an Indian family. Barry got to the Euston Road and hailed a black cab. It was an expensive mode of transport, but Barry liked to support the working man, plus he had an idea that he could now afford it.

Not until he was ensconced in the taxi did he dare to retrieve his phone from his breast pocket. Not to check his bank balance – too soon, surely – but to check that his recording app was still whirring away. Indeed it was. Barry smiled gleefully.

'Where to mate?' the driver asked for the second time; even with his meter running, he was a little impatient.

'Oh, yes, sorry, mate. Brick Lane, please.' Barry instructed. He had a number of contacts along from Brick Lane who could do quick translations. Thanks for the job offer Mr Sharma, but Barry Shenfield works solo. He sat back and breathed easily.

Chapter Seventeen

Noah plonked the beers down, and Jonson grabbed his hungrily. This was his first drink since his disastrous Friday night, adding to the occasion of being in his local pub with his eldest son.

'Where's the crisps?' Jonson asked.

'You didn't say you wanted crisps.'

'No, because it's obvious. We're having a pint. We're going to need crisps.'

Noah tutted. 'Fine. What flavour?'

'I don't care. Surprise me.'

Jonson slurped his beer again. He loved being in the pub, but particularly with his son. Noah threw two bags onto the table.

'Three quid. Can you believe that?'

Jonson chuckled as he opened both bags and laid them open in sharing mode.

'So, how you been then?' Jonson asked more generally but with enough inference for Noah to realize that their 'pint' had a purpose, namely his future. Noah gave his dad a weary look.

Everything would be reported back to Anna, of course, so she might as well have joined them.

'Yeah, you know. Pretty good.'

Jonson waited patiently.

'Football's going well.'

Noah had decided against attending university, which Anna worried about. Naturally, Jonson agreed with her, but privately he sided with his son. It was their little secret but meant he felt an extra responsibility over Noah's next move.

'Other than football,' Jonson prodded, knowing he couldn't go back to Anna empty-handed. Noah sighed.

'Dad, it's difficult, you know. I'm going to travel. Thailand and then down to Oz...'

Jonson glazed over at this. Great news, Anna. The boy wants to travel. Last time he checked, there were no vacancies for travel writers, and there was no shortage of Instagram accounts depicting beautiful beaches.

'And what about your music?' Jonson finally asked.

'Yeah, you know.' Noah shrugged.

'No, not really. What does that mean?' Jonson asked. 'Come on; I can't take travelling back to Mum.'

Music was one thing his parents were united on.

'You don't have to be a teacher,' Jonson began.

'Yes, dad. I know that. I don't have to be a teacher. But that's likely what I'll end up doing.'

'Right, but you won't know that unless-'

'Dad, how many times? I get it. Unless I try, right?'

Jonson understood his pain and took a moment. 'Listen, son, the thing is-'

'Is that I'm just not that good,' Noah stated and gestured with his hands, 'not like you and mum think I am, anyway.'

'That's bullshit. You play beautifully.'

'Dad, to you, I play beautifully. But I'm a better footballer than pianist, and you're not telling me to try football again.'

'No, because it's so tough.'

'Oh, and you think music isn't? Dad, there are kids who play all day. Every day. That's all they do.'

'I know that. And we're not expecting you to be a concert pianist.'

'Good. Because I've got more chance of playing for Arsenal.'

'Right, and we're not saying you'll be the next Billy Joel...'

'So, what then? Becoming a teacher?'

Jonson tutted heavily. 'It's just a wonderful thing, that's all. And who knows where it might lead?'

'And I'm not giving up. I love my piano. But it's just a hobby.'

'Okay, fine.' Jonson raised his hand. 'But your mum's been on about university again-'

'Ah, man'

'Yeah, well, maybe she's right. She normally is.'

Noah didn't respond.

'Well, anyway, you're gonna need a plan. And good ideas. Not travelling. Or else we're both in the shit.'

Noah chuckled. 'So this is about you then?'

Jonson laughed. 'Hey, listen, I'm still figuring shit out. I got lucky when I met your mum.'

'And anyway, speaking of music?' Noah asked.

Jonson finished his pint. 'What?'

Noah tutted. 'How's the violin?'

Jonson grimaced. 'You see what you've done there?'

'What's that?'

'Here we are; father and son having a pint, and you've gone and ruined it. What is wrong with you?'

Noah chuckled.

. . .

On their flight to the United Kingdom, Milly read the document that she had been working on for the last hour or so. It wasn't a script per se but more like a series of ideas that had been percolating for a while, and she had rather hoped that one or two might have evolved into something a little weightier. But nothing really leapt out. They all felt a little forced or contrived, and none of them were 'vulver', so Cynthia would be disappointed. Milly closed her laptop, determined not to feel despondent. Mitch and the girls were all watching movies. Isla had chosen a Tom Holland film, but Mary remained loyal to Zac Efron, while her husband was enthralled watching Gerard Butler wage a one-man war and somehow winning. Mitch hadn't taken any persuading to take the impromptu trip. It had been two years and was overdue. It was his idea to surprise Jonson and Anna. The prospect of seeing Jonson's face would make the long flight seem shorter. Surprising people is one of life's great joys, and now it even sparked a neat idea. Milly wondered. She opened her laptop again and began to type.

Sidhu re-wrote her text one more time.

"Hi, Mum and Dad, it's me. You'll be angry, I know, but I am fine. I am with a friend, and I am going to stay the night. Please don't worry, because I am safe and well. I just need to figure some things out. And please don't worry about the violin either. It has all been a big mix up.'

Ms Heinzog insisted on reading it before it was dispatched to ensure that Sidhu hadn't re-inserted another power-sapping apology. Now was not the time to cede any hard-fought gains.

'Can I?' Ms Heinzog asked. Sidhu nodded and watched her add a line of text before firing it on its way and then passing the phone back. Sidhu read it and blanched.

"I love you both, S x"

Just four short words, and yet so powerful.

'Now turn it off again before they call you.'

Sidhu duly obeyed.

'Happy now?' Ms Heinzog beamed.

'He will be so furious-'

'Yes, and we have discussed this already. And what can he do?'

Sidhu tilted her head and widened her eyes.

'Er, he can shout at-'

'Fine. Then I will go with you. Do you think he will shout at me?'

Sidhu chuckled at such a prospect.

'He had better not.'

Sidhu stared in wonder at the tiny but extraordinary lady before her. Battle-hardened and formidable. No one in her experience had ever faced down her father. No one.

'Now, I am starving. And you must be too.'

Sidhu nodded. 'Yes, I'm famished.'

'Good. Then, let's eat. Is there anything you don't eat?' Ms Heinzog asked.

'Er... beef.'

'Oh, yes, of course. But you do eat fish?'

Sidhu nodded.

'Excellent. We will eat, and then we will play together. When I finally meet your father, I will assure him that you are now an even better musician.'

Sidhu smiled. Finally, Ms Heinzog had said something which made perfect sense.

Sanjeev Sharma read Sidhu's text on his wife's phone again. If it was good news, then he did not let on. It appeared that Nihal had been correct. It was certainly good timing for his trip to

Moscow, which he now might not need to postpone after all. The deal had been in negotiation for years. The copper mine would still be there if he missed the trip, but its owners would think less of him for postponing something so important. His wife Prikash wept quietly, and he tried to console her as best he could.

Barry could not contain himself any longer and logged on to his online banking as the taxi neared his destination. He spied his balance, and he yelped like a child on Santa's knee. Mr Sharma might be used to buying people, but he hadn't encountered an alley cat like Barry before. His money was welcome, but Barry saw it more as a down payment with more to come.

'Anywhere, special?' the driver called out as he neared Brick Lane.

'Er, anywhere here is fine, pal. Thanks.'

Barry gathered his belongings and fished in his wallet. The taxi had card payment facilities, but the driver would prefer cash, so Barry pulled out two twenties and a ten.

'You can keep that mate.'

'That's great, pal. Thanks very much.'

Barry smiled. Happy to spread the love. He could afford it, after all.

Vippin Singh ran a number of businesses from his long-standing family newsagents shop a little along from Brick Lane. He had inherited the shop from his father, who was now semi-retired, and quickly Vippin saw opportunities far beyond selling newspapers and fags, which had kept his old man busy for forty years. The shop hardly shut, and he was currently doing very nicely from the vaping bonanza, in particular the sale of 'legitimate' CBD oils. Using Vippin to translate Sanjeev's conversation was certainly a risk. A petty crook, he was not trustworthy, but he was always available, and Barry needed to act immediately. The two men agreed a price of £500 cash, significantly up on Barry's original offer.

Vippin dispatched a customer from his shop with a box of illegally imported cigarettes and then bellowed in his native language for someone to relieve him. His old dad emerged, stooped and bedraggled from years on his feet and working all hours. His three other children had all become professionals and had made their parents terribly proud. Vippin hadn't shown any capacity for schoolwork, and yet it was Vippin making all the money. Together they made for the back office, a tiny space packed with cigarettes and pornographic magazines, the only vices his dad had dealt with and done very well from. Barry opened his app on his phone, but Vippin shook his head.

'Money first, mate.'

Barry handed over five envelopes, surely the easiest money he had ever made. Vippin knew Barry well enough and checked each envelope in turn while Barry opened his app.

'You getting a pen and paper, or what?' Barry asked impatiently.

'I will, yeah. But I need to listen to it first. You know, to get a feel...'

Barry didn't like this, but he relented.

'What am I listening to, by the way?' Vippin asked.

'Just two blokes talking.'

'Which blokes?'

'It doesn't matter. Just shut up and listen, and let me know what they say.'

Barry hit play, and Sanjeev and Nihal quickly filled the room. Vippin listened as Barry stared at him intently for clues, any hints at anything that might be valuable. After four minutes and eight seconds, the voices reverted to English, and Barry stopped his app. Vippin's face remained neutral, giving nothing away.

'Two blokes having a row. Do you want it word for word because that might take a while? You could leave it with me-'

'I need it now.'

'Okay, but I need to listen to it again.'

'Fine. Get a pen.'

Chapter Eighteen

At just after 10am, the Carmichael family breezed through immigration with Milly's British passport. They quickly retrieved their luggage and found the car that Milly had booked. En route to their hotel, Milly enjoyed taking in views of home. It was so grotty in and around the airport, with so many buildings in need of a damn good wash, but it felt wonderful to be home. A light drizzle hung in the air like a threat, and she even hoped it might rain. 'Good for the gardens,' Milly thought. She had chosen a boutique hotel called Rushes in fashionable Barnes. Everyone needed a shower, a quick bite and maybe a nap. Later this evening, they head to Ealing to surprise Jonson and Anna. Milly couldn't wait, and, with nothing planned, she wondered if she might head into town to another hotel: an old haunt of hers where she might surprise some other people.

Vippin sat with his pen and paper, his mind frantic with thoughts and considerations. What to give up; what to retain for himself. Both men were highly educated. One was middle-aged, powerful and missing a violin and a daughter, and Vippin only dared to imagine who he might be. He repeatedly stopped and started the app to appear thorough, but it was really a ploy to buy himself some time.

MAN #1: '...but sir, I have met with our broker already and spoken with our lawyers...'

MAN #2: 'Fuck the insurance and this fuck-shit violin. Up his fuck-arse. Do you hear me?'

MAN #1: 'Yes sir.'

MAN #2: 'Fuck, fuck, fuckety, fuck. Fuck-shit them all. Every last fucking one of them. Am I clear?'

MAN #1: 'Er... yes sir.'

Vippin chuckled as he hit pause and casually looked at Barry.

'Do you want every word?'

'Yeah, why?' Barry snapped.

'Just there are a lot of F words.'

'Whatever he says. I need it all.'

'Sure. Who is this guy anyway? The angry dude?' Vippin asked cheekily, but Barry shook his head. Nice try.

'Just translate what he says. Five hundred quid's worth.'

MAN #1: "...How fuck-shit dare you... Sidhu might be kidnapped."

MAN #2: "Sir, no, that's not the case."

Vippin stopped the machine with a quandary. Sidhu is pronounced in Hindi with a P, not an H, and the name was said quickly and only once. This made it a possibility to omit the name, but it was a risk. Hindi for kidnap is Aparan Kna, which offered Vippin a safer alternative. Barry looked like a man whose knowledge of India and its culture did not extend beyond Chicken Tikka Masala, and so he decided that he could withhold this information for now. Finally, Vippin handed over the complete transcript and waited while Barry read it.

What Barry read was not what he had been hoping for. Mr Sanjeev Sharma would not be welcome on the BBC. His fruity vernacular and odd phrasing was fun, however. 'Fuck-shit' was new to Barry. But he wondered if he might be missing something. He read it again. Something felt off. He eyed Vippin, but then his phone beeped. An internet alert on one of his Google searches which he read.

"...*$15 million violin remains missing and is believed to be owned by a student at the Royal College of Music and the daughter of a wealthy foreign businessman...*"

Barry grimaced at this development. Just clickbait, laying out morsels and providing rabbit holes to swallow up surfers into lucrative labyrinths. Barry noted the ever-increasing valuation of the violin and the hint at the owner. Naming the Royal College was troubling, though. Other hacks would be sniffing about, and this new clue might force his hand. It narrowed things down, but not so much. A majority of the college's students were female, practically all their dads were wealthy, and a healthy majority were foreign. Nonetheless, Barry needed to up his pace.

He had a call in to Karl Hibbert at the Evening Standard. He had an array of good photos of Mr Clarke and was waiting on a ruling from his legal team, a firm of solicitors in Luton who were obliging and cheap. A photo of Sidhu Sharma would be very useful, but Karl would never run it. And the same for her old man. Speculative. Litigious. Career ending. Unless that is, Barry had a photo of his own.

Chapter Nineteen

The Carmichael's spacious electric taxi turned silently into Roseberry Gardens, as though it too was in on the surprise in-store for the Clarke family. Jonson looked at Anna when their doorbell rang. They had eaten already, and it was late for a delivery. Jonson appealed to everyone. Anyone expecting someone or something? No takers. He felt a growing paranoia that it might be that weird policeman or the creepy guy from outside his work.

'I'll get it,' Noah offered.

'No, man. It's fine. I'll go. But stay here. Your mum and I aren't finished with this little chat about your future.'

As Jonson left the room to answer the door, the bell rang again, adding to the tension. Anna, Noah and Ella heard their front door open, followed by an almighty scream. Anna leapt to her feet before Noah could even twitch, keen to defend her husband from whoever had darkened their home.

Jonson continued to wail as he held Milly aloft with her head buried into his neck. Mitch and the girls beamed as Anna struggled to join the embrace. Jonson finally put Milly down and scooped up the two girls for an equally enormous group hug. Mitch marvelled at Noah's growth spurt, and they hugged like brothers before they all smashed their way into the lounge. Immediately the kettle was put on, more out of habit than need. Anna opened a bottle of fizz, and Jonson cracked some beers, dispatching Noah for more supplies. And crisps!

Their catch up was brief and hurried. Milly omitted her writing woes, and quickly the only topic of discussion was Jonson's latest tribulation. Milly had already gleaned the important information, but there were gaps, and typically Jonson wasn't the most helpful in filling these in. Anna stared, waiting for Milly's verdict. Was her husband going to jail? It was all very Jonson. Mitch had also listened and wanted to laugh his ass off, but the moment wasn't right; he could feel Jonson's anxiety. Milly mused a moment, conscious that everyone was waiting on her judgement, as though she were a lawyer or some kind of wise elder. She smiled at her old friend

'Jonson, really. What the hell is it with you?'

Jonson exhaled heavily. 'I know; it's like I'm jinxed.'

Anna was pleased that Milly wasn't panicking.

'I mean, who leaves something like that on a bloody train?'

'Yes, exactly. Thank you, Milly.' Jonson looked pointedly at Anna.

'And all the people who must have seen it but didn't pick it up,' Milly continued.

'Doing the right thing, you mean,' Mitch added helpfully.

'My man.' Jonson held up his hand, which Mitch duly slapped. It made a loud and very satisfying sound. Jonson was delighted. He wrapped his arms around the shoulders of Mr and Mrs Carmichael.

'Man, I can't believe you guys came over. I am so stoked that you would do this for me.'

'Well, we were due, right?'

'Overdue, I would say.'

'And when Isla saw the violin on the news...'

Jonson's eyes widened. 'Are you serious? I'm on the news in America. Me?'

Ms Heinzog was full of surprises as she expertly prepared their meal in her pristine kitchen. The room was not large, but it was surgically clean and fabulously well-ordered and stocked. Every surface was stainless steel or ceramic, with a central marble island that sat below a hanging frame with pots and all manner of utensils to hand. Sidhu watched carefully and felt humbled by her capability. Sidhu's mother didn't prepare any food. In her home, their food was prepared, served and cleared by staff, and Sidhu sat comfortably in the 'can't boil an egg' category. Ms Heinzog hummed as she dexterously sliced a clove of garlic. She withdrew a magnificent looking fruit or a vegetable from her walk-in cold store, which Sidhu didn't recognize and was too ashamed to ask.

Their dinner was superb: grilled halibut with roasted vegetables. As they ate, the two women chatted vibrantly about life and music. Sidhu enjoyed a glass of wine, and all her woes seemed to rescind.

'This is delicious, thank you.'

Ms Heinzog smiled.

'You are such a great chef.'

'You sound surprised.'

'I am.'

'Really, why?'

'Erm...'

'Cooking is easier than music.'

'Yes, but...' Sidhu faltered, unsure how to explain herself.

'I am a great violinist. I am not a great chef.'

'Well, I am neither.'

'No. But you are young.'

'Yes, I suppose.'

'Which is why you are here and why we are doing this.'

Sidhu nodded.

'I enjoy cooking. It's all-encompassing and distracting. And I like eating, too.'

'So, do I.'

'I used to live with a very brilliant chef in Zurich, although he was French. Have you been there?'

Sidhu shook her head.

'I was playing in Vienna, and I used his villa as my base.'

'You were friends?'

Yes, I suppose we were. But we were lovers, too. And I insisted on him teaching me to cook. Everyone should know how to cook. It's very cathartic.'

Sidhu could only imagine. She thought of Zurich and Vienna and this man in her life, a fleeting lover. How exciting and daring. This brilliant musician with the whole world as her playground.

Ms Heinzog dabbed her mouth with her brilliant white napkin.

'I don't eat dessert. And I don't enjoy clearing up.' Ms Heinzog grinned as she pushed her empty plate forward a little. 'This will be done by my pixies.'

Sidhu nodded. Finally, something she was more familiar with.

'I think we should go and play, don't you?' Ms Heinzog suggested.

Sidhu took a moment.

'Our violins.' Ms Heinzog clarified, and Sidhu chuckled. After a normal day at college, Sidhu would play for two hours at least. Mandatory. This was the bare minimum expected if she wanted to fulfil the dream of her parents. The prospect of playing with Ms Heinzog in her own home was exhilarating.

'I would love to play with you.'

'Very well then. I have a studio in my basement, which I think you will like. I need to run my Shostakovich.'

Barry read his rather grating text message again.

"*Starbucks. The Strand. Along from the Savoy on the left. Tomorrow. 8am. N*"

Barry had Nihal's number saved as 'Audi Man'. The text felt more like an order than a request, which Barry didn't care for, but he didn't see that he could refuse. He already had Mr Sharma's money, and this made him a little anxious. Rich people guard their money closely, paranoid that everyone is ripping them off. And, in Barry Shenfield's case, Mr Sharma was absolutely right to be paranoid.

Barry needed to be cautious. The story in the mainstream media appeared to be dwindling. No doubt his PR team had finally pulled their fingers out and got to work. But Barry calculated that he could take some credit for this also. Show his value. He smiled. As always, he survived on nothing more than his wits and guile. He was looking forward to seeing Audi Man again. Or N, as he called himself.

Back at their hotel, Milly wiped down her face in the bathroom, her mind still running over the evening with Jonson. The girls were exhausted and settled down quickly, and Mitch was in the lounge catching up with some sports online. Milly sipped her tea, which was probably a mistake if she wanted to sleep. Tomorrow she would visit her parents, although it would not be a surprise this time. Her folks were not big on surprises.

'Crazy, though, what people leave behind.' she called out.

'Yeah, I guess,' Mitch replied, distracted by his laptop, 'damn it. They lost. Jee-sus, come on.'

'Who lost?' Milly asked.

'The Bulls. Fuck,' Mitch moaned.

Milly appeared at the doorway in her pyjamas.

'Honey. We're in England now.'

'Right?'

'So we're not doing American Football.'

Mitch's face dropped.

'Are you being serious?'

Milly looked at him curiously.

'What do you mean?'

'The Bulls?'

'Yeah, what about them?'

'They play basketball. How can you not know that?'

Milly got it now and laughed.

'Yeah, who cares?'

'Who cares?' Mitch asked, 'er... millions of people.'

'Okay, I'm sad the Bulls lost.'

Mitch shook his head in disgust. 'McIlroy won in Texas, though.'

'Oh, good. The golfer, right?' Milly smiled, and Mitch chuckled too.

'I was just thinking about Jonson.'

'Love that guy.' Mitch lay back on their bed.

'I mean, who leaves a priceless violin on a train?' Milly mused. 'That's what I can't get my head around.'

But Mitch shrugged.

'Well, people are tired, I guess,' he suggested, but Milly didn't buy this. It didn't feel very logical. She thought of the owner and their story. Do rich people even ride trains?

'You think Jonson's in the clear?' Mitch asked hopefully.

'I don't know. I hope so.'

'Yeah, me too. It'll be better when it turns up, though. That's for sure.'

Milly agreed although something else was niggling her.

'And Jonson always comes through, right?' Mitch added, hoping to draw this chat to a close. Mitch had checked that the girls were asleep in their adjoining room, and there was just something romantic about a hotel. Mitch pulled back the duvet on her side as a kind of non-committal invitation, but Milly grabbed the hotel stationery paper and pencil. It always helped to write things down. Milly wasn't ready for bed.

'I'm going to have another cup of tea. Do you want one?'

'Sure,' Mitch sighed.

Chapter Twenty

Out of habit, Barry arrived early on the Strand and watched the Starbucks from a café across the road. He looked at his wristwatch. The arranged time had almost arrived, and he hadn't seen 'N' or anyone he might associate with Mr Sharma. Barry ran through his array of options again. Much would depend on them, but Barry backed himself on the hoof. This was life on the streets and not the boardroom. Barry liked his odds.

He waited for a bus to pass before he crossed the famous street, conscious that he might be being watched. He pushed the heavy door open and entered the branch of the ubiquitous coffee shop. The familiar smell of the place enveloped. It felt phoney, pumped in through the air units, and had no doubt been workshopped by people in sneakers and made by people in lab coats. Barry looked about easily. The place was relatively quiet. A few customers were dotted about the place, but none that Barry recognized, and certainly not the regal-looking N. Barry joined a small queue for coffee and surveyed where he might sit. He wanted somewhere quiet and where he could see any comings and goings.

Barry got his coffee just in time to snatch a window table from a young couple, one of whom was about to sit down as the other joined the line. Barry practically barged the young lady out of his way and plonked his coffee down to confirm his prize. He took a seat and glanced about the place again. He didn't appreciate tardiness. Barry Shenfield was a busy man.

At a little after 8am, Nihal breezed into the branch. He spotted Barry immediately. He was alone, which suited Barry, and he looked as groomed as ever. His beard was newly trimmed, and he wore an immaculate crisp white shirt under a navy cashmere coat. He sat opposite Barry and looked at him coldly. Barry half smiled. He was prepared for anything, intimidation included.

'Good morning,' Barry began cheerily.

'Is it?' Nihal asked.

Barry shrugged. He took a slurp of coffee to give him some time and to demonstrate how relaxed he was.

'Well, you asked me to attend,' Barry began casually.

Nihal's eyes narrowed. 'I don't like you, and I don't trust you.'

A bold and aggressive opening; Barry needed to adjust a little. Nihal's nostrils flared. His patience evaporating. He gestured at something over Barry's shoulder. Barry didn't have time to turn as two men joined them. One sat down next to Nihal and the other next to Barry. A cozy table of four. The new arrivals were the two men Barry had spotted outside the Sharma residence. Mr Sharma's security detail: ex-military and now earning more money than they had ever imagined and without much risk, apart from the boredom. Neither of them said a word, and Nihal did not introduce them. The man opposite had the dark ink of a tattoo poking out from under his shirt sleeve, covered by his heavy watch bracelet. Barry liked to remain one step ahead, but judging from the glare of the man sitting opposite, one false move and he might never walk again.

'Everyone okay for a drink?' Barry ventured.

'Shut up,' Nihal hissed, and Barry complied.

'Give me your phone,' Nihal added coldly. Barry eyed the young man cautiously. He wondered if his face betrayed his alarm.

'You want my phone? Because-'

Under the table, Barry felt a heavy foot press up against his, and it wasn't a game of footsie. So much for being in control. Barry wondered what might have happened to make everyone so angry. Quickly he thought of Vippin. Barry quickly calibrated his options. Running was certainly appealing, but the whippet-thin killers would run him down in no time. And running implied guilt. Barry felt in his pocket for his device and handed it over. Nihal passed it to the goon on his left.

'Code?'

Barry held up his index finger. The goon made the phone available. Barry got the impression that this was not the first time they had forcibly accessed another person's phone. And possibly not always with fingers still attached to the owner. On Barry's touch, the phone came to life. He waited now, his mind thinking of a possible explanation. He would know soon enough if Vippin had betrayed him.

Nihal skilfully manipulated the device, his fingers a blur and his eyes finally off Barry, darting about his screen as he opened and manipulated apps. Barry's mouth dried, but he didn't feel he could go for his coffee. Finally, Nihal turned his attention back to him and then showed Barry his phone with the voice recording app active and whirring away. Barry was going to kill Vippin if he wasn't dead already, of course. Now though Barry had some explaining to do and, unable to do so, he smiled instead. Come on, guys, a man's gotta eat, right?

Nihal produced a laptop and plugged in Barry's phone. No protests from Barry. Anyone observing this meeting might have suspected that something untoward was occurring, but no one was watching. Just four blokes enjoying an early breakfast, although only one of them had a coffee.

'You have our money...'

'Which I can return,' Barry suggested.

'You work for me now, 'detective'.'

Nihal emphasized his job title to indicate that Barry's ruse was finished. The man opposite flipped the lid off Barry's coffee and slowly emptied it in to his midriff. It wasn't hot enough to scold, but the man couldn't have known that. Barry didn't say a word.

'The family name gets mentioned anywhere, just once...' Nihal stated. This was a real threat and one which Barry understood.

Nihal edged closer. 'You like to tell stories?'

Barry nodded, unsure what to say.

'If this goes against you, my people will snap your fingers and cut out your tongue.' Nihal might have watched a few too many films, but Barry didn't doubt him. His options were narrowing by the second.

Milly chatted with her dad while the girls made a fuss over their grandma, and Mitch flitted between the two. Milly had booked tickets later to visit nearby Kew Gardens and to have a spot of lunch in one of their eateries. Milly never tired of visiting her parents and the house she grew up in. It was not too large for the two of them to rattle around in it, and Milly hoped that they might avoid the dreaded downsize. Every nook and cranny was packed with possessions and family memories, photo albums that rarely got opened and even Milly's old school projects.

They moved through usual pleasantries about how much the girls had grown and swiftly got onto the second cup of tea for everyone, with the exception of Mitch, who had never warmed to the national drink.

'Your mum misses you too,' her dad said quietly so that they couldn't be heard.

'I know, dad, but I do keep offering to pay for your flights. Big seats as well.'

'I know, and you're very kind. But it's such a long way, and you know she worries about her veins.'

Milly sighed. She had long given up encouraging her parents to become more adventurous.

'How is it out there?' her dad asked, 'still good?'

'Yeah.'

'Oh, good. That's good to hear. You always seem so happy on the phone.'

'I am. We all are. Although work is a little tricky.'

'Oh, really...'

'Yeah, you know, that tricky fourth album.'

Her dad laughed. 'It'll come. I have every confidence in you.'

'I know dad, thanks. And what about you?'

'Yes, okay. I'm still busy with the volunteering.'

'Oh yes, you said. That's great.'

'I don't know why more people don't do it.'

Milly was pleased that he had found something. He had started working with adults with Down syndrome, and she had no doubt that his patience and warmth made him a perfect carer.

'Oh, and that reminds me,' he remembered, 'how is Jonson?'

'He's fine.'

'Only, I see he's in trouble again.'

'Well, not really. You mean the violin.'

'Yes, it's in the evening paper with his photo-'

'It's just a misunderstanding.'

'Oh... because I think I heard his name on the radio.'

This stopped Milly.

'Really?'

'I think so. I was flicking channels and-'

'In what context?' Milly asked.

'I don't know. It was a split second and just his name. But it's an unusual Christian name, Jonson, because it's a surname, of course. But people will fiddle with names these days...'

Milly zoned out and grabbed her phone to do a search. Quickly, she found a site with a photo of Jonson and a library shot of a violin.

'Does he have it?' her dad asked mischievously.

'No, dad, of course, he doesn't.'

'Bloody marvelous this technology. Everything at your fingertips. What amazes me is just how many cameras there are now. People don't realize it, but we are being filmed now practically all the time.'

Milly thought of something now. She needed to call Georgina.

Chapter Twenty-One

A golden rule of professional journalism is integrity and the protection of one's source. Lucky then that Barry never claimed to be a professional, so he sang like a canary. He gave up Vippin instantly, helpfully providing his address also in the hope that they might chop off *his* fingers first. But Nihal had more pressing problems, such as the failure of Mr Sharma's expensive PR team to keep a lid on the story. Jonson Clarke had been named by one of his ex-students DJ'ing on a dance music radio station, and soon Jonson's name was all over the web. Barry's first call was to Nigel at Transport for London.

'Barry. You can fuck right off!' Nigel screamed into the phone.

'Nigel, please, just calm down and listen to me.'

'Calm down! That's easy for you to say.'

'Nigel, I've told you there's nothing to worry about.'

'Right. And I trust you, why?' Nigel seethed.

Barry ignored the insult. It paled in comparison to the prospect of losing his tongue, and he needed Nigel on side. Barry put it as casually as possible and got his answer immediately.

'What? No way. Fuck off, Barry. Absolutely not.'

'Nigel, it's just-'

'No, Barry. No. I'm not doing that, ever.'

'But Nigel, listen-'

'No, you listen: it's not right.'

'Fine. Okay, fine. But all I'm saying-'

'I know what you're saying. And it's a big fat fucking no.'

Barry heard a door slam in the background. He imagined that Nigel had found somewhere quiet to continue their conversation.

'Now you listen to me,' Nigel began. He had lowered his voice, and he sounded muffled, like he was cupping the phone or he had taken to a broom cupboard.

'I can't just wipe tapes.'

'Yes, I know that-'

'Because right there, that's my career over. Plus, it draws attention.'

Nigel made a decent point here.

'Yes, Nigel, I know this, and you're right. I would never ask you for such a thing.'

'You just did,' Nigel barked.

'I was just mooting it.'

'Oh fuck off, mooting.' Nigel was about to hang up now.

'All I'm saying is (here Barry exhaled heavily for effect) if anyone comes along wanting images, especially of the girl who left the case-'

'What girl?' Nigel quipped.

'Yes, exactly. Good. What girl? No one needs to know. And let's keep it like that. That's all I'm saying. Let's not allow any images of her to appear in the newspapers.'

Nigel went quiet now, and Barry knew precisely why. He grimaced, the greedy bastard.

'Five grand,' Barry offered.

'Ten?' Nigel countered.

Barry shook his head in disbelief, without due consideration that it was Mr Sharma's money he was spending. But it was in Barry's bank account, and the thought of Nigel getting one over him still hurt.

'Fine. Check your account in an hour.' Barry hung up and saved the recording of their conversation to his phone's recently freed up hard drive.

Qnctd PR, with their offices on Shaftesbury Avenue and an army of Julian's, Imogen's and Jocasta's, had a struggle on their hands to keep the highly lucrative Sharma account. No one could have foreseen the online dance station leak, but the client would not see it this way. Since then, they had worked the phones and now needed to demonstrate just how connected they really were. Saskia Reeves, the very head of the agency, called Nihal herself and offered her assurances that no mainstream media would be running anything about any violin or the Sharma family. But Saskia could not have anticipated the ambitions of Officer Gareth Dibble, who was determined to see his name in lights. Gareth noted the involvement of the Royal College of Music, laden with class, kudos and wealth; it fitted perfectly with his vision. He scrolled the college's website, looking for a suitable member of staff to approach. It did not take him long.

Not even the world-famous botanical Kew Gardens in full greenery could distract Milly from her new-found mission.

'Oh, Milly, look, the Magnolia trees. I love Magnolias...'

Her dad sighed, knowing what was coming next.

'I've always wanted a Magnolia tree.'

'Yes, well, we have one.'

'Yes, but you didn't feed it.'

'I did feed it.'

'Then why doesn't it look like this?'

'Because this is Kew bloody Gardens, darling. I was an accountant, remember.'

Milly enjoyed their little tiff and took her opportunity to share an aside with Mitch.

'...if there are photos of Jonson with the violin, then there must also be images of the person who left it. There has to be.'

Mitch smiled. 'So, you find this person and Jonson's off the hook.'

'Right. But you'd think they'd have done this already?' Milly reasoned, 'This is a fifteen million quid violin we're talking about.'

'Yeah, I guess.'

'Mitch, I need to head off to see Georgina,' Milly said apologetically because leaving Mitch with her parents in an English garden was definitely a short straw. But he smiled that he was up for the challenge. Milly hugged him.

The principal of Jonson's college Dr Judith Venter had requested to see him urgently, which, in his experience, was never good news. Dr Venter terrified Jonson. They had spoken about matters already, but, with his name being released, Dr Venter needed to go over things again. Yet again, Jonson explained the series of events and confirmed that he did not have a bloody violin. Being drunk was a flimsy defence, but no matter because Dr Venter believed and backed him absolutely. Jonson thanked her and felt a little awkward doing so.

'Don't you worry. This is ma area.' Dr Venter said confidently and a little too gleefully. Jonson sighed his thanks, which she misinterpreted as woe. He could see how his circumstances could compromise his college, particularly as he was a mentor to young men.

'So what do you suggest I do?' Jonson asked.

'Not I.' Dr Venter smiled. 'We. What will WE do?'

Jonson did his best to smile. Dr Venter looked like she might burst into tears. By 'ma area', she meant her life. Her PhD had trained her for this. Her thesis had been 'Ethnographic research into the societal trauma caused by the overrepresentation of Caucasians in the arts, media, politics and education.' On graduating from Cape Town University, the newly qualified 'doctor' hot-tailed it to England. Her mission was to make England pay, and not just her salary either.

Later in his own office, one of Jonson's charges, Stefon Taylor, smirked at him knowingly. Jonson sighed.

'Listen bro,' Stefon began. He liked Mr Clarke and had been thrilled to see him in the papers. 'About this violin bro-'

Jonson tried to stop him, but Stefon needed to be heard.

'All I'm sayin' is... when you is ready... I know people.'

Really? You know fences in the classical music market. For an instrument, I don't have. But Jonson couldn't be bothered to explain himself. Easier to just acknowledge the offer. He would keep it in mind.

Chapter Twenty-Two

On Wednesday morning, over breakfast of fresh fruits and pastries, Ms Heinzog could see that Sidhu's situation had changed with the naming of the man who did not have her violin. Sidhu was aghast and wanted to quickly exonerate the poor man, but Ms Heinzog headed her off.

'But this poor man, Mr Clarke. Everyone will suspect him.'

Ms Heinzog agreed that this was an awkward reality.

'But only for a short while.'

'But still-'

'Just until you explain to your parents, and then everything will be fine.'

'You always make it sound so simple.'

'Well, in some ways, it is,' Ms Heinzog replied without much conviction.

'How will I explain it?' Sidhu asked, 'I reported it missing, and suddenly I have it again? And meanwhile, people have suspected this poor man, Mr Clarke.'

'You could really get rid of it.' Ms Heinzog suggested.

'What, my Guarneri?' Sidhu looked across the breakfast table in disbelief.

'Well, your dad is rich, plus it will be insured.' Ms Heinzog faltered at the prospect of fraud, theft... 'Okay, scrub that. Bad idea.'

And with this, they both burst out laughing.

'Unless you give it away.'

Sidhu shook her head. 'Really? Who to?'

'I don't know. A charity, maybe?' Ms Heinzog suggested, still clutching at straws. Sidhu looked at her oddly.

'No, and it's not mine to give away.' Sidhu added.

'No. There is that.' Ms Heinzog conceded.

'Then what should I do?' Sidhu asked, 'I can't leave Mr Clarke on the hook like this.'

Sidhu began to reach for her phone.

'No, I wouldn't do that. Not just yet.'

'Then when?'

But Ms Heinzog didn't know.

'Why don't we go for a walk and mull it over.'

'Really?'

'Yes, why not? I find it often helps.'

It was a beautiful morning, warm enough to need only a sweater, but with a little bite of cold as a reminder of the bitter days behind and the warmer days ahead. Milly and Georgina carried their coffee as they walked in London's Hyde Park. Her old friend Georgina had finally given in to her kid's demands and acquired a dog, a beautiful blue Staffordshire bull terrier called Tess. She promptly declared her London office as dog friendly, which gave her an excuse to get out of the office more regularly. Like a smokers break without the health risks. The two friends quickly caught up on the business of the day: namely, Jonson Clarke.

'Thanks for that number, by the way,' Milly said.

'No problem, did you call him?'

'Yep. I'm seeing him later.'

'That was quick. Do you want me to send someone? Or I can try and move things...'

'No, no, I'll be fine.'

'It's just that this story is growing...'

Milly beckoned for more.

'Well, I mean, there's pressure to kill it.

'Oh, really, by who?'

'I don't know, but that's the point, right?'

'Can they do that?'

'They can try. And money talks. Always.'

'Be handy for us to know. For Jonson, I mean.'

'I'm hearing a wealthy foreign family. Which hardly narrows it down.'

'But for now, everyone thinks that Jonson has it.'

'Or had it,' Georgina corrected her. Milly sighed.

'How's he holding up?'

'Yeah, you know, good. He's used to this kind of thing. His family are well. Anna almost got cast in a TV thing.'

'Almost, ouch.'

'I know.' Life in the arts. 'But I think she's more worried about her husband at the moment.'

'And what about that son of theirs. The eldest.'

'Noah?'

'Is he still beautiful?'

Milly smiled. 'He's a worry for her, too. He's still in-between things and not going to university.'

'Yeah, well, he'll be fine, that one; believe me.'

Georgina's dog found a piece of grass that was suitable and emptied its bowel.

'Finally!' Georgina exclaimed, 'Milly, we'll do this again. Get the families together, huh? And I'll keep my ears pinned.'

'Brilliant; thanks, George.'

'And let me know how that meet goes.'

'I will.'

The two friends hugged and went their separate ways. Georgina headed for the gates at Hyde Park and Milly towards Park Lane. Neither of them had seen the unlikely couple also walking in the park; the two women who had passed them earlier, and one of them, the older regal-looking lady, had remarked on Georgina's beautiful dog.

'...no, I can't adequately explain it. Not yet anyway,' Ms Heinzog said flatly as their conversation continued, 'it just seems a shame to end something so exciting, that's all. And without any real gain.'

'You keep calling it exciting,' Sidhu repeated, 'it might be exciting for you, but not for me. I'm terrified.'

Ms Heinzog nodded. 'Yes, of course, I'm sorry.'

Sidhu waved her hand.

'Look, I get your terror. I understand it.'

'Really?'

'Yes, of course.'

'When were you last terrified?' Sidhu challenged her.

'Er... when I played last year in Rome. In St. Peter's Square, for the Pope.'

Sidhu could not imagine such a thing.

'Will you be nervous this week? For the Royal Albert Hall?'

'My Shostakovich? Not the easiest piece I have played, but no, not really.'

Sidhu was excited about the concert and imagined such a spotlight.

'And anyway, it's not terror or nerves: it's excitement,' Ms Heinzog continued, sensing some logic and a theme emerging, 'and you're excited because you're in a position to strike out for change.'

Sidhu dwelled on this as yet another dog walker passed them.

'Men like your father are difficult.'

Sidhu said nothing.

'They Men are expectant. They don't tolerate criticism. They just hear "yes".'

Sidhu nodded along.

'"Yes, sir. Yes, sir. Three bags full, sir." Because people are afraid to lose his patronage.'

Sidhu grew impatient with this build-up and hoped she might get to her point.

'But this is not normal.'

'What isn't?' Sidhu asked quickly.

'To never hear "No". In some ways, it's the most important word because it creates boundaries and constraints.' Ms Heinzog seemed happier now and more confident. 'Have you ever been wrong?' she asked her young student. Sidhu nodded.

'Of course, you have. We all have. When you reported your violin stolen. When I involved myself by inviting you to my house.'

'And not returning home,' Sidhu added.

'Yes, quite.'

Sidhu agreed and almost laughed.

'Which is why you must do something different now. Something brave.'

'Like what?' Sidhu asked impatiently. Ms Heinzog had

promised much from their walk and so far, had not delivered anything but more platitudes.

'I think I should go home.'

Ms Heinzog paused briefly and then agreed.

'Fine, then I will drive you.'

Sidhu sensed her disappointment.

'Ms Heinzog, you must understand. In my culture-'

'Oh, please, spare me the culture speech. That is too frequently used to justify unjustifiable behaviour.

'But no, you don't understand.'

'Young lady, there is almost nothing that you understand that I don't. Hindi perhaps. But I have lived far longer than you have, and I have been all over the world. I know all about this culture and that culture. A family is a family wherever they are on earth.'

Sidhu absorbed her painful rebuke.

'Ms Heinzog, I am already unpopular enough because of who I am.'

'And who are you?'

Sidhu grimaced. 'A little rich girl. And if I don't hear it, then I feel it. That is what they will write about me. No one will understand. Damn it, how could I have been so stupid?' Sidhu scolded herself.

'Impetuous, yes, but you are certainly not stupid.'

'Well, it doesn't matter anyway because it's the same outcome.'

'Leaving your privilege aside,' Ms Heinzog began, more calmly now, 'You are just like everyone else. Same needs and hopes to be happy.'

'Fine, then what should I do?' Sidhu demanded. 'I keep asking you, but you don't seem to know.'

Ms Heinzog faltered.

'How old are you?'

'Nearly twenty.'

'A young woman. In her prime.'

'My one life.' Sidhu added, using her oft-repeated words.

'Yes, quite. And with so much ahead, we hope. You will experience many things which will seem so very important at the time. Things that will feel absolutely crucial. And yet, you will come to forget them completely. Recitals. Examinations. Parties. Interviews. Holidays. Boys you meet. Men you sleep with...' Ms Heinzog was more fluent now, warming to her theme. Sidhu blushed at matters so personal but said nothing, giving tacit permission for her to continue.

'But this event.' Ms Heinzog gestured to her surroundings. 'This whole mix up with your violin...'

'Not a mix-up. A cry for help.'

'Okay, even better. Knowing that is good. It is progress. Or it can be...'

Sidhu considered this.

'You will never forget this, ever. As an old lady, even older than I am now, you will always remember these last few days.'

'Yes, I expect I will. But-'

'And this means it is important. Maybe even pivotal.'

Sidhu nodded.

'I don't like the word fate. I don't believe in it, not really. We make our own paths. But this doesn't mean that things don't happen for a reason. Sometimes, at least.'

'And this is such an occasion?' Sidhu asked.

'Maybe, yes. It feels like it to me.'

'But how? And why?' Sidhu pleaded.

'Ah, that I don't know. But neither will you unless you try to find out. Earlier, what did you say, something about, it doesn't matter...'

'...because it's the same outcome.' Sidhu completed for her.

'Yes, that's it. So everything depends on how you react and

what you do. And I am involved, too. Look at us here. Why have I prolonged your problem? Because it felt right for me to do so.'

Back at her home, Ms Heinzog gathered her things and located her car keys.

'...so before you show your hand, to use a ghastly American expression; sorry, I used to live with an American rock star,' she added casually, which caught Sidhu's attention.

'Really, which one?'

'Oh, it doesn't matter. He's fat now and bald, and he still has a ponytail.'

Sidhu chuckled at this image.

'And you are right; I don't have the answers for you. Nobody does – except you. So, you just need to kick up the leaves and see what emerges.'

Sidhu stared at her heroine.

'Otherwise, this will all be for nothing. Things will be the same, and you will be unhappy. Who knows, maybe forever.' Ms Heinzog clicked her mouse and the website loaded with the photograph of Jonson Clarke snapped outside his college. Ms Heinzog stared hard at it. She imagined his current turmoil. Sidhu certainly owed him an apology, and suddenly something occurred to her. She dwelled on it for a moment. She scanned the text and noted that he lived in Ealing, which was not so far.

Ms Heinzog wondered. Sidhu sensed something was afoot.

'What is it?' Sidhu asked.

'For all the reasons we have discussed, your father can wait. He should wait. Can we agree on that at least?'

Sidhu shrugged. Yeah, I suppose.

'But not Mr Clarke, the non-thief. Perhaps he cannot wait.'

Sidhu shook her head. 'I'm sorry, but I don't follow.'

'You said so yourself: it's the right thing to do and the kind thing to do,' Ms Heinzog continued obliquely, but now with a wicked glint in her eye. 'Plus, it would ease your conscience and buy you some time.'

'Ms Heinzog, what the hell are you talking about?'

The violin maestro smiled mischievously.

'You could go along and explain yourself to him.'

Sidhu stared hard at Ms Heinzog.

'Go along and see who... Mr Clarke?'

Ms Heinzog shrugged. 'Why not?'

'Is that what you call kicking up the leaves?'

'Well, it's definitely different. And unexpected.'

'And what if he's angry with me?'

'Well, he probably will be. But not for long.'

'How do you know?'

'I don't. I don't know. But he has a kind face.'

Sidhu shook her head. 'No way.'

Ms Heinzog held her hands aloft, unsure if any real progress was being made. But then her phone rang. Her landline.

Chapter Twenty-Three

The Shelton Tower had not changed very much since the day Mitch had finally opened Milly's package containing her script all those years ago. The reception had been spruced up somewhat but otherwise remained exactly as she remembered, as did the ensconced general manager Mr Mahmood, still at his post and still hopelessly devoted to his hotel and to its guests. The tiny man remained a hive of energy. He was a little heavier around his middle and thinner on top, but he had held up well. Even his thick Turkish accent remained.

'Mill-ee, I am delighted to see you again.'

'Thank you, Mr Mahmood.'

'I miss you, Mill-ee. Why so long?'

Milly smiled and apologized again. Her time working for him had been her nadir, and yet she recalled it so affectionately.

'You want to come back?'

Milly laughed as the thought of returning firmly put into perspective her writing block and current woes.

'Not just yet, I don't think. How are the toilet flushes?' Milly asked. His little eyes blinked and flashed as his memory made the connection, and finally, he smiled as his memory cranked into gear.

'The flow-tas!' he bellowed, and they both laughed.

'You must come for dinner. You and your family.'

'Yes, we'd love that.'

'No booking required. I will give you staff discount. Fifteen-per-cent.'

'Deal.' Milly smiled.

'And today?'

'I have a meeting.'

'Ah, very good. Someone I know? Not, Mr Jonson. The man with the hair?

Milly smiled again.

'The black man,' Mr Mahmood added just in case there could be any confusion.

'Yes, I remember. His hair has gone now. But he's still black.'

Mr Mahmood roared with laughter, but then something caught his eye, and he stopped. A bellboy was leaning against a pillar staring at his phone. Mr Mahmood glared in disbelief.

'Mill-ee, please, if you will excuse me. I have to give a bellboy his final bloody warning.'

Phone calls to the Heinzog residence were as rare as visitors, particularly from the Vice-Chancellor of the Royal College of Music. She made her excuses to Sidhu and took the call in her adjoining library, closing the highly polished, heavy mahogany door after her. Apparently, an officer Dibble had called the RCM requesting a meeting with Ms Heinzog, and the Chancellor could hardly refuse.

'Why me?' Ms Heinzog enquired.

'He didn't say.'

'Didn't you ask?' Ms Heinzog snapped. She did not defer to anyone, even the VC of the RCM.

'No, I'm sorry, I didn't think to. But I can see now that I should have done. I do apologize.'

Ms Heinzog's silence was enough response.

'And because I saw that you have a class today at 2.30...'

This jolted Ms Heinzog. With the excitement of having Sidhu to stay, she had almost forgotten.

'...er, so I suggested that 1.30 might be convenient for you?'

'Well it isn't.'

'Oh...'

Ms Heinzog sighed. Could she refuse a meeting with a police officer?

'But since you've put it in my diary.'

'Yes, I am sorry about this. But I didn't know what else-'

'Where?'

'Er... well, here at the college. He was quite insistent, actually.'

Ms Heinzog took a moment. This was at least better than meeting at a grubby police station.

'Fine, then.'

'Oh, good, thank you.'

'But 2pm. Not 1.30. He's only getting ten minutes.'

A troubled Sanjeev Sharma looked down on London from his private jet. Sidhu's timely text had been his permit to fly, yet it still caused him pangs of guilt. His mood could not be improved, even by the brilliant sunshine and the clear views of the bustling city below, with old River Thames bisecting and snaking its way through and without a care. It would survive everyone and every drama playing out around it. Companies soaring and then failing. People being fired. Individuals jumping from bridges.

Crises that are overwhelming in the moment but in the great scheme of things and from the vantage of his jet seem trifling and immaterial.

Sanjeev always peered down every time he flew, picking out famous landmarks from the medieval to the ultra-modern; this time, he thought of Sidhu, down there somewhere below with a 'friend'. Soon, any guilt he felt turned into ire. Her behaviour was impossible to understand. It was unforgivable. Sanjeev stared at the Shard below with contempt. Owned by the Qataris who he had never managed to do any business with. The building looked isolated and out of place.

Barry Shenfield, unbeknownst to them both, was directly in Sanjeev's eye-line as he rushed from seeing a wounded Vippin and was now worried about his next meeting. It seemed like a nice venue, at least, but this was little comfort judging by the state of Vippin's bruised face. He thought to call N just to check in but decided not to. Barry chased up the stone steps as the heavy doors were opened for him by a smiling man wearing a ridiculous suit complete with top hat.

'Welcome to the Shelton Tower, sir,' the man greeted Barry warmly. Subtext: that will be five pounds, please. Barry was met by a blast of warm and scented air. He took in the impressive reception, with its enormous vases full of pungent Stargazer Lilies. He recalled what the lady had said to him on the phone and veered to his right for the cocktail bar. Milly was just finishing up with Mr Mahmood, who sized up the scruffy man approaching. Milly stood up and smiled. She was the only person in the bar, but Barry had already searched her up online and knew who to look for.

'Mr Shenfield. Hi, I'm Juliet Millhouse.'

Barry shook her hand.

'Can I get you a drink?'

'No, too early for me, thanks.'

'A coffee? Something soft?' Milly asked.

Barry shook his head, still shaken by his earlier meeting. 'So, how can I help you?'

Milly smiled easily, appreciating his economy.

'How did you get my number?'

Milly ignored the question. Unusual for a journalist to ask for a source.

'I'm a friend of Jonson Clarke.'

Barry eyed her carefully now.

'Ah, the man with the violin.'

Milly didn't care for his description of her friend.

'Or not.'

'Is that right?' Barry countered, unnerved by her confidence.

'Yes, and I think you know this already.'

'Is that right?'

'Yes, but don't let facts ruin a good story, eh?'

Barry absorbed her insult easily enough; it was far less painful than what Vippin had endured. But he was intrigued now. 'And these facts,' he replied, 'would you care to share them with me?'

Milly gestured. 'Not really, no. It's more a feeling I have.'

Barry relaxed a little now.

'What, like a hunch?' Barry sneered.

'If you like. And that there's no reward. Which is odd for something so valuable, wouldn't you say?'

Barry said nothing and just shrugged, their game of chess continuing. Milly considered him. He was adept and competent. But he wasn't a professional. Georgina had said as much. And his cool exterior belied something within: something was bothering him.

'As you can imagine, Mr Jonson is under some considerable pressure.' Milly nodded for good measure, and this prodded at him.

'Yeah, well, aren't we all?'

'Particularly since he was named.'

Barry took a moment. 'Yeah, well, not by me; he wasn't.'

'But you did write the story.'

Barry smiled.

'You're quite the storyteller yourself. What was that movie, Untitled? My wife loved it.'

Milly half smiled.

'No offence, but it wasn't for me.'

'None taken.'

'Must have been an earner, though.'

'Wrong tense, I'm afraid.'

This wrong-footed Barry.

'Still is.' Milly's turn to smile now. If she was unsettled by his research, then she didn't show it. She'd done her homework too.

'Your story about this violin... it's all pretty speculative,' Milly suggested.

Barry shrugged. So what?

'I'm surprised they even ran it,' Milly continued.

'Dunno. Maybe it was a slow day. Maybe you should ask them.'

'Oh, I will. Karl and I are friends,' Milly lied. They had met when his newspaper covered a London premiere, but 'friends' was a stretch. Barry made a mental note to call Karl, and he forced a strained smile.

'That seems to be a theme to your work,' Milly pressed.

'What's that?'

'Speculation.'

He shifted now.

'I read your piece on teachers doing cash-in-hand tutoring...'

Barry bit his bottom lip. What the hell did this woman want?

'Or the Chelsea player, Marco Rochelle and his affair.'

Barry was losing patience now. 'Yeah, well, all in the public interest.'

'Oh, absolutely. The fans pay his wages, right? So they deserve to know who he sleeps with.'

'Yeah, something like that.'

'And, speaking of which... Congratulations, by the way.'

Barry faltered again. 'On?' He asked, teeing her up.

'On you getting married.'

Milly had his full attention now. 'What the fuck do you want?'

'Barry. I want lots of things. But what I really want right now is to absolve my friend.'

Barry sneered. 'Yeah, well, you know. I'm sure it'll turn up.'

'I hope so. Better for everyone. The owner must be climbing the walls.'

Barry's eyes narrowed. 'Yeah, well, I wouldn't know.'

'That's a shame because that really would be a story worth telling,' Milly suggested.

'Yeah, well, you do stories. Maybe one for you,' Barry snapped back.

'I think we both make up stories, Barry.'

His mind was back on Nihal now and his thugs. Juliet Millhouse entering the fray did not help his cause. She added a touch of Hollywood: something the press would enjoy.

'Who is the owner, by the way?' Milly asked, but Barry just sniggered.

'It won't be long. People own these things for a reason. Perhaps we can all meet up?'

'Yeah. Maybe a picnic somewhere?' Barry joked.

'Yes, how about Regents Park?'

Barry did not like Milly at all. She was far too assured.

'The footage of Jonson on the train with the instrument,'

Milly began, 'there must also be footage of the person who left it, right?'

Barry didn't respond.

'And presumably, it was reported missing?'

He remained silent.

'And wouldn't someone have to leave their name? So that they could be contacted?'

More alarms and klaxons. Barry made another note to call Nigel.

'I could always get in touch with Transport for London.' Milly smiled.

'Yeah, just give them a call. They're a piece of piss to get a hold of.'

'And I've already put a call in to Officer Dibble. Rather unfortunate name.'

Barry was reeling now.

'You have my number?'

Barry nodded. 'How long are you over for? You said you were visiting?'

'That's right. I am. As long as it takes.'

Chapter Twenty-Four

Mitch and the girls had found plenty to keep them occupied in London while Milly took on her new-found duties of amateur sleuth. Mitch was delighted to see how animated Milly was on her return, making notes, updating anyone who would listen and putting further calls in to Georgina. He was equally enthralled that Mr Mahmood was still at The Shelton.

'Jeez, man. The little guy?'

Milly chuckled.

'Wow. With all his rage, I had him in a box years ago.'

Milly nodded. 'Mr Mahmood's a force of nature. He's not going anywhere.'

'Mom, is Uncle Jonson going to jail?' Isla butted in, clearly worried.

'No, of course not, honey,' Mitch answered on Milly's behalf, 'well, not for this thing, anyway. But this being Jonson, the prospect of some eventual jail time is a distinct possibility.'

Milly laughed and assured Isla that Dad was joking.

'But he's in trouble, though?'

'Yeah, kinda. But he's always in trouble,' Mitch answered, 'and Mom's helping him now.'

'Can I help, too?'

'Er-'

'He called, by the way,' Mitch said, 'inviting us out tomorrow evening for dinner. Does that work?'

'Yeah, I spoke to him. We should book a car.'

The story had it all: a fifteen-million-pound prize and an ongoing treasure hunt. A world-famous musician with a saucy history. An elite college. Some unknown rich bloke missing a violin, perhaps an oligarch with a super-hot model wife. And now, an attractive star writer added to the mix. Manna from heaven for Officer Dibble. But he would need to be cunning. He parked a little along from the Royal Albert Hall and carefully arranged his police ID on his dashboard, waiting for his text. He checked his watch: ten minutes until he was due to meet Ms Heinzog and his launch of Operation *Paradise Island: The Oldies*. He had already called the surgeon and fixed a date for his next procedure. The producers would be begging him to join.

Sidhu was relieved to hear that her father was outbound again. Prikash was delighted to receive her phone call, and both of them took a moment as their tears flowed freely.

'Sidhu, please, where are you?' Prikash asked.

'Mum, I've told you already. I'm at a friend's house.'

'Damn you, Sidhu. What has got into you? Whose house? Where and why?'

Sidhu sighed. 'Mum, I'm sorry, but you know why.'

'My God, the trouble you have caused.'

'I know, and I am sorry.'

'Then come home. Come home now, so we can talk.' Prikash demanded, a little more angrily now.

'When is dad back?'

Prikash grimaced as a member of staff entered with a pile of laundry. She was sent scurrying away with a scowl and an angry hand gesture.

'I don't know. I never know his plans. But when he finds out you are still not home-'

'He still went off again, though,' Sidhu pointed out.

'Sidhu, do not judge your father; he is phoning every half hour worrying about you.'

Sidhu admonished herself.

'You said you were coming home,' Prikash continued, 'please, let's talk and then we can call him.'

This appealed to Sidhu but for Ms Heinzog's plans to extend her adventure for one more day.

"Tomorrow we go to college together, and then I take you home?"

It seemed like such a good idea, and Sidhu had agreed. It seemed neat, and it gave her closure and a timeframe.

'Mum, I promise I will be home tomorrow after college. You have my word.'

But what then? Sidhu wondered. She weighed the wisdom of Ms Heinzog against the reality of her father's wrath. Most likely, she would be confined to home and college only, with no phone and Nihal accompanying her everywhere. This thought made her shudder.

'And have you been playing your violin?' her mother asked, which made Sidhu smile. She had much to explain and share with her. She was even tempted to come clean now. It might make everything okay.

'Yes, I am practicing, and this is not going to affect my music at all. It might even help.'

'What do you mean?' her mother asked curiously.

'I will explain everything, Mum, I promise. How is dad?'

'How do you think he is? He is furious. But he blamed Nihal, of course.'

Sidhu felt a pang of guilt. 'Please tell him I called. And that I am fine. Everything is fine.'

'No, it isn't Sidhu, not until you are home.'

'And I will be tomorrow. I promise.'

'Sidhu, whatever this is, it must remain just a family matter. Then it can be fine, and we can deal with it.'

'Yes, mum, I know this, of course.'

'Then come home before there are more stories. If our name is mentioned in the newspapers...'

Sidhu nearly relented but for the persuasiveness of Eleanor Heinzog. She trusted her and wanted to believe in her sense of adventure.

'Tomorrow, Mum, I promise.'

'I love you, Sidhu.'

'I love you too. And, I am sorry. I am sorry for worrying you as I have.' Sidhu felt relieved with her apology and relief that Ms Heinzog did not witness it. "Apologies, cede power". She would hit the roof.

In the boardroom of the Royal College of Music, with its walls adorned with imposing oil paintings of previous Chancellors, Ms Heinzog could scarcely countenance the man sitting before her. Ms Heinzog listened to him carefully. Officer Dibble smiled at her as a child would smile at its favourite pop star.

'So you don't know anything about this priceless violin?' Dibble repeated his question. Ms Heinzog glared at her inquisitor. Few people, if any, had ever asked her a question a second time.

'Do you think I am stupid?' she asked.

'I beg your pardon?' Gareth continued to smile.

'You are either suggesting I am stupid or that I am a liar.'

'I don't follow you,' Gareth said.

'You don't strike me as a policeman.'

Gareth took this as a compliment. He almost thanked her.

'I know everything there is to know about the Guarneri, but I know nothing about a violin that may or may not be missing.'

Dibble scribbled something in his pad. Maybe a doodle?

'Why have you asked to see me?' she asked pointedly, her eyes narrowing. Dibble chuckled, although he couldn't give the real answer, of course: that her fame and infamy were part of his quest to appear on *Paradise Island* and a raft of other reality shows. On his computer, he had a comprehensive spreadsheet of all the TV shows he was eligible for, with progress columns on his current applications. Ms Heinzog looked at her watch. Her masterclass was due to begin, and then she had a young lady to drive home.

'You are not to contact me again. Do you understand?'

Dibble nodded. He had no intentions of doing so. He just needed this meeting and a photo of him entering the august college. His journalist contacts would do the rest.

'Well, thank you very much for seeing me. It's been a pleasure.'

'Has it?'

Gareth got up to leave, but Ms Heinzog stayed in her seat. There would be no send off, or hand shake.

'It's been an honour-'

'Really, would you like a photograph with me?'

Gareth now beamed at the elegant lady. He scrambled for his phone.

'Get out,' Ms Heinzog said wearily.

Nihal was also relieved to see Sanjeev take to the skies again. Good fucking riddance as far as he was concerned. For all his acumen, he had been a liability in this entire fiasco, flying off the handle and bringing in people off the blinking street. And since it was Sanjeev himself chasing his daughter away, his being out of the picture might entice Sidhu out from her hiding place. Nihal shuddered at the prospects of the eventual family reunion. By then, everything had to be resolved, with the family name in good order, and hopefully, the stupidly expensive bloody violin returned. This would be enough for his gleaming reference, which he needed to get out of this family and back to a Mumbai law firm.

On Sanjeev's orders, Nihal had not been informed about Sidhu's latest phone call. Better to keep him on his toes and alert to any possible threats and opportunities for the Sharma family. And once this matter had been resolved, Sanjeev would indeed dispense with his services.

Chapter Twenty-Five

Jonson slurped his cold beer and savoured the moment. The two families were sitting at the largest circular table in his favourite Indian restaurant. For a man under such scrutiny, Jonson appeared to be very relaxed. Amazing what great company and the prospect of an Indian meal can do. A mountain of poppadoms arrived for the nine hungry people. Always a magnificent moment. The chutneys and pickles followed, people already cracking the giant crisps and retrieving stray pieces for themselves. The full complement of the Clarkes and the Carmichael families made it a bonanza booking for the restaurant, and the waiters duly fluttered about. Milly and Jonson sat next to each other; he was grateful to hear her updates on the situation and also her assurances.

'Which is no real surprise,' Milly explained, 'because if this had been an ordinary violin, this wouldn't even be a thing.' Jonson nodded. Just my luck, huh.

'But we don't know who the owner is?' Jonson asked.

'Not yet, no. But the possibilities are narrowing, and it won't be long.'

'Which will be a good thing, right?' Jonson wondered.

'Someone rich though,' Anna added, overhearing their conversation.

'And powerful.' Milly explained the press black out courtesy of Georgina. Jonson nodded again.

'Well, my phone hasn't stopped. First, it was journalists calling, but now it's my mates taking the piss. They're loving it, of course.'

'Then they're not your mates,' Anna remarked.

Jonson tutted. 'Anna, not now please, it's what blokes do.'

Jonson grabbed a whole fresh poppadum and plonked it on Anna's plate, along with his best smile.

'Anyway, Noah, what are you up to?' Milly asked to change the subject. Noah looked knowingly at his mum.

'Yeah, you know. University maybe and a few other possibilities.' Noah answered vaguely, avoiding Anna's gaze.

'And what about a girlfriend?'

'Milly, come on, leave him alone.' Mitch chipped in.

Noah blushed. 'Not at the moment. But there are options,' he added, and everyone laughed.

'Man, these chips are the best.' Mitch snapped another piece of poppadum, and no one bothered to correct him. 'Hey, buddy, can we get some more of this mango ketchup?'

Milly shook her head; Noah wanted to high five him for diverting attention away from him.

'My dad says that Uncle Jonson isn't going to jail just yet,' Isla announced too loudly and promptly brought the house down and the laughter quickly became a cheer when the onion bhajis were presented.

'Any more beers, sir?' a waiter asked expectantly.

'Why not...'

. . .

Gareth Dibble did not have much patience in his locker, particularly so with his impending fame at stake. To work on his cause, he called in sick and convened a meeting with his fame team in his 'luxury' apartment in the heart of Dagenham. It was a streamlined team: just himself and Yvonne, who also handled his PR as well as his 'socials'. Before Yvonne got to her bad news, she needed to soften the blow.

'Your latest Instagram post, the one with your cat, has 78 likes already, which is really good.'

'Maybe I should get a dog? I think dogs are more popular.'

'You mean online?' Yvonne asked.

'Yeah, of course; where else?'

Yvonne made a note to investigate the popularity of cats against dogs.

'And you have 22 new Twitter followers overnight after your retweet of @Scobey_Bee_Man.'

Ordinarily, this would be good news but not today.

'What about my story?'

Yvonne grimaced as she explained the resistance she had met. There had not been much traction for the images of Officer Dibble entering The Royal College of Music.

'But I had a violin with me.'

'I know. It's ridiculous.' Yvonne shrugged.

'A police officer. A detective. A well-known detective. Entering the Royal College of Music with a violin...'

Yvonne continued her encouraging nods.

'...while there is a missing Stradivarius...'

Yvonne didn't bother to correct him.

'How did the meeting go?'

'What meeting?'

'With the famous violinist.'

'Oh. You mean the rudest cow I have met. Do you know what she called me?'

Yvonne wasn't sure if this was rhetorical.

'Huh?' Gareth prompted for an answer.

'I don't know.'

'Stupid. Can you believe that?'

Yvonne didn't answer.

'I'm a fucking detective.'

Yvonne forced a smile.

'So nothing then. No one's interested?'

Yvonne blew out her cheeks.

'I don't know, it's strange. But it's gone quiet.'

Gareth sighed. He held his upper arm, which felt too soft for his liking. 'Do you know about these gyms where you don't have to work out?'

'Er-'

'They use electric pads which contract your muscles for you.'

'No I haven't, sorry.'

'Don't worry about it.' He clicked his fingers repeatedly, snapping himself back to more immediate concerns.

'Right, so what now then? What are you thinking?'

'Er...' Yvonne sighed.

'Come on; you're the expert.'

This didn't flatter Yvonne. She was in her last year at Middlesex University doing Media Studies, and she didn't feel very expert. Gareth paid her a retainer of £175 a month, up from £150 when she first started, which was not much money, but it was a lifeline against her rent and the near-certainty of not getting a job in the media.

'Well,' Yvonne began.

'Yep, let's hear it.'

'It's a good story. It's a great story.'

'Yes, it is. Thank you.'

'So it might indicate that the owner of the violin, whoever it is...'

Gareth prompted her impatiently.

'That they don't want any publicity.'

Gareth dwelled on this. His nostrils flared. Who were these freaks who didn't like publicity?

'Then why buy such a violin? And they don't get to decide. This is my publicity. Not theirs.'

'Well, if they're rich, they might have spiked the story.'

'Oh, is that right?'

'Well I don't know. But people with power, you know, rich people... they can probably control certain things. Things like this.'

'Well it's disgusting. One rule for them, eh? Bloody Russians coming over here. Buying up everything they want, rigging our elections...'

Yvonne didn't know how to respond to this. 'The owner might not be Russian.'

'Yes, I know that. I'm just saying. But they'll be foreign.'

'Maybe-'

'Bound to be. No British person in their right mind is going to spunk ten million quid on a violin.'

Yvonne panicked now that he might tweet such a thing. This would be a big mistake, although Gareth didn't tweet as himself. He used the handle @_hot_cop37. He had insisted on 'hot cop'. All part of his brand and mission statement. But the singular handle hotcop had long been claimed, so he had been forced to include the credibility-busting underscores and the arbitrary number 37 because even _hot_cop69 had gone. So many hot cops: who knew?

But even so, a mere mention of the word 'foreign' on any of his socials would not play well for him. Yvonne had gained Gareth's trust. She liked him, but she worried about him.

'Okay, fine, then we take it online. Fuck 'em.'

Yvonne chewed her lower lip.

'Yvonne, this is what the internet was invented for. This is what Twitter is for. To allow people to become famous. And I am not letting this opportunity slide. This Heinz woman is famous. Apparently, she slept with Lenny Kravitz...'

Yvonne tilted her head to process this new morsel of information.

'Really?'

'Yeah, Lenny Kravitz.'

'Right, but I'm thinking she's probably not alone...'

'Sure. But this lady plays the violin for the fucking Pope.'

An unfortunate choice of language. Yvonne filed this 'fact' in her never-to-be-used-ever column.

'So what websites can we get it on?' Gareth asked, energized now, 'we just need it out there. The photo of me with the violin. Plus my headshot, the one that TOP PIX did for me. The photo of Heinzog and a shot of the Stradivarius or whatever the fuck it's called.'

Yvonne scribbled in her notepad.

'There's gotta be sites that will lap this shit up. Blogs even. I don't care. Get it on the blogs. Those losers always need something to write about. And do that thing you do with stuff online.'

'You mean SEO?'

'Yeah, that's it. SEO the shit out of it. Tag it. Hash it. Fuck it. Do whatever it takes. Just get eyeballs on me and my Twitter.'

It was almost too painful for Barry to look at: a CCTV image of Sidhu Sharma on the underground train with her violin. It was not lost on Barry how beautiful she was and what a story that might be slipping through his hands. He had made mistakes, but now was not the time for an audit. Nigel had called the meeting, which was opportune for Barry, but he had a bad feeling, and he hoped that his suspicions were not correct. Nigel put the image back in his folder and smiled at his ex-colleague.

'Believe me, Nigel, that photo really needs to stay in your bag. In the dark, so to speak.'

'Blimey, you've changed your tune.' Nigel smiled greedily.

'Yeah, well, things have moved along a little.'

'Is that right?'

Barry didn't answer, so Nigel prompted him. 'Anything I should know?'

Barry shook his head.

'It's just that I'm getting a lot of calls. You know, interest,' Nigel added casually.

'Nigel, please listen to me. This isn't like normal.'

'How so?'

'We could get hurt.'

Finally, he had Nigel's attention. Barry hated losing his story, but, ever the pragmatist, he was choosing health and salvation.

'Barry, are you threatening me?'

'No, I'm informing you. There's a difference. A big difference. There are people who do not want that picture ever to be seen by anyone...'

'Right?' Nigel probed.

'And I've been threatened to keep it this way.'

Nigel's eyes narrowed. 'I see.'

Barry said nothing, feeling more vulnerable now.

'And you're being paid; I take it?'

The two men stared at each other, contemplating this implied threat and veiled extortion. Unspoken but apparent. Just business, as Barry would say. Nigel smiled, and Barry joined him.

'How much do you want?' Barry asked.

Nigel shrugged. 'Well, that depends. I don't want to be greedy.'

Barry scoffed. Is that right, you bastard?

Barry retrieved two phones from his pocket. One handset was recording their current conversation, and the other was in Barry's hand while his fingers flashed across the screen. Nigel's bravado collapsed as their previous conversations on the subject began to play.

'These are serious people, Nigel. Trust me; you don't want that image appearing anywhere. You can't play golf from a wheelchair.'

Chapter Twenty-Six

Yvonne did as she was instructed and 'hash tagged the shit out of it', which had gained the story some online coverage. She managed to place the story on a few gossip websites with IP addresses in Romania, and things gradually built from there. But the real breakthrough came with a RT from a verified Twitter account of an American 'influencer' by the name of @pimpitbitch, even though all the attention was over the handsome kid holding a football trophy standing next to his dad, Jonson Clarke. The influencer's tweet made no mention of a Hot-Cop, which was disappointing, but no matter, as two hundred new followers joined Gareth's church and nudged him through 8000 followers and closer to the hallowed 10k. Common thinking is that celebrity status begins with ten thousand followers on three different platforms. Twitter would be Gareth's first, and TV celebrity bookers would no doubt take note. Yvonne was quick to capitalize on possible trending opportunities, conducting a thorough audit on @pimpitbitch. The bio for this account was economic but profound: 'They/them. Black, Gay and Fucking Furious'. An account with 2.1m followers, the most recent of which was one @_hot_cop37. A follow-back would be extraordinary but unlikely, and so Yvonne dampened his expectations.

'It's all about the moment,' Yvonne explained.

'Great. What does that mean?'

'Well, at the 'moment', it's all about this handsome kid in the photo.'

'Okay, good. And what else?'

'So we find him, and we follow him.'

'What if he's not on social media?'

Yvonne scoffed. The sooner Gareth gave up his detective duties, the better for everyone.

'Gareth, he's young, attractive and good at sport. He's on social media, and you're already following him.'

It would help if Noah could recall how many Twitter followers he had the last time he checked. But not being an avid phone watcher and a passive social media user, he couldn't recall, but he felt sure it was fewer the last time he'd been on his account. Noah clicked on his notifications, and his eyes widened at a succession of notices, many of which were just a series of red love heart emojis. Unerringly, many of these appeared to be from men. He scrolled down, wondering what might have caused this. He was used to occasional romantic overtures, but this was another level. He read one comment and blanched. What the hell was happening?

One of the many new people eyeing Noah Clarke's account was Sidhu Sharma after her internet alerts for Jonson Clarke had started to ping. The photo of father and son was a very happy one, and it held her attention. From his smile, Mr Clarke's son was clearly on the winning side that day, and he might have even bagged the winning goal. She noted his name, Noah. A nice name. Who doesn't like a man who saves animals? She had never met a Noah before. She clicked through to the accompanying story, an unlikely tale that took her a moment to understand. It featured an unusual looking man crossing a road with his shoulders pinned back, his head tilted upwards and carrying a violin case. The street was familiar, and she realised that it was outside her college. Her heart started beating faster now; her eyes frantically scanned back and forth as she saw a stock photo of Eleanor Heinzog. But no photo of Sidhu, thank goodness, nor mention of her name. Her heart pounding now. The only other photo was of poor old Mr Clarke snapped outside his work, and she felt responsible and guilty. She preferred the other much happier photo of him and his son, who just so happened to be beautiful. Sidhu looked at her watch and thought of Ms Heinzog, who would be home soon.

That evening, they played violin together for three hours ahead of Ms Heinzog's appearance at the Albert Hall, and they hardly discussed matters at all. Sidhu didn't mention the new online story, preferring to sleep on it instead. Similarly, Ms Heinzog did not mention her encounter with Officer Dibble. The man was a fool and would not trouble her again. After a simple meal, they retired to bed early and agreed that tomorrow Sidhu would finally return home.

Breakfast the next morning had a fateful feel to it. After college today, Sidhu would return home to face the real music of the day. Ms Heinzog assured Sidhu that she would accompany her. The breakfast table was laid out beautifully with fresh berries, yoghurts, honey and pastries. Ms Heinzog had enjoyed having an impromptu house guest, although it had also reminded her of her loneliness. It had been an unexpected and extraordinary few days. She looked at Sidhu. Her anxiety was palpable. She felt a pang of disappointment because it appeared she had been wrong about the opportunity and the moment for young Sidhu. Nothing magical had occurred as she hoped. No spark of inspiration. Sidhu would be admonished, and things would quickly return to the way they were.

'What are you doing today?' Sidhu asked, trying to sound casual, which caught Ms Heinzog's attention as she poured herself another cup of tea from the solid silver pot.

'Why do you ask?'

Sidhu shook her head a little too vigorously. 'Oh, you know, no reason.'

But Ms Heinzog was intrigued. There was something else. Sidhu was as easy to read. But she didn't push because she felt, whatever it was, it was forthcoming, and it might be fun to wait. Sidhu finished her granola, her mind whirring.

'It's just... I was thinking we might do something after college?'

Ms Heinzog looked at her curiously. 'But you're going home?'

'Yes, I am. I know.'

Ms Heinzog didn't reply.

'But before I go home, I mean.'

Ms Heinzog now felt a small jolt of excitement. 'Go on.'

'It's just... I was thinking...' Sidhu paused.

Ms Heinzog tilted her head, all ears.

'That we might visit Mr Clarke, after all.'

The older lady smiled curiously. 'The man with the violin?'

'Well, no, the man without the violin.'

Ms Heinzog was delighted, but she was also confused. 'But you were so against it.'

'Yes, I was.'

'Then what's changed?'

Sidhu blushed. Being honest was probably the best option, so she reached for her tablet. Finally, she turned the screen to present Yvonne's story. Ms Heinzog's eyes flitted back and forth, up and down, her slim finger scrolling. Sidhu watched nervously, noting when her eyes widened and narrowed. Ms Heinzog recognized Officer Dibble and felt a wave of anger as things began to fall into place. She looked at Sidhu and breathed slowly to calm herself, the way she did ahead of a recital.

'You said that it would be easy to set up?' Sidhu asked quickly.

'No, I said it wouldn't be difficult.'

'Right.' Wasn't that the same thing?

'I don't appreciate appearing in tittle-tattle stories like this.'

'No, I understand. And I apologize. It's a website I haven't heard of...'

'No, but you found it. Which means others will find it also. This afternoon, we could be on the bloody BBC.'

Sidhu looked ashen. 'I hope not.'

'But you haven't explained why?' Ms Heinzog stated. Something in Sidhu's face betrayed her. She reached for the tablet and began to scroll again as Sidhu tried to back pedal.

'Please, forget it. It's silly. I'm being stupid.'

Ms Heinzog's finger stopped on a later part of the story. A photo of Mr Clarke with his son. She looked at Sidhu and smiled warmly.

'Ah, I see-'

'Forget it. Let's just go home. I promised my mum.'

'You want to meet his son.'

This stopped Sidhu.

Ms Heinzog felt a rush of energy. This was precisely what she had hoped for. Something silly and daring. But so simple and natural also. Officer Dibble might have served a purpose after all, not that she would ever thank such a grubby little man.

'Then we should go together,' Ms Heinzog announced, 'it's what Mr Clarke deserves, right?'

Sidhu beamed at her new best friend. 'Really? Can we?'

'Of course we can. We can do whatever the hell we like.'

Chapter Twenty-Seven

It didn't take Noah very long to locate the source of his new-found popularity, and he sat down with his dad before he headed off to work. Jonson read the story with creeping alarm. He looked at the photograph on his mantelpiece and recalled polishing the silver just a few days ago before any of this nonsense began. Anna read it, too, while Jonson got on the phone to Milly for some crisis mitigation. Milly had already seen it, having been alerted by Georgina. She assured Jonson that it was just clickbait and wouldn't appear on any official sites or any newspapers. Jonson still fretted, though.

'Jonson, try not to worry. This will all blow over soon.'

'Yeah, I guess. What are you doing today?'

'Oh, you know, London stuff with the girls. Mitch is taking them on the world's biggest hamster wheel while I have a few meets.'

'That's good. Nice day for it.'

'Yeah. Last night was fun. Mitch is talking about opening an Indian again in LA.'

Jonson chuckled. 'We're around this evening if you're stuck.'

'Okay, cool. Let me see how the day pans out.'

. . .

The first of Milly's meetings was a hastily convened breakfast in Notting Hill with Georgina.

'When are you seeing them next?' Georgina fired, her phone constantly beeping.

'Er, today maybe, but later on. We haven't planned anything. Why?'

Georgina fixed Milly with an earnest look.

'I had my assistant make some calls...'

'Right.' Milly said warily.

'I'm hearing there's going to be a piece about Noah.'

'Jonson's son?'

Georgina tutted. 'No, the one in the Bible.'

Milly didn't laugh. 'What kind of piece?'

'Oh, you know, the usual. Eligible, shaggable hottie. That kinda thing. I've been through his Instagram-'

'And?'

'Yeah, there's a few snaps they'll grab. All things online are indelible. Kids have no idea.'

Milly made a note re: her two girls.

'Well, I'm sure he won't mind,' Milly suggested, but Georgina shook her head and clutched at her friend's expensive cashmere pullover.

'Noah needs to go through his entire online life and delete anything that might be awkward.'

'Like what?' Milly asked, alarmed now.

'Anything that could embarrass him. Anything of a sexual nature. Women in lingerie. Girls...'

Milly fumbled for her phone. 'Right, but you said it was indelible.'

'Yes, it is, and they'll find it anyway, but at least make it difficult for them.'

Milly nodded, waiting for her call to Anna to be connected.

Nihal knew that Prikash was lying to him because her newly-acquired sense of calm could only be explained by Sidhu's further contact with her. A positive which he welcomed, but this story online and the mention of the Royal College were unsettling. With Sidhu being homeward bound, it would be awful now if the family name was mentioned. Terrible for the family but worse for him because he would be blamed, so he needed to take matters into his own hands.

Nihal waited for the buzzer, pushed the heavy door of the Royal College and entered, climbing the few steps of the highly polished mosaic floor. The lady on reception recognized him and smiled warmly. Nihal was frequently discussed by the middle-aged ladies of the RCM office, and they had enjoyed seeing his handsome face in the newspaper. Nihal held up his violin and smiled.

'Good morning ladies, I work for the Sharma family,' Nihal began modestly, in the unlikely event that she might have forgotten him. The receptionist nodded enthusiastically.

'And Sidhu Sharma, of course is a student here.'

'Yes, she is indeed.'

'Sidhu called home today to request that this specific violin be dropped off to her. Don't ask me why. I know nothing about violins. They all look the same to me.'

'Me too!' the lady shrieked, and they all laughed.

'Well, I expect there's a good reason.' The lady's voice faded as she pulled her spectacles down from her hairline to consult her computer screen. Her plump fingers tapped her keyboard.

'Yes, Sidhu Sharma: here she is, but she's in class at the moment.'

Nihal felt a jolt of energy on hearing this.

'Would you like to leave it for her?'

Nihal smiled again as he handed over the instrument that Sidhu had not requested. He congratulated himself on his instincts as he thanked the ladies. He made for the exit with his phone in hand, dialing Sanjeev Sharma to share the good news. No doubt he already knew, but it showed that he was on point at least.

'What are you reading?'

'Oh, nothing important,' Gareth lied to his colleague in the police canteen. His colleague looked bored. 'You want another brew?' Gareth didn't, but he needed to read Yvonne's email, so he agreed and hoped he might fill the kettle up to the top.

Dear Gareth

Traction to your site/s remains strong, which is great news. Well done. I will send the Google Analytics data separately, but I know you don't like them, so, for now, you have another 120 new followers on Twitter – amazing – plus 60 likes and 9 RT's. Well done you. As expected, the handsome son - Noah - is driving the most traffic, and I suggest that if you are planning on any further meet/photo ops, then it is with him. He was on Chelsea and Brentford's books, and he played for London and England schoolboys. Two of his teammates have become professionals – possible angle? Have you heard of Troy Bateson? At Arsenal now but on loan to Burnley. He is verified and has over 400k followers – Amazing! You follow Troy now. There is also decent traffic for the Hollywood writer you mentioned, Juliet Millhouse. This is her writing name. She wrote the famous film Untitled. She is in London at the moment and defo worth meeting. And the journalist also, Barry...

. . .

His colleague returned and sat down heavily. 'Good news, is it?' his colleague chirped. Gareth smiled. It was indeed, but nothing he could share. Yvonne was a bloody marvel. Her idea of playing the journalist particularly appealed. In his experience, journalists were often happy to share and exchange information. Today the drab canteen and piss poor tea were particularly depressing and a good motivator for Gareth to finally get out. This afternoon he had his first session booked with a gym using electrical muscle stimulation. Things were looking up for @_hot_cop37.

Noah spent a frantic hour purging and sanitizing his online life, made more difficult by needing to fend off his mum's offers to help.

'Mum, if I'm looking for stuff that's embarrassing, then it follows that I won't want you to see it either.'

'Well, what sort of stuff are you talking about?' Anna asked a little huffily.

Noah gestured angrily. 'Mum, seriously, you need to leave. Just let me do it, and we can discuss it later, okay?'

Half an hour later, he was done. He had deleted only two Facebook posts, he stopped following a raft of Instagram models and, as instructed, he began following a few more wholesome accounts, including The National Trust.

'How'd it go?' Anna asked.

'Yeah, fine. Any calls?' he asked.

Anna shook her head. 'Anything online?'

They had both set internet alerts and so far, nothing had appeared. Anna put the kettle on. More out of habit than need. 'Bloody hell, imagine being actually famous,' Anna mused, and Noah shook his head.

'Milly's famous, right?'

'Yeah I suppose. By today's low bar anyway. But she doesn't get written about. Or followed.'

'Papped you mean?'

Anna shuddered at the prospect of people outside her house.

'Troy gets it a bit. Although not so much now he's at Burnley.'

Noah was confident there was nothing in his locker to worry him, but still, he didn't relish being written about.

'Hey, mum, listen. I know this isn't dad's fault, right, but...'

'You don't have to say it.' She handed Noah a cup of tea he hadn't asked for. 'This is all on him. Whether he meant it or not. This could only happen to your bloody dad.' Anna's phone began to vibrate.

'Speak of the devil.'

Chapter Twenty-Eight

Barry decided he could not let Vippin's beating deter him. Everything is a balance: a delicate equation between risk and reward. And something in his marrow told him that he was missing a trick in this story and possibly something that needn't incur Mr Sharma's wrath. Just an inkling as he peered at his notepad. He looked at the list of protagonists' names within a diagram, with arrows back and forth and a violin in the centre. He circled Milly and Noah Clarke. He got off the phone with Karl at the Evening Standard. They were not running anything, and Karl was even more terse than usual. Sharma's expensive PR team had finally woken up. But Barry fretted over the snippets of information that kept recurring online.

'Who the fuck is Hot Cop?' Barry made a note on his schematic and did a doodle of a cartoon penis next to his name. He listened to his messages: people wanting to chat and being ever so polite, including Detective Dibble. Barry circled Hot Cop on his pad. He wondered if he hadn't seen him before somewhere. Something about him felt familiar.

An hour later, in the Sharma palace, Nihal and Barry eyed each other carefully. They didn't like each other, but so what? Teammates don't need to be friends. They needed each other, and so far, so good. The story had gone quiet. Barry listed a long line of half-truths and blatant lies about how he had made this happen. He appeared less confident now and more contrite, which Nihal approved of.

'I threw some stuff out about his son as a distraction. Don't know whether you saw that?'

Nihal nodded. Shenfield was certainly cunning. Maybe Sanjeev had been right to trust him after all. The instincts of a billionaire?

'Yeah, thanks,' Barry muttered, although Nihal hadn't thanked him. But still, he could sense he was softening and that he might wish to share something. A little victory that was eating at him, perhaps.

'His daughter is coming home today, after college.'

Barry processed this quietly. 'No longer missing then?'

Nihal pulled at his immaculate beard.

'Well, that is good news. Well done, Nihal, you must be delighted.'

Nihal half smiled.

'Mr Sharma will be delighted.'

'It is a relief. She was at a friend's house. We will have a car waiting for her.'

'Yeah, that's a good move. Smart. Well done.'

'Thank you.'

Their mutual appreciation was slowly growing.

Barry picked the moped up from his usual hire place in Shepherds Bush. It was speculative and a risk, but one he had finely calculated. He would know soon enough if Nihal was having him followed, and subconsciously he began to prepare an explanation. He'd been in similar scrapes before and enjoyed the anonymity afforded by a helmet. He merged easily into traffic on Kensington High Street, where rich people like to shop. But Barry wasn't rich yet and was just passing through. He found a parking bay a little along from the Royal Albert Hall at just after 3pm. He paid the exorbitant fee for the maximum stay of two hours, which he hoped would be enough. He swapped his helmet for a baseball cap, pulled on a large overcoat and, with his training shoes, he looked just like one of the super-rich residents of the area out for a stroll. It wasn't very long before he spotted a conspicuous car, another large dark Audi, but different from the previous car, Barry thought. He pulled his cap down as he approached. The car was parked on the street and down a little from the college but not in a parking bay. Barry eyed the private plates. The windows were obscured, but the windshield afforded just enough light for Barry to make out a man in the driver's seat, one of the men he had met for an unfriendly coffee not so long ago. He who dares... Barry walked by; his speed and gait didn't alter at all. In the car, two men trained to kill, to spot adversaries and anything untoward, and Barry Shenfield walked right under their noses.

All-day at college, Sidhu fielded questions about her absence. She stuck to her ruse of a twenty-four-hour stomach bug, although it hadn't affected her brilliant musicianship. She played so beautifully in the afternoon that one of her tutors singled her out for glowing praise. This bolstered her confidence, which would be needed if she was to proceed with her madcap plans for the rest of the day. It would all hinge on Ms

Heinzog, a woman who she had completely misread until this week. Her austere façade and robotic personality were just a cloak, hiding a wise owl and a mischievous child in equal measure. She was waiting for her Sidhu, just as she had promised.

'My driver is waiting.'

'You still think it's a good idea?' Sidhu asked.

Ms Heinzog didn't answer this.

'How did you get the address?'

More silence.

'I'm just asking.'

'Well don't. It's not important.'

'And have you called ahead?' Sidhu asked, forcing Ms Heinzog to stop now.

'No. I think it is best that we don't forewarn them.'

Sidhu nodded, barely.

'It will be some surprise,' Sidhu added anxiously.

'Good. People like surprises.'

'Do they?' Sidhu wondered. But Mr Clarke would like her message that he was in the clear, and she could return home with a clear conscience. Sidhu started for the front door of the college, but Ms Heinzog held her back. Like Barry, she, too, had walked the block earlier in the day and spotted the car waiting for her protégé.

'Not that way. Your father's car is waiting for you.'

'How do you know?' Sidhu asked. Another pointless question.

'My driver is at the back. We can go through the kitchen.'

Safely in Ms Heinzog's car, they had much to discuss.

'What if they are not in?' Sidhu asked.

'Then it is not meant to be,' Ms Heinzog stated flatly.

'I thought you don't believe in fate.'

'I don't.'

'I could always go again, I suppose,' Sidhu suggested hopefully.

'No, I don't think so.'

'Why?'

Ms Heinzog chuckled. 'We have just sneaked out using the tradesman's exit?'

Sidhu looked quizzical.

'I think after today, you will be under 24-hour surveillance. No more tube journeys.'

Sidhu sighed, and now she really did hope that Mr Clarke was home. And his son too. It was becoming cold as the sun called time on another day, as the gleaming Jaguar eased through the traffic using all available shortcuts and back routes. Neither the driver nor the two passengers saw the single light that followed them all the way from their college. Barry Shenfield could barely breathe with excitement as he kept a safe distance behind the story that might finally cough up some real dough.

Just as Georgina had warned, the story on Noah appeared quickly on two gossip websites and was just as she predicted. That he was hot and had girls fawning over him, which was news to Noah. The copy carried a photo of him, Noah, in Ibiza looking suitably rippling. Jonson read it when he got home and gave his son a look of tacit approval. Well done, son, although he didn't say this, of course.

'Bloody disgrace' is what he said to Anna, who was busy searching some of the Instagram profiles mentioned that Noah had been following. Noah sighed wearily. He would explain later. Mitch made a mental note of some of the names.

'So, what does it mean?' Jonson asked, 'the story is over, but they've moved on to Noah?'

Milly shrugged. 'Who knows? It's all bullshit anyway.'

Mitch opened a beer and handed one to Jonson. 'Hey Noah, you want one?'

'Yeah, but I'm gonna jump in the shower first.'

'You know we've got pizzas coming,' Anna added.

'Sure, I'll just be five.'

'Hey, don't forget to moisturize.' Mitch joked and took a hit from Milly for his efforts.

'What? He's a sex symbol.'

Noah grinned as he left the room. He could see where this was going, and right on time, the doorbell rang. He scurried up the stairs, and Mitch grabbed his wallet to tip the pizza delivery driver.

'I'll get 'em.'

He opened the front door expectantly and was surprised to be confronted by two women. One was old but striking, and the other was young and very beautiful. They did not look like delivery drivers, and there was no sign of any steaming boxes.

'Can I help you?' Mitch asked.

The older lady spoke first. 'Is this the home of Jonson Clarke?'

'Er... Is he expecting you?'

'No. Not really.'

'Oh.' Mitch wondered how 'not really' was in any way an answer.

'Is he home?' the lady asked.

Another alarm rang in Mitch's head now. Mr Clarke? Who calls Jonson, Mr Clarke?

'Would you mind just waiting here for a moment? I'll just... er... I need to check... Sorry, you are?'

'My name is Eleanor Heinzog.'

'Right.' Mitch waited for a little context or more information, but nothing was forthcoming. He had forgotten her name already and didn't feel he could ask again.

'If you just wait here a second.'

As soon as Mitch reappeared in the lounge, everyone realised something was wrong.

'Where's the food?' Jonson asked.

'It's not the food. It's someone to see, Jonson.'

'Who?' Milly asked.

'Not journalists?' Jonson asked.

'I don't know. Maybe. They don't look like-'

'Who are they?' Milly snapped.

'I don't know. Two ladies. A Miss Hedgehog or something.'

'Who?' Jonson asked.

'I don't know. It's foreign, and she said it quickly.'

Milly stood up purposefully and gestured to Anna and Jonson that she would handle things. She walked past her flat-footed husband and headed for the hall, leaving Mitch to explain as best he could.

'What do they want?' Jonson asked.

'I don't know. I didn't ask. I thought they would be the food.'

Jonson could hear Milly in conversation. Whoever it was, there were no raised voices, and it all sounded cordial. It was great that Milly was present yet again. Milly would know what to do. Suddenly, his lounge door was pushed open. Milly appeared first and with a wicked smile. Jonson looked at her quizzically, but Milly's smile just broadened, and she was not alone. Two people shuffled into the room after her. Both looked rather awkward and sheepish.

'Jonson, this is Eleanor Heinzog.'

'Hello, Mr Clarke. I am sorry to trouble you.'

Jonson stared at the two women in his lounge, trying to make some sense of who they were and what they might want.

'This is Sidhu.'

Sidhu smiled as best she could, her eyes taking in everyone in the room briefly and noting that Mr Clarke's son was not present.

'Hey ladies, how are you both doing?' Jonson smiled warmly. 'How can we help you?'

Chapter Twenty-Nine

Throughout his difficult journey on an undersized moped, Barry had delighted in his guile but now was not the time for self-congratulations because, on this darkening residential street, Barry faced a truly momentous decision. Possibly a life and death situation. Should he call in his highly valuable information to Nihal, thereby gaining the trust and affections of one of the world's wealthiest men who also happened to have threatened his life, or should he strike out on his own and risk absolutely everything for his own greed and ego? As ever, Barry Shenfield did not hesitate. His first task then was to establish who lived in the house that violin girl and weird violin woman were visiting. Barry had a number of contacts in various agencies, including the police, essential for the intrepid investigative journalist and part-time detective.

By the time Ms Heinzog had finished her explanation for their impromptu visit, the lounge was full, with the exception of Noah. Maybe he does moisturize after all? Everyone was rapt. Sidhu had barely said a word and did not know where to look. Jonson ran things through in his mind one more time just to be sure that this was good news.

'You see: I was right all along.' Jonson beamed as Anna wiped her eyes dry and squeezed her lovable but infuriating husband's hand.

'I never doubted you,' Anna whispered into his ear as the quiet was broken again by the doorbell.

'That'll be the pizzas, and now we won't have enough. You guys are staying, right?'

On this kind invitation from Mr Clarke, Ms Heinzog deferred to Sidhu, it being her 'situation' and her timeframe. Sidhu nodded that she would like to stay, and Jonson beamed yet again. Good decision. They could always order more, or Noah might even run out and get some fish 'n' chips. Jonson darted for the hall to retrieve the pizzas, and, as the excitement began to grip the busy lounge, Milly tapped her glass and appealed for some quiet.

'Just to say, even though it's obvious, no posting about this on any social media.' This was received with a groan of approval and mirth. 'And absolutely no photos,' Milly continued. But unfortunately, it was too late for this appeal, with Barry already in position; he snapped clear images of a smiling Mr Jonson Clarke as he received the pizza boxes and handed the rider a tip.

As well as the extra doorbell, the rising noise levels in the house, plus the infectious excitement all drew Noah from his shower. He pulled on a pair of trackie bottoms, a vest and jumped into a pair of flip flops. He was starving and intrigued to know what the noise was about.

Noah entered the lounge and was immediately over-whelmed. Slices were being claimed, and boxes hastily passed about with napkins and drinks. Empty stomachs rumbled, but this was no match for the excitement brought by their visitors. Noah spotted them immediately. The older lady was sitting down in front of what looked like her first-ever slice of pizza, but his gaze was held by her friend or colleague who was standing with Mary and Isla.

'This is Noah. Our eldest,' Jonson announced proudly.

'Noah, a vest?' Anna screeched.

'I didn't know we had visitors.'

'Doesn't matter, Anna; he looks fine.' Jonson reasoned, and Sidhu agreed. She liked Jonson instantly. He was warm and infectious, and Mrs Clarke seemed lovely as well. Jonson was obsessed with the way Ms Heinzog was sitting ramrod upright and gingerly going about her slice.

'Nice, eh?' Jonson held his thumbs up for good measure. Ms Heinzog just smiled politely, which was all the encouragement that he needed.

'We're gonna need more pizzas.'

'On it.' Mitch stepped up. 'What, two more?'

'Yeah, two large. Noah needs fattening up.' Jonson laughed as Anna got on with the practicalities of clearing space and bringing in extra chairs so that everyone could sit down. Jonson filled Noah in quickly and predictably got some crucial facts wrong.

'Wait,' Noah appealed for clarity, 'the violin is yours? So, it's not lost?' Sidhu nodded gently and looked rather embarrassed.

'Well, that's great news.' Noah smiled and looked just like his dad. 'And we thought Milly was the best surprise visitor we could have,' Noah joked, and everyone laughed, including Sidhu, although she didn't understand the joke.

'Turns out, I was right all along. How about that, eh?'

'He was drunk,' Noah added.

'Hey,' Jonson fought back again, and Sidhu chuckled and enjoyed the atmosphere.

'I am so sorry,' Sidhu began.

'No, what-' Jonson protested, but Ms Heinzog interjected

now with one of her hand gestures, and everyone fell silent. Now she deferred to Sidhu again. This was most definitely kicking up leaves. Sidhu took a deep breath.

'I do need to apologize for many reasons and to a good number of people. It's been a crazy few days for me and for us all, by the sounds of it...'

Milly watched the young woman carefully. She could sense her anxiety and trepidation, made worse with everyone staring and hanging on her word. It was quite a tale and felt more like a confession than an explanation. Milly also considered Noah. He hadn't taken his eyes off her and hadn't even touched his pizza. Perhaps he wasn't hungry, but Milly knew better. She had made a career from imagining romantic scenarios with 'cute meets' just like this one.

Shielding himself from the cold as best he could, Barry checked the images on his camera of Mr Clarke. He didn't need to hear from his contact now about the ownership of the house as the plot thickened. What a blinking thing. Barry wracked his memory but could not make any connections or sense of this visit. Certainly, he hadn't expected it. His attention turned to Nihal and his new and ad hoc employer. Providing such information to Mr Sharma might be very lucrative. He stared at the attractive front door of Mr Clarke's house. Downing Street black with a stained glass insert, illuminated from within. The street was attractive, lined with trees and German cars. Barry put the house at well over a million. Not bad for a glorified teaching assistant and an unemployed actress. Barry drummed his fingers, deliberating what to do. Maybe he could play both sides. Or at least hedge for now. For any real purchase, he decided that he needed a photograph of the girl exiting the house: the money shot. If the media blackout continued, then Mr Sharma would pay handsomely for this image never to be seen.

Chapter Thirty

Nihal met with the security detail and ran through events one more time: Sidhu had attended school but had not appeared at the end of the day. Any moment he expected a call from his boss to fire him. Right on cue, his phone rang. But it was not Mr Sharma calling: it was Barry Shenfield.

Noah listened carefully to everything Sidhu had to say. He asked questions politely and did not ask her for any awkward explanations. Sitting nearby, Ms Heinzog kept an ear open on all of Sidhu's utterances as she fielded questions more generally about her life and work, some of which were less tactful than she was accustomed to.

'Are you famous?' Isla asked.

Ms Heinzog blushed. 'Well, in certain circles, yes, I probably am.'

'Which circles?'

'Isla, stop asking so many questions,' Milly rebuked her daughter.

Ms Heinzog smiled and shook her head politely.

'Darling, Ms Heinzog is a very well-known violinist-'

'Please, call me Eleanor.'

Isla turned to face her again and readied for her next question.

'Are you rich?' Isla asked, and now Eleanor Heinzog whooped with joy. The wonderful abandonment of childhood.

'Er, well, yes, I suppose I am.'

'My mom and dad are rich. And my mom is famous.'

Milly tutted. 'Honey, why don't you go help Auntie Anna with all these boxes.'

Isla did as she was told, with a lingering and knowing look at Sidhu and Noah as she passed the young couple.

'You have an enchanting child,' Eleanor said softly.

'That's one way of putting it, but thank you.'

'You're lucky to have your family and such friends.'

Milly took in the room around her. 'Yes, I am, thank you,' she conceded, her troubles a distant glimmer already.

'And your fame.' Ms Heinzog smiled. 'You're a writer?'

'I am. Although I wouldn't say famous.'

'Good for you. Being famous isn't so wonderful, as I'm sure you're aware, living in Los Angeles.'

'You've been there, of course?' Milly asked.

'Many times, yes. But I have always rushed home. We now know just how bad Saccharin is for us.'

Milly laughed.

'For the soul at least,' Ms Heinzog added.

'Well, I must say, this has all been a remarkable chain of events,' Milly stated in the hope that Ms Heinzog might elaborate.

'Yes, it certainly has.'

'And how did you become embroiled?' Milly pressed. A

perfectly reasonable question, but one which Ms Heinzog needed to be careful answering.

'A quirk of fate, I would say. But a happy one, I think,' Eleanor replied as she took in Sidhu, who was still chatting with Noah.

'Do you believe in fate?' Ms Heinzog asked, and it was Milly's turn to scramble a little.

'That's an interesting question,' Milly answered evasively. Once Milly had been connected to the lost violin, Ms Heinzog had researched the 'glamorous Hollywood writer'. She enjoyed the enchanting story of how her screenplay *Untitled* had been discovered and became a hit movie and her subsequent marriage to the 'handsome Hollywood hunk'. Milly sighed, still pondering. Mr Mahmood flashed in her mind, and here she was now with her husband and daughters.

'Well,' Milly began, 'the romantic in me wants to, absolutely. But the rationalist prefers to believe that we make our own outcomes.'

Ms Heinzog demurred politely and made a mental note to recall this logic the next time she was confronted by a disappointed parent.

'But you live in London now?' Noah asked. Sidhu nodded, a little worried now by this reality and how long it might last. Travelling the world from city to city and palace to palace. The apparent glamour but the less obvious loneliness. A life without roots can be a life without nourishment and the fear that her father might punish her with yet another move. Instinctively, she looked at her watch.

'Do you need to go?' Noah asked kindly. She did of course. Days ago. She needed to see her mum, and she wanted to also.

To apologize and begin her repatriation and penance. But she also wanted to stay chatting to this boy whom she hardly knew.

'And is that what you want? To be a violinist like Ms Heinhog?'

Sidhu chuckled. 'Zog... Heinz.'

'Oh, sorry.'

'Don't worry. I don't think she heard.'

Ms Heinzog smiled at young Noah, and he knew otherwise. He smiled back his apology.

'My parents want me to be a violinist.'

Noah smiled ruefully. 'Then maybe we have the same parents.' Sidhu took in the riotous scene before her. Too many people in too small a room, taking in two strangers so quickly and sharing a meal. The Clarke and Sharma households were hardly similar.

'I play the piano,' Noah clarified.

'Oh, wow. That's great.'

'Well, no, not exactly great. Not like you can play, anyway.'

'But you study music?'

'Oh, yeah, I've done the grades: the tantrums and tears.'

Sidhu laughed.

'Grade eight was when my mum cried.'

Sidhu cackled at this.

'But I'm not good enough to make a living at it. There are loads of pianists, and some of them are playing all day, every day.'

Sidhu raised her eyes.

'Right, but I bet that you're awesome.'

'Well I should be. I play all day, look who my teacher is, and you know about the violin I have.' Noah nodded. This statement raised more questions than answers, but Noah's instincts were not to pry. Another time perhaps? He hoped. Sidhu was unlike any girl he had ever met before, as beautiful as she was beguiling, and he lost track of everyone about him as they chatted. Of course, he was happy that his dad would not be going to jail, but, for now, anyway, he was more excited that Jonson was inadvertently responsible for putting Sidhu in his orbit.

Barry was becoming impatient now. With a further order of pizzas delivered, he wondered if they might even be settling down for the night. Nothing would surprise him anymore. And still, he fretted about his decisions. Nihal had been short on the phone, but he was under considerable stress, with Mr Sharma rampaging and blaming him for everything. Barry assured himself that everything was going to be fine. He just needed to trust his instincts.

Just then, the Clarke front door cracked open. A thin strip of light appeared, and, whippet quick, Barry was ready with his camera, concealed behind a suitably large SUV. And there she was: Sidhu and the weird violin woman standing bathed in light, and, as if directed by Barry himself, Mr Clarke now entered the frame. Barry clicked and had his shot. He watched the two women disappear into their waiting Jaguar. At this hour, they would head back into London on the motorway, and Barry would not follow. Too dangerous, and he had what he needed already. Plus, his energies are needed elsewhere.

Noah waited in the lounge for the front door to click shut and the inevitable inquisition to begin. He noticed Milly's demeanour and that Mitch was itching to hold up his high-five hand. His mum, too, looked at him wryly but had said nothing, of course. Anna knew that Jonson would oblige on behalf of them all. His dad would be the litmus test, and, right on cue, the lounge door burst open. Jonson appeared, beaming ear to ear.

'Oh my God... how beautiful is she?'

Noah closed his eyes slowly.

'I think Sidhu and Noah like each other.' Isla announced and an almighty guffaw spread through the room.

Chapter Thirty-One

Sidhu and Ms Heinzog said little in the car bound for Regents Park, both lost in their own thoughts and trying to make some sense of everything. Ms Heinzog also noticed the fledgling affection, but she said nothing. Their car swept off the Marylebone Road at some speed, a matter of moments from the Sharma palace. Ms Heinzog reached for her student's hand. She could feel her anxiety and gave her a reassuring squeeze.

'I will come in with you.'

'Thank you, Ms Heinzog.'

'Eleanor.'

Sidhu smiled.

'And as we discussed, you must be honest. Completely honest.'

Sidhu sipped at her water; at least her father was away from home. Yet she was still terrified.

'Just here, Ms Heinzog?' Her driver asked.

'A little along,' Sidhu corrected him, 'the white house at the end.' The enormous property was illuminated. It looked magnificent and intimidating, and even Ms Heinzog's eyes widened.

Sidhu punched the code into the keypad, then applied her index finger to a black pad and waited for the mechanism to release before she pushed at the heavy outer door. A house maid was already alerted and would be on her way to open the internal door. Her mother was close behind and in tears already on seeing her daughter, which was followed by shock and surprise when she caught sight of her illustrious companion.

Sidhu embraced her mother warmly and apologized over and over as Ms Heinzog stood by and said nothing. Nihal hovered at a respectful distance. Ms Heinzog eyed him carefully, and somehow, they seemed to understand each other. He, too, was relieved to have Sidhu home. He noticed Sidhu's two violin cases immediately, and he began to piece together possible explanations.

Sidhu broke off from her mum and nodded at Nihal, an apology of sorts before she introduced her companion, who really did not need any introductions. Nihal watched her closely. He would be fully enlightened later, but the presence of the famous violinist was a surprise and already illuminated matters. Mr Sharma might be thousands of miles away, but he always saw everything. He would have been notified already of Sidhu's arrival home, and Nihal expected an imminent call. His phone vibrated, and he backed away to take it.

Gareth Dibble was nil by mouth for his operation, having booked a further week's sick leave with stress and partial recurrent PTSD, his favourite acronym of all time. It was a fortunate and even fateful sign that his in-demand surgeon had received a last-minute cancellation, and he'd been persuasive about the upsides of what he called a hybrid operation: a moob reduction, tummy lipo and some stomach sculpting combo. Gareth did not hesitate. It had to be easier and less painful than doing the plank. It was very expensive, though, at an eye-watering £25,000, but Gareth concentrated on the bigger picture: *Paradise Island* and becoming an influencer. Newly inducted celebrities are most potent in their first year and can expect to earn as much as £500,000. Gareth intended to head off to LA, the Mecca of celebrityhood: where @_hot_cop37, with a cute accent and tight butt (he would have to get this done also), would take the reality shows by storm. Gareth sucked his stomach in as best he could and pushed up a moob. Not long now.

It was the middle of the night in Moscow, but Sanjeev Sharma would not be able to sleep with the news that Sidhu had arrived home safely. And even more remarkable and curious, her new 'friend' was the one and only Eleanor Heinzog, one of the few people whom he truly admires. The recovery of his violin had been relegated to a mere footnote.

'She is with Sidhu?' Sanjeev had choked. 'Ms Heinzog is in our house?'

'Yes, and she tells me they have been playing violin together.' Sanjeev's heart soared, but why hadn't Sidhu explained this? Although her behaviour remained egregious, Ms Heinzog's involvement changed things, and Sanjeev needed to reflect this.

'It has ended beautifully, Sanjeev. Sidhu is fine. No harm has come to her. There is nothing for you to worry about.'

Sanjeev was mightily relieved and said a prayer of thanks to God. His daughter had returned, his good name remained intact, and his daughter had made a new friend to whom it would be hard to refuse sleep-overs with.

Nihal confirmed all of this and added with some confidence that this whole unseemly episode had now drawn to a close. He left an appropriate pause that Mr Sharma could have filled with some gratitude, but the bastard chose not to.

'How is she?' Sanjeev asked.

'She seems fine. A little emotional. Some tears, but I think she is fine.'

Sanjeev had not been referring to his daughter, but he didn't want to admit this and hung up.

Sidhu explained matters and recent events to her mum as best she could, but concerning her epiphany at her masterclass, she deferred to her mentor. After all, much of this drama has been at her behest, and so it was reasonable that she might explain.

Noah shut his bedroom door and barred his excitable dad so that he could reflect on his unexpected encounter with Sidhu. New territory for him; he felt bewildered and equally excited. The internet had plenty on Sharma Chemical Inc and its illustrious founder, but very little on his family. Sidhu did not appear on any searches, and there were no images of her either. He thought of her smile as he thumbed his phone and pondered the golden rule that everyone knows: not to be too keen. But somehow, this felt different. How Sidhu appeared and held herself, not to mention her peculiar circumstances. Perhaps it was appropriate that she left so abruptly, like Cinderella hemmed in by a deadline. Noah felt his cool exterior rapidly crumbling.

Prikash was putty in Ms Heinzog's hands, who herself was clearly revelling in the obvious awe she commanded at Chez Sharma, an upside she hadn't factored in when she suggested such a bold play. As Prikash continued listening to Ms Heinzog's explanation, she was interrupted by Sidhu's phone beeping. Ms Heinzog had a fair idea who the text might be from, and, if so, then Mr and Mrs Sharma's problems might just be beginning. Sidhu spied her phone. She put it down quickly and looked at her mother, her face flush with excitement.

'Everything all right, Sidhu?' Prikash asked.

'Yes, mum, everything is fine,' Sidhu gushed, surprising Prikash. Her daughter was not normally prone to such verve.

'I just wish that dad was home so I could see him too.'

Prikash sat up now, sensing something afoot, and Ms Heinzog did the same.

'Because I have something else to tell you...'

Ms Heinzog's eyes widened. They had agreed on candour, but not everything at once. Ms Heinzog assumed the metaphorical brace position ahead of impact.

'I think I might have met someone.'

Prikash's face fell. Had she heard correctly? And just when things had been going so well. She looked at Ms Heinzog for an explanation, and, for the first time in this entire saga, Eleanor Heinzog was lost for words.

Chapter Thirty-Two

The next morning, after practically no sleep and with the magic of Ms Heinzog's presence over, Prikash read Sidhu her very best riot act about responsibility, respect and the arrangements for her attending college and returning home each evening. Sidhu nodded compliantly. She had not slept either but for very different reasons.

'The car will be waiting for you. And you will jolly well be there.'

'Yes, Mum, I promise.'

'Good. Otherwise, I dread to even think-'

'Have you told him?' Sidhu asked boldly.

Prikash shook her head. Her nerves were already jangling without Sanjeev taking to the skies again with this new situation in his mind.

'But you're going to?' Sidhu pressed, and Prikash snapped, resentful of the position Sidhu had put her in.

'Sidhu, for goodness sake, this is a boy you have only just met.'

'Yes, I know. But...'

'But nothing. What is this? You have only met him once? And you want me to tell your father, really?'

Sidhu nodded and said nothing. Her mother made good sense. But it wasn't Noah per se, more that she had met a boy she was attracted to that she wanted this prospect taken to her parents and specifically her dad.

'I will decide if I speak to your father,' Prikash huffed, 'do you understand?'

'Yes.'

'Yes, what?'

'Yes, Mum.'

'And do you have any idea how angry he will be?'

Sidhu nodded.

'Good, then you will allow me to handle this in my own way.'

Sidhu did not respond. There was not much to add, and, as upsetting as this all was, she rather enjoyed the power that had come with meeting Noah.

Milly would not have chosen *Hairspray* herself, but the girls had been adamant. They took a taxi into town and were dropped off just shy of Piccadilly Circus so that they could walk along Regent Street and up Shaftesbury Avenue. The show began noisily and did not relent as Mary and Isla shrieked and clapped in delight, so evidently, it had been worth every cent of the astronomically expensive tickets. After the show, Milly was due to have a quick coffee with her agent Lyal, but a text and an urgent phone call from Georgina in the interval changed her plans. They settled back in their seats for the second act with their ice creams. Mitch could sense that something was awry. He gestured for news.

'Georgina's been in touch. We're seeing her afterwards.'

Mitch smiled. If it had anything to do with Jonson, then it was highly likely that things were not okay.

In the coffee shop a little along from the theatre, Georgina hugged Mitch.

'Hey, dreamboat... you still putting up with her?'

'Yeah, I call her a stop-gap,' he joked, and Milly smiled demurely.

Mitch took everyone's drinks order and joined the queue, leaving the ladies to get to whatever it was. Georgina looked after him approvingly.

'I see he's got fat then,' Georgina said bitterly, and Milly chuckled.

'He wouldn't dare,' Milly joked, 'how's David?'

'Oh, you know, he did dare to get fat. And bald, actually, which is nice.'

Milly shook her head at her incorrigible friend. 'But still lovely and kind, I presume?'

Georgina shrugged. 'Yeah, I guess there is that.'

Milly tutted.

'How was the show?' Georgina asked casually.

'Er, noisy, but we were right at the front. My God, how hard do they work?'

'The cast? Oh I know, and for nix.'

'No way.'

'Yeah, the people in the chorus? The extras you'd call them, darling. Five, six hundred quid a week.'

Milly felt guilty now and a little fleeced also.

'Wow, we just did almost a grand on four tickets.'

'But you guys loved it, right?' Milly appealed to her girls, and they duly beamed their approval.

'I want to be an actress,' Isla announced. Milly raised her eyebrows, and even Mary sighed.

'So, come on, what's up?' Milly asked.

'There's a new photo of Noah.'

'That was quick.'

'But it hasn't been placed yet. I have a mole at Qnctd. They're going to kill it.'

'Which they can do, right?'

'To an extent. But there are other ways it can get out. Online.'

'Okay, well, what is it? This photo?'

Georgina took on a more serious air now. 'When you were at Jonson's house last night. They arrived by car, right?' Milly thought quickly.

'Er... yeah, Ms Heinzog has a driver. He dropped them off and waited outside.' Georgina considered this for a moment. It could be the driver, but she doubted it.

'What's she like, by the way, the maestro?'

Milly widened her eyes. 'Oh, you know, terrifying. She has this air.'

'Oh, I know. My dad fancies the pants off her.'

Milly shrieked with laughter.

'And did you see anyone outside?' Georgina asked.

'No, why?'

'Because the photo is of Noah last night with Sidhu Sharma.'

Milly struggled to take this in. So quick.

'Someone must have been watching the house.'

Milly tried to connect some dots.

'And you don't think someone in the house-'

'No, no way. I even warned people as a joke,' Milly began.

'You should let Noah know. And Jonson and Anna.'

Milly nodded.

'And what about Sidhu?' Milly asked. 'Do you have her number?'

Georgina shook her head. 'Okay, let me think about that. And maybe tell Noah to lie low for a few days. Stay off-line at least.'

'Really?'

'Yeah, I would.'

Noah arrived way too early for his impromptu meeting, so he decided to take in the Natural History Museum. A cultural interlude his mum would approve of. He had visited many times before on school trips, and now it seemed like a great place to kill an hour. The first few cases of fossils captured his attention, but quickly they began to blur. His mind was occupied with the living creature he was about to meet and in such odd circumstances. But in truth, even if he had not been so anxious and distracted, Noah would probably not have noticed the scruffy man watching him.

Sidhu, too, felt fretful and conflicted. Her mother had reacted predictably at her unlikely pronouncement, and she daren't imagine her father's response. Her mother might also be correct that she was being naive. And yet it still felt like the right thing to do. Her recital class this morning had dragged interminably ahead of her meeting with Noah at the café along from South Kensington tube station. Noah had suggested they meet after college in the West End, but Sidhu declined. At first, he interpreted this as a rebuff until Sidhu elaborated a little about her familial circumstances, and he understood.

Ms Heinzog was also enduring an unproductive morning with a Chinese protégé who was not as good as his parents had insisted he was. She wondered about her favourite student and what further adventures might be in store for her. Happiness, she hoped. She noted that Sidhu had, in fact, not been entirely candid with her mother. She had met a boy, yes, but she concentrated on his music and dodged the likely hurdle that he was not Indian, and her mum had been too afraid to ask.

Ms Heinzog recalled her short but highly-charged time with Sidhu. It had been an extraordinary few days, thrilling for them both, and Ms Heinzog felt certain that there was more to come. Ms Heinzog, very much a woman of the world, had been firm with Sidhu when she raised her culture, but this would be front and centre when her father returned. Ms Heinzog was not given to love at first sight but she had witnessed many times the pains of unrequited love, and she resolved to help Sidhu wherever she could.

Chapter Thirty-Three

I n a bustling nondescript cafe in South Ken, an odd meeting was playing out between two young people.

'This is a bit weird, huh?' Noah ventured nervously.

'Yeah. It is, I guess.' Sidhu agreed although she wondered what 'this' really is.

'Mad, when you think about it. You know, your violin and my dad. Who you are.'

'And how we met.'

'Yeah, exactly, in my lounge one minute. And now, here we are.'

'Just having a coffee.' Sidhu added as a claim to its innocence.

'Right. But do your parents know?' Noah asked.

'God, no.'

'No, same.'

They both burst out laughing; a very welcome release.

'It hasn't been great for your dad, though.'

Noah smiled dismissively. 'Oh, I don't know; he loves attention. And it had us all thinking. Or guessing, at least.'

Sidhu went to speak, but Noah held his hand aloft.

'No, don't apologize.'

'It's just-'

'You've done that already. And it's all okay.'

Sidhu nodded gratefully. 'Okay, that's kind, thank you.'

Noah shook his head. 'What for? No one got hurt. And we haven't done anything wrong.'

Sidhu liked his use of 'we', although she couldn't agree with him on this. She imagined her father's reaction if he could see her now.

'Don't worry about my dad. My whole life, he's been getting into scrapes.'

'Well, I think he's very cool.'

'Mmm...'

'My dad, on the other hand... not cool.'

'Oh, I don't know. I looked him up.'

'You didn't?' Sidhu shrieked.

'Yeah, I did. There's pages on him, but nothing on you.'

This flattered Sidhu on both counts, and she smiled.

'And excuse me, but he's a remarkable dude.'

'Oh yes, he's remarkable all right, but he's definitely not a dude.'

Noah's turn to laugh.

'And he likes to win,' Sidhu added with a more serious tone. Noah nodded knowingly.

'How's college?' He asked, changing the subject.

'Er... yeah, great normally.' Sidhu took a slight beat. 'But it was a little slow this morning.'

'Oh yeah?'

Sidhu's heart approaching a flutter now. 'Yeah, I can't think why.'

Noah beamed at her. 'Well, funny that, because my morning dragged a little too.'

This felt like a breakthrough, and they both laughed cautiously.

'Look, I hope you don't think I'm a crazy person. Because I know, we've only just met...' Sidhu began, her voice faltering a little.

'Yeah, like yesterday.'

'Right. And this does sound crazy, I know. But I told my mum about you.' Sidhu squeezed this out with her own embarrassment.

'No, you didn't.'

'I did. I don't know why, but I did. And what does that make me?'

Noah didn't know, and he didn't care. He just chuckled and thought he understood. He recalled his parent's excitement over their meeting. He took a moment and then reached out across the table for her hand, and thankfully she responded. They held each other briefly and smiled at one another.

'Yep, this is definitely weird.' Noah quipped to break the tension as he pulled his hand away.

They made such a handsome young couple that other diners might even have noticed them. One certainly did: the ever-resourceful and thorough Barry Shenfield, sitting a few tables over. He returned to the Clarke's address, in his car this time and on a hunch. He watched Mr Clarke leave for work, but he didn't follow because his nose told him the story had moved on. Mrs Clarke walked their dog but equally was of no interest. It was the son who Barry focused on, and when he appeared at just after 10am and headed for the station, Barry decided to head into town by train as well. Just on the off-chance.

Jonson was under strict instructions not to mention any of the current developments to anyone, especially not to Dr Judith Venter, the principal of his college and arch justice warrior.

'Thanks, Judith, that's very kind of you, but it all seems to have gone away.'

'Really?' She asked, unable to mask her disappointment.

'Yeah, I've gotta rush. I've got a meeting at Haringey council about two of my students,' Jonson lied; his meeting was with his eldest son in Kensington.

'But if there is anything you need...'

Jonson nodded as he backed away.

The café was much quieter when Jonson arrived, or at least it was until Noah shared his news about his earlier meeting.

'Are you serious?' Jonson screeched, Milly's warning prominent in his thinking.

'Yeah, why, what's up?'

'Well, you've only just met her.'

'So?' Noah added. 'You met mum, once.'

'Wow, man, what are you saying...'

'No, I'm not saying anything.' Noah protested, sensing again his dad's concern. 'Dad, what's up with you?'

'No, no, nothing...' He liked Noah's confidence, and he decided that Milly was probably being overly cautious.

'It's cool you've met up. And why not? She's lovely, man. Nice girl?'

'Yeah, really nice.'

Jonson nodded, his mind still a little frazzled.

'Well, there you go. And gorgeous. Fit as...'

Noah glared at his dad disapprovingly.

'No, dad, she's not fit.'

Jonson looked confused now. She isn't?

'She's beautiful.'

'Oh, okay. Copy that.' Jonson said kindly. He needed to explain about the photo, but it didn't feel like the right time. He smiled broadly and clapped his hands.

'Dad,'

'What?'

'Do not do the love speech.'

Jonson pulled a face. What love speech?

'But you like her, though?'

Noah suddenly looked much younger.

'There's just something about her.'

'Yeah, she looks like a movie star.'

Noah shook his head. 'No, not that. It's something else.'

Jonson nodded knowingly, dying to be asked, but Noah did not oblige.

'She's rich?'

'Dad...'

'I'm just saying.'

'Well don't. It's ugly.

Jonson scoffed.

'Okay fine, they're rich.' Noah conceded. 'But that's not it.'

'No, because that would be wrong. Even though you see it a lot. Although usually, it's the other way around, you know, ugly blokes and...'

'Dad.'

'All right, I'm just saying.'

'Well don't. Why are you so upset anyway?' Noah asked.

'I'm not upset.'

'Oh, leave off. Something's off. I can tell.'

Jonson frowned. 'You do know who her dad is?'

Noah said nothing and just waited.

'One of India's richest men. The key word here being 'India'.'

'Right, meaning?' Noah asked. Jonson tutted heavily and tilted his head. 'In case you haven't noticed, but I'm black, and so are you.'

Noah glared at his dad. 'Dad, you can't make assumptions like that.'

'Okay fine. On being black, fine. Maybe. But you not being Indian, that's gonna be a problem.'

Noah chewed his lip.

'Well, there's nothing I can do about that, is there?'

'Right, which is why it's a problem.'

Noah nodded. 'Well, like you said. We've only just met.'

'Exactly.'

'It's not like we're getting married. We're not even going out.'

Jonson made a fist, and they bumped.

Sanjeev Sharma sat in yet another meeting in yet another luxury hotel with his beleaguered battery of lawyers, his team from Mumbai, plus an array of local fixers, all pitted against a similar team sitting opposite. A huge game of chess. At stake, after three years of work, was the acquisition of Russia's leading mining and minerals company, and yet his mind was elsewhere. His immediate thoughts were in London with his family, reunited in his beautiful home. Prikash and Sidhu would enjoy their time together, and he had been assured that making this trip was the correct play. Getting the deal done was certainly worthwhile, but, more importantly, he could feel his anger slowly abating, which had to be a good thing. Earlier, he received an update from Nihal that all was well. Sidhu had been dropped at college, and there were no more reports on websites or elsewhere. Good news. The Russians countered with higher demands, but he knew this was just bluster. They would inevitably agree on his price, but so what? He would have given anything right now just to be at home with his family.

Chapter Thirty-Four

Barry waited in the very agreeable luxury of the bar at the Soho Hotel. He enjoyed people-watching his fellow diners. They were mainly beautiful people and a few wizened types on their final laps of the corporate block. He sipped his drink and imagined the contrasting mania in the Qnctd offices a mile up the road. Emergency meetings hurriedly convened about a photo they had received of two young people enjoying an innocent coffee.

Barry's issue now was who to trust. Obviously not Vippin or Nigel at his old workplace. Nigel didn't have the nerve. It needed someone with a certain temperament for something so daring. And a need. He knew plenty of hacks who could eavesdrop, sift through rubbish and set up stories with prostitutes and cocaine, but none he could trust. He noticed Nihal approaching with the host and fortunately alone this time.

Barry brought him up to speed with a succession of well-rehearsed lies and half-truths, and Nihal did the same, including the rather cruel news of Sidhu appearing to be smitten.

'Violin problem solved then,' Barry gushed, 'Mr Sharma will be delighted.'

Nihal shook his head.

'Mr Sharma doesn't do delighted. Not for his staff anyway.' His eyes were heavy and red as though he had not slept. Calls at all hours from his boss, no doubt. A young waitress appeared at their table. Barry gestured to his empty glass and appealed to Nihal. 'I'm having another one. This is a celebration, in my book anyway.'

Nihal took a moment and sighed. Why not?

'Very good. Two more, please, my darling.'

'A celebration for you perhaps. But not for me.'

Barry nodded sympathetically.

'I'm guessing that Mr Sharma can be difficult?'

Nihal chuckled at such an understatement.

'Well, he's a billionaire,' Barry suggested. Nihal scoffed. 'After everything I've done for him.'

Barry's mind flickered. 'How long have you been with the family?' he asked to keep on the subject of his employer. The drinks arrived, and Nihal took a long sip.

'Coming up for three years. If I make it, that is.'

Barry felt a jolt of energy and gestured for him to continue.

'I hear them on the phone. Him and Prikash.'

'His wife?'

Nihal nodded. 'Apparently, this is all my fault.'

'How so?' Barry asked, heavy on empathy again.

'He's a billionaire, right. He's never wrong. So I'm out. I'm getting fired.'

Barry's heart leapt at this. This might be tremendous news.

'Well, I'm sorry to hear that,' Barry lied.

'Yeah, thanks.'

Nihal drained his drink.

'Another one?' Barry offered, but Nihal shook his head. He would be at the college for Sidhu's pick-up, and being pissed would not play well.

'So, what will you do?'

'Not sure. Head back to Mumbai, I expect and hopefully with the reference I deserve.'

'Hopefully?'

Nihal nodded.

'Like I said, he's difficult. He has a tendency for jealousy, and he's not known for his sense of forgiveness.'

'But you've come through for him. And this is resolved.'

Nihal sighed. 'Do you want to tell him that for me? Me being in the newspaper was probably the end. Made his family vulnerable.'

Barry nodded, looking suitably chastened.

'That's on me then, and I am sorry. I really am.'

If there were any budding dramatists in the bar right now, they would do well to sit back and observe Barry Shenfield giving an acting masterclass. His apology played right into his hands. Nihal had a grievance, and Barry had a debt. What better way to compensate the man who has made everything possible and with so much to lose? But Barry wouldn't reveal himself just yet. Too many mistakes are made in haste. He needed time to plan, plus he was already a bit pissed.

'What are you doing now?' Barry asked casually.

'Picking up Sidhu from college and taking her home.'

'Very good. Well, let's maybe get a proper drink-in-some-time. Maybe I could buy you dinner. To say thank you.'

Nihal pushed his thick mane of hair off his face and smiled as best he could.

Prikash sat across from her daughter and tried to process what she had just been told, and this time there was no Ms Heinzog to shield her.

'The son of the man with the violin?' Prikash repeated in disbelief.

'Mr Clarke?' Prikash added just to be clear.

Sidhu nodded, her mouth drying.

'But Sidhu. He is not Indian.'

'Yes, mum, I know that.'

Prikash looked panicked now.

'He is English.' Prikash said diplomatically.

'Yes. He is English, and he is also...'

'Yes, mum, I know what he is.'

Prikash clutched her breast, barely able to breathe. Sanjeev would explode.

'And mum, remember, we are just friends.'

'Then, why bring it up at all?' Prikash countered.

'You know why. And at college, I have friends from all over the world.'

'Yes, but he is not at your college, so it is different. And what will your father say? He will never allow it.'

Sidhu knew this already, of course, but it still stung her.

'And what about you?' Sidhu asked, just as Ms Heinzog had instructed her. The two of them had spent an entire masterclass without touching their violins, and for this very moment.

"Enlist your mother's support. You must have her as an ally."

Sidhu's question took her mother by surprise.

'What I think?' Prikash faltered. 'Sidhu, it doesn't matter what I think. It isn't important what I think...'

'It is to me. It's important to me,' Sidhu replied promptly. Ms Heinzog had hit the bullseye once more. She might as well have accompanied Sidhu home again.

'Sidhu, stop it, please. You know full well that it is your father who decides-'

'Yes, I know. But he wants your favour as well.'

'But this is not-' Prikash deflected.

'Mum, I want to know what you think of him.'

'But I've never met him.'

'You know what I mean.'

Prikash felt ambushed and steadied herself as best she could. It was all a considerable shock: first a boy, then a boy who was not Indian. And now a black boy.

'But Sidhu, this is madness; you have only just met him.' Prikash pleaded.

'Yes, and it's probably nothing.'

Prikash seized on this. 'Good, then it is not something to bother your father with. It is best-'

Ms Heinzog had covered for this contingency also.

"You need to be firm here, Sidhu. Your father must know, or else this is all for nothing."

'No mum. That is not an option, and you haven't answered my question.'

'But Sidhu, you've only just-'

'I know, which is why it's so important.'

'Why? What is so important?'

'That I have might have some charge over my life.'

'Do you like this boy?'

'I don't know. But yes, maybe I do. I think so. But that it is not the point.'

'Then, what is? Because you are not making any sense to me. So, please explain, tell me what you want me to do.'

Sidhu took a moment.

'I need you to tell dad.'

'Tell him what?'

'That I have met a friend called Noah. A boy who I think I like. And the truth. And if you can't find the words, or the word, then you can send him a picture. But I want him to know whether or not I ever see this boy again.'

Prikash was taken aback by Sidhu's composure. And her eloquence. Almost like a speech that had been written and rehearsed. Prikash was weeping now, a weapon she often called upon.

'But Sidhu, he will take you back to India. Or worse.'

'What? What do you mean? An honour killing? He will kill me?'

A flash of anger now caught Prikash, and her face changed.

'How dare you!' Prikash spat venomously. 'Don't be so ridiculous. Your father would never do such a thing. He loves you.'

'Good, then we shall see.'

Prikash slapped Sidhu's face hard. She had never raised her hand to her daughter before, so it duly hurt them both. Sidhu's tears flowed freely. Both of them, for a moment, were terrified.

'But mum, my question remains.'

'Oh, what question?' Prikash thundered. 'Puppy love and nothing more. You're being ridiculous.' Prikash watched her daughter and saw her hurt and anguish.

'Sidhu, all I ever want is for you to be happy.' She reached for her daughter's hands. They held each other. 'Yes, I have preferences, of course. That you meet an Indian boy like yourself. Like your brothers. A boy from a good family. And with our culture. A Hindu...'

Tears now cascaded down her face.

'But you are young and naïve.'

'Yes, but I have feelings and my own mind.'

'Of course, I understand this; I do.' Prikash softened now. Sidhu felt her heart might burst as they hugged each other.

'But Sidhu, your father.'

'I know.' Sidhu wiped her eyes. 'But what can I do? Because this is my life and my future.' Sidhu whispered, without explaining that when the mighty Sanjeev Sharma arrived for his showdown, the equally mighty Eleanor Heinzog was intending to be present, and she had taken down bigger buffalo than him.

Chapter Thirty-Five

Prikash mulled for a little while before deciding that she had to act quickly: the longer she left matters, the more inflamed they would become. Undoubtedly Sanjeev would explode, but the sooner this happened, the better because it would give him more time to recover. That it was just a friendship played in her favour. But whatever threats he made and sanctions he had in mind, Prikash was determined that Sidhu would not become a prisoner in their beautiful home, Dubai style. Prikash closed her office door and did a quick calculation of time zones. She stared at her phone and steadied herself.

Sanjeev was in another pivotal meeting. His aide explained that it was not a good time, but, all revved up and committed now, Prikash insisted on speaking with her husband. Given what sums were at stake in this meeting, this was a gross imposition, but Sanjeev took the phone and walked to a corner of the large board room. After cursory pleasantries with his trembling wife, he heard only two more words from her and promptly fainted, sending his staff scurrying for medics. It didn't take him long to come to. Just a few seconds. One of his aides was assuring a frantic Prikash that he hadn't died.

'He is fine. He just fainted. He's very tired. But can I just clarify what it is that you told him...'

The meeting was now over, and a new itinerary was redrawn immediately, with his jet prepped, refuelled and bound for London.

Nihal had been in the Sharma household long enough to establish ways of hearing everything he needed to. Sidhu had finally met a boy she was attracted to, and he relished the problem this posed for the man who was about to fire him. Although Nihal was Indian born, he had been educated abroad and was as much a product of the West and the twenty-first century. A man abreast with modern sensitivities and attuned to accusations of racism, to which no one is immune, not even the English royal family. Sanjeev Sharma, however, was a man from a different generation and a vastly different place in the world. Born and educated in India, Sanjeev Sharma, for all his worldliness, the strident global capitalist, he remained as far removed from the tenets of progressive politics as it was possible to be. He would explode at Sidhu's news, and Nihal could not wait.

Yvonne was pleased that Gareth had opted to go under the knife because it would give her a break, if nothing else. Annoyingly, but typically, Gareth had texted the moment he came around from his multiple procedures.

'Any news? How is my Twitter?'

She didn't reply. She hoped his convalescence was as protracted as possible. Perhaps he might get an infection. She admonished herself for such cruel but wishful thinking.

As a rule, Barry didn't much care for PR professionals. A profession largely comprised of posh people doing favours for one another. He, therefore, enjoyed ruining their latte-filled days with his little digital intrusions. Barry had a raft of contacts and various phone numbers of notable people, including people within Qnctd. His strategy had now changed, however, and he needed to contact them again, using one of his many pseudonyms.

He re-read his email that he had sent, which was now being pored over and setting hearts racing in the Qnctd house, and indeed also in a much larger house in Regents Park. Barry was very specific in his email that he had no intentions of publishing his new story or any of the photos. A winner needs to be adaptable, and, despite his weight, Barry was as nimble as any. The image of the two young 'lovers' in the café was probably the piece to complete his dangerous jigsaw: Mr Sharma would pay handsomely to keep it buried. Barry smiled. He had to hold his nerve now and somehow bring Nihal on board. Timing and wording would be key. Barry opened his pad, clicked his pen and began scribbling down odd words, thoughts and ideas:

N's loyalty, just desserts, racist bastard... (possible future story on S's racism???), N has worked his ass off (balls off?), it's not stealing if it's money owed (due??), over and above... extra mile (no, avoid shit clichés like this)

His tone would be crucial. Later he would open a word document and write it all out properly. Hone it and then learn it. For now, he fired Nihal a friendly text. Just checking in on his new buddy. A soft start if you like. And, ever efficient, Nihal was onto it immediately. Barry's phone pinged.

'S inbound from Moscow. ETA 6 hours. Good news from Qnctd just in – the story is dead.'

Barry chuckled at the wonders of technology. Things were coming together. He was playing all sides and always staying ahead. He had a good feeling about this. A really good feeling.

Chapter Thirty-Six

Noah and Sidhu exchanged a flurry of texts ahead of her showdown with Sanjeev. Noah felt ambivalent that Sidhu was so insistent on mentioning him to her old man. He was flattered that she would want to, but he was also concerned by her urgency. As everyone kept reminding him, they had only just met, and he didn't want her running into trouble on his behalf. And if her father was anything like Sidhu had described, then he would undoubtedly try to put a stop to whatever their fledgling friendship is? He might even prevent them being friends. Bravely, he offered to be present himself before the great man, but Sidhu declined his offer. Privately, he was mightily relieved, although he didn't say this as they continued to text.

'What time is he home?'

'Landing in 1hr. Then 40 mins by car.'

'OK, good luck. You got this. Let me know.'

'Sure.'

'Maybe, tell him my family are huge curry fans. Like, huge.'

The three dots appeared in Noah's window, and he received

just an emoji of a laughing face. The sign-off text. He hoped it wouldn't be their last conversation. And yet none of this felt very real. It was all rather bewildering. Yesterday he was unencumbered and trying to make plans for his trip abroad, and now he could think of nothing else but her. Sidhu had explained her family life and circumstances: the travelling, the business and her parents' ambitions for her. It was left unsaid that he would not be a welcome addition to her life in any form. He glanced at his watch and made some quick calculations.

His phone vibrated again, this time alerting him to an internet search he had set, and he panicked that it might be the story Milly had warned him about. But fortunately, it was about his footballing buddy, Troy Bateson. They hadn't spoken for so long, and, needing a distraction, Noah placed a rare phone call.

'Yo man, wha's up mo-fo?'

Noah smiled, happy to hear his voice, in high spirits and understandably so. 'Hey, man. I saw your news. Congrats, bro.'

'Been ages cuz. You gone cold on me cos I'm at Burnley, fam?'

Noah chuckled. Troy was the best football player Noah had ever played with or against, and that he made the professional ranks was an eternal sense of pride for them both. 'Yeah, that's it, Troy. I'm not hitting you up again until you play for England, you hear me?'

Troy's booming laugh filled his phone. His exuberance as infectious as ever.

'But I saw your news about Arsenal. Man, that is so dope.'

'I know, man and about time too. I'm back now, and this time, let me tell ya, I'm breaking through. I'm playing, for real.'

Noah shook his head at such a thrilling prospect. 'That would be so sick. I want tickets though.'

'Course, man. I'm gonna get you in a box.'

Noah chuckled. 'When are you back?'

'Soon. My agents are on it. They're making it happen.'

Noah smiled. Troy had people now. 'That's great, man. I'll swing by.'

Noah ended the call, delighted for Troy, but quickly his thoughts reverted to Sidhu. He looked at his watch and hoped she was okay. She didn't seem the football type, but she might like to see a match. Troy would be thrilled to meet her, and Noah smiled at the prospect. Six foot three Troy Bateson, his muscles covered in tattoos. Noah would put Troy in any team, apart from the one charged with winning over the confidence of Mr Sanjeev Sharma. Noah glanced again at his watch. Mr Sharma must have landed and be in his car now. And with his terrified daughter waiting for him.

Sanjeev was on the phone to Prikash as his jet touched down, and somehow Sidhu just knew without needing to be informed. Her mother emerged after an hour in their in-house beauty salon in the property's cavernous basement, and she looked stunning. But her immaculate make-up was unable to mask her anxiety. Sidhu nodded her reassurances. Everything was set up. She had the text to confirm it all just as they had planned. But Prikash fretted at her duplicity and whether she could hide it from her husband.

'Nihal is with him in the car. He will fill him in properly.'

Nihal would not be able to assuage him. Only Sidhu could do this, and she was ready. From her fourth-floor apartment within the Sharma mansion, Sidhu watched the gleaming Rolls Royce Phantom round the corner and quickly disappear below ground. She peered nervously in her mirror and dabbed both her eyes with a tissue. Her mouth felt dry. She opened her text app and fired off the message she had already written.

Nihal emerged first from the elevator onto the spacious landing, which let onto the large drawing room. His face was pinched and strained from his torrid car journey. He had phoned ahead to reiterate his strict instructions for the entire domestic staff that Mr and Mrs Sharma would meet in the drawing room and that they were not to be disturbed under any circumstances.

Sanjeev now appeared from the elevator. He looked exhausted. It had evidently not been a good flight. His eyes found his wife first, and he smiled as best he could. He deliberately did not yet take in Sidhu. His other children were present, who he greeted briefly with quick hugs and kisses and then dispensed them back to their nannies to quickly vacate the room. The heavy double doors closed, and finally the only business on the itinerary could be attended to. Sanjeev looked at Sidhu. He looked wounded, like a warrior returning home from battle. But even worse, he looked disappointed. Disappointed with Sidhu, his foolhardy daughter who had no idea of the trouble she had caused. Disappointed with her naivety or stupidity to dream up such a plot which threatened everything that was important. Putting things right could be ruinously expensive, but his daughter's honour was worth any price, as was his good name. And until a suitable solution presented itself, he instructed Sidhu not to use her Guarneri.

'But Sanjeev,' Prikash had protested, 'this will only alarm people-'

'Damn it, woman, do as I say!' Sanjeev thundered down the phone, tired of being questioned and compromised by other people's foolishness. Sanjeev had thought of nothing else for days, and finally, he was able to confront his daughter.

'Sidhu, how can you treat your mother like this?' he asked quietly.

'Father, we have a lot to discuss.'

'Oh, do we?' Sanjeev replied.

Prikash went to speak, but Sanjeev held his hand aloft.

'So, now my daughter is so grown up that she discusses things with me? Is this right?'

Sanjeev had used his flight to think of his opening.

'I would like to discuss things,' Sidhu corrected herself.

'Ah, so a request then? And not an order.' Sanjeev eyed Prikash carefully as he said this.

'Yes, Dad.'

'But why would I discuss something with you when you do not listen to what I say?'

'Sanjeev-' Prikash appealed.

'Please, Prikash,' Sanjeev snapped, 'not another word from either of you.'

And just at this moment, the doorbell chimed. Sanjeev was momentarily distracted but quickly regathered himself and reverted now to Hindi to remonstrate and vent his fury. Sidhu tried to interject but was never permitted. Suddenly there was a knock at the door of the drawing room. At first, Sanjeev looked confused. He stopped shouting and waited for silence as he glared at the door. And then, sure enough, there was a further knock at the drawing room door. He assumed it was Nihal, who he should have fired already. There was one further timid knock at the door, and Sanjeev could not ignore it any longer.

'Yes, who is it?' Sanjeev bellowed.

The doors opened slowly. A tiny maid appeared with her head bowed in apology. Sanjeev glared at her, but then the maid moved aside. Ms Heinzog had made many entrances in her long and esteemed career, but this one topped them all. She appeared to be tall by comparison to the maid and taller again by her balletic pose with her head held high. Like a knight in armour. Sidhu could have burst into tears on seeing her. Ms

Heinzog took a step into the room, and, without saying a word, her gaze took in the three people present in turn, landing finally on Mr Sharma himself, who was staring agog and completely lost for words.

Chapter Thirty-Seven

Two floors above the drawing room in the Sharma mansion, another meeting was taking place, one every bit as important and just as tense. Nihal's private office adjoining his suite was well appointed and presented. Nihal slumped glumly in his comfortable leather chair; Barry faced him and appeared calm and assured. He retrieved his mobile phone from his pocket and ceremoniously laid it on the low glass table between them, holding his hands aloft in the surrender pose for good measure. Nihal chuckled.

'But how do I know if that's your only phone?'

'You don't,' Barry grinned, and they laughed, a welcome release for them both. It felt peculiar that they might become allies. But pragmatism always dictates, and if Barry were to prevail, then it would be highly lucrative for them both. It all hinged on whether he could bring Nihal onside.

'You want a drink? A coffee, tea?' Nihal asked.

Barry waited, his eyes expectant.

'Or a beer?'

Barry clapped his hands. 'But only if you'll join me.'

Nihal shrugged. Sure, why not.

'Good lad.'

Nihal leaned forward and hit a button on his desk.

'Yes, Mr Khan, how can I help you?' A voice emanated from the bowels of the house.

'Hey, Binu. Two beers please.'

'Certainly sir. And anything else?'

Nihal looked at his new colleague. 'You want anything? Snacks or something?'

Barry gestured: hell yeah. Never in his life had Barry Shenfield turned down snacks. They weren't dancing quite yet, but they were breaking bread, which was a step in the right direction.

'Yes please, Binu. Beers and snacks for two.'

'No problem Mr Khan, sir. They will be along in a few moments.'

Nihal cut the call and then stopped for a moment to think of his circumstances.

'I wonder how it's going down there?' Nihal asked.

Barry shrugged. 'Who cares? It's not relevant,' Barry replied, deliberately being open and also a little suggestive. His master play had begun.

'What do you mean, not relevant? Relevant to who?' Nihal asked.

'To you and me. To us. The underlings,' Barry quipped. 'The daughter is home. The violin is safe. So now it's just a bruised ego that needs fixing, but he'll survive.'

Nihal wondered. 'Although, this is a very big ego we are talking about.'

Barry chuckled. 'Oh really, a billionaire? And that's why you're getting the big heave-ho...'

Nihal shook his head, a little confused.

'You're getting fired because you know...'

'Because I know what?' Nihal asked.

'That he's been humbled by his daughter and her skinny teacher.'

Nihal considered this.

'And this makes you dangerous,' Barry added mischievously, 'he can't have the business world knowing about such things, now, can he?'

Barry had Nihal's full attention now, and he gestured for more. Barry turned his head to one side. 'Knowledge is power, my friend. It's valuable.'

Nihal's eyes narrowed, his mind assessing and calculating.

'What do you mean, exactly?'

They were like two poker players eyeing each other warily.

'Like I said, I'm assuming he's got more enemies than friends. Real friends anyway.'

Nihal half smiled but said nothing.

'There's good value to keeping things quiet.'

'Right, so what are you suggesting?' Nihal asked curiously.

Barry shrugged. 'That we might stick it back to him?' Barry said defiantly and emphasizing 'we'.

'Blackmail, you mean?' Nihal asked coldly.

Barry was well prepared for this. He reacted as if hearing it for the very first time. 'Well, that's a strong word.'

'Well, what would you call it?'

'Not that, anyway. That would be suicide,' Barry answered, 'career suicide anyway, because, with his influence, you'd never work again.'

Nihal nodded. 'What, then?'

Barry took a moment now. 'Sharma has more money than Billy-O.'

Nihal shrugged.

'He buys whatever he wants.'

Nihal nodded again.

'This house, that car. A new jet. Yacht... Whatever he wants, yeah?'

'Yep, that's about right.'

'And this is no different. He's just buying something he wants. And it's something that we have.'

With this, Barry was finally exposed. And just then, there was a knock at the door. Refreshments, presumably. Well done, Binu. Perfect timing.

Sanjeev was completely wrong-footed by the arrival of Ms Heinzog. He was simultaneously angry at his daughter's temerity, admiring of her cunning and bedazzled by the woman herself. Most of all, he was humbled that she should deign to visit his simple home.

Bedazzling was a good word to describe her masterly oratory, which was every bit as polished as her wizardry with a violin. Sidhu had to stifle a smirk when Eleanor explained to her enormously powerful father that he should refer to her as Ms Heinzog.

'Your daughter has a remarkable gift.'

Sanjeev clutched at his breast at this and from someone so esteemed.

'I have always said she can play with the very best,' Sanjeev gushed.

'Yes, and she will.'

Sanjeev's heart soared at this.

'If you allow her to.' Ms Heinzog added, and Sanjeev's face fell.

'Sidhu is a brilliant musician. But she is more remarkable for her spirit and her verve.'

Sanjeev tried to process.

'Sidhu is exceptional, and you are right to be very proud of her.'

Prikash noted that she posed this as a statement and not a question.

'As parents, you are to be congratulated.'

Sanjeev nodded again. Such praise.

'I have encountered young people from across the world and often from families like yours: shall we say, families with means.' Eleanor continued to heap praise on the great man with the great ego. 'And yet Sidhu remains completely adjusted and normal.'

Does she? Sanjeev wondered. Sidhu continued to blush and watched her father continue to soften.

'I see myself in her,' Ms Heinzog continued, 'if I had my time over, I would want to be Sidhu Sharma with the world at her feet. With your support, I have no doubt that she will achieve great things. Greater things than anything we can buy.'

Sanjeev could not recall a meeting where he had listened so much and spoken so little.

'But you are right to be angry also.'

Sanjeev continued to nod in agreement with this remark-able woman.

'You are angry with Sidhu, but you should also be angry with me.'

Sanjeev shook his head, but Ms Heinzog gestured for him to be quiet.

'Because it is me who extended Sidhu's little excursion.'

Sanjeev understood now, and he was grateful for her candour.

'And we must all attempt to understand and reconcile why Sidhu did what she did.'

Yes, of course. Nods all round.

'So that positive outcomes emerge. Mr and Mrs Sharma...'

Ms Heinzog fixed Sanjeev with her most earnest look, and she paused.

'A man can only be a great man if he allows his children to become their best selves.'

By the time Nihal had finished his second beer and polished off his plate of warm prawn crackers, things had moved along nicely. On the table lay a photograph of Sidhu and Noah holding hands in the Kensington café. Barry had shown his hand now. He felt that Nihal was hooked, but could he land him?

'But it's still blackmail.'

This time Barry didn't correct him.

'And risky,' Nihal added, 'because he's no dummy.'

'No, but he's desperate, and he wants this to go away. And quickly.'

Barry had all the answers. Nihal considered the image again. The prospect of it being published made him shudder.

'But it's illegal, and I'm supposed to be a lawyer.'

Yet again, Barry had anticipated this point.

'Technically, yes. You are correct.'

Nihal waited expectantly for Barry to continue, only he didn't. He said nothing.

'Go on,' Nihal demanded from him.

'Well, the law is blind, right? Equally applicable to us all?'

Nihal scoffed at this.

'Exactly. It shouldn't favour the rich; only it does. Rich people get a different law. The law they want. And who writes the law?' Barry asked. 'In general, I mean. Is it poor people or rich people who make up the rules?'

Nihal had heard this many times already. 'It's not perfect, but humans are flawed, and it's the best we can do.'

'Fine. The best we can do, maybe. But this doesn't mean it works, and it's why you're about to get screwed. Because Sharma owns you, and he has every right to screw you.' Barry delivered this line word perfect, and it shook Nihal accordingly.

'So, this isn't theft. This is money due. Your just desserts,' Barry added confidently, 'And...' Barry raised his finger now and paused, just as Ms H did in the meeting below a moment ago. '... it will never come back on you. Ever. Because I've got everything in place.'

Nihal rocked back and forth, his mind rushing with opportunities and threats. Riches. Revenge. Prison. Even death. He looked at Barry, a man who was entirely untrustworthy, and yet he sounded so plausible.

'Take me through it again. Particularly, these safeguards you keep mentioning.'

Barry didn't smile yet. Too early. Now he adopted a serious tone because extorting money from billionaires is a serious business.

'Right, first thing, forget money. He has so much; he doesn't care. Not really. Not as much as he cares about his honour, anyway.'

'And Sidhu's,' Nihal added acidly.

Barry snapped his fingers and pointed at the photo. 'Yes, good. Even better. That's why this photo is worth every penny of what we take him for?'

'But they've only just met-'

'Doesn't matter. It's all about now, how it looks and what he thinks of it.'

Barry made a good point, and Nihal smiled at the man with all the answers. He started to believe now, and his eyes began to twinkle.

'How much?' Nihal asked. A vulgar question, but one that needed to be asked.

And finally, Barry smiled. 'Two million.' he said casually, as though it were a bargain. They could ask for more, but no need to be greedy.

'Jesus. Pounds?' Nihal gushed.

Barry tutted. 'No, rupees, you doughnut. Yes, of course, pounds. And it's worth every blinking penny.'

Nihal could hardly believe his ears. Presumably, they would split it, enough money to fully re-establish himself in Mumbai and to clear all of his family's debts.

'But we need to work quickly.'

'How quickly? Before I am fired, you mean?'

Barry shook his head. 'Quicker than that, I'm afraid.'

'Really, like when?'

'Now. Immediately.'

Barry's thinking was that they had to act in case the 'friendship' turned out to be precisely this and thereby invalidating his photo.

'Nihal, my man, I say it's your turn. Fuck him. And I can help you.'

'What do you need me to do?'

Barry held up his hand, and Nihal slapped it.

'First up, you can get on the blower to the lovely Binu. Because I think we deserve another drink.'

Chapter Thirty-Eight

Sanjeev sat up in bed as Prikash removed her make-up in her dressing room. His mind was a flurry of mixed emotions: confusion, hurt, anger, of course, but also tinges of pure elation. He hadn't succumbed to the new American dependency on 'wellness', but if Ms Heinzog ever tired of being a musician, then he felt sure she could occupy herself with counselling. The world had no shortage of lost rich people who might avail of her wisdom. Prikash reappeared in a short silk negligee, looking every bit as attractive as she did on their wedding night, putting his paunch and jowls to shame. He felt humbled to have such a loyal and beautiful wife. Prikash nestled next to him and held his swollen belly, and he pushed his arm under her back so that she could rest her head on his chest.

'I am sorry Prikash.'

Prikash instantly raised her head so that she could look at him. She could not recall the last time he had said such a thing. She looked at him closely. He looked mournful.

'Sanjeev, you don't need to apologize for anything.'

'Yes, I do, and I will. I must, my dear, because I have been so angry with her.'

Prikash nodded. 'And I have too. But only because we love her. And we want what is best for her.'

Sanjeev nodded briefly.

'She is young and strident,' Prikash began to explain.

'And clever too, to involve Ms Heinzog.'

Prikash shook her head. 'But she says that this was not planned. It is just what happened.'

'No, I meant this evening. Having her come to the house for when I arrived,' Sanjeev added.

'Ah, I see.'

'My dear, answer me something, please.'

Prikash fretted a little now.

'Did you know?'

Prikash faltered a moment.

'That Ms Heinzog would be attending this evening?'

Prikash did not need to answer.

'We discussed it, yes. But it was Ms Heinzog's suggestion, and we both agreed that it might be a good idea. Sanjeev, I am so sorry.'

He half smiled. He was both pleased and relieved that his wife had not lied to him.

'And they were right. It was a good idea. She is a formidable woman. How old is she, do you think?'

Prikash chuckled. 'I don't know. Sidhu and I discussed this. Maybe seventy.'

'Yes, I suppose. But she looks well.'

'She looks amazing.'

'And such a remarkable musician.'

'As we will see very shortly.'

Sanjeev looked confused. Prikash tutted at her husband and his frantic life.

'We discussed this before you left for Moscow. The concert for the college. At the Royal Albert Hall.'

Suddenly, he joined the dots. 'Ah, yes, of course.'

'Which we can attend now.' Prikash smiled and looked at him suggestively. Sanjeev nodded, but his attention wandered, and he appeared distant again. His mournful look returned. He sighed and rubbed his tired eyes. Being so angry was exhausting.

'Sidhu is worried you might take us home to Mumbai...'

Sanjeev sighed wearily.

'I could. I thought about it.'

Prikash shook her head.

'And for what? To have my daughter hate me?'

'Sanjeev, she doesn't hate you. She loves you.'

Sanjeev dwelled on this. He sniffed and shook his head. As well as exhausted, he felt bewildered with so much to acclimatize to. His team should have closed the deal in Russia already, and yet he had not even checked.

'And you like him?' he asked quietly.

'Sanjeev, I have not met him. They are young and just friends, so please, you must keep things in perspective.'

'And his family, Sidhu has met them already?'

Prikash nodded, and his face hardened.

'Where?'

'That is where they met. When she went to Mr Clarke's house,' Prikash explained.

'She went to his house?'

'Yes, Sanjeev, we have discussed this already. She went to explain what happened with her violin. They even went in Ms Heinzog's car. And they were not alone together.'

Sanjeev recalled now and looked somewhat appeased. She hadn't gone alone, at least.

'Ms Heinzog has been remarkably kind to Sidhu.'

'Yes, she has. She seems to really care for her.'

'We should thank her in some way,' Sanjeev suggested.

His phone pinged, most likely with the notification of

tomorrow's itinerary, which usually began with a breakfast meeting at 8am. But this evening, he ignored it. It could wait. Prikash nestled into him and began to stroke his chest suggestively. But it would be for nothing. His mind was elsewhere. Prikash turned out the light and rolled over onto her side. But then a voice came from the darkness.

'Prikash...'

'Yes, Sanjeev.'

He paused, and the silence pushed down on them both.

'I am delighted that Sidhu is home.'

'Yes of course.'

'That we are a family again.'

'I know.'

'And it is her happiness that I want.'

Prikash said nothing. Her eyes were wide in the dark, waiting for him to finish.

'But she cannot see this boy, Noah. It is impossible. I will not allow it.'

Sidhu showered in her private bathroom if only to wash away all the tears she had shed. Even her father had cried, which was a first, and, fittingly, only the ice-cool Ms Heinzog remained entirely dry-eyed. Sidhu put on a new set of night clothes and leapt into bed as happy as she could ever recall being, bursting with excitement to communicate with Noah. She didn't call him, though: that would be too much pressure and is not the modern way when messages can be typed and garnished with emojis. The tantalizing three dots, the modern version of flirting. Noah shared her joy and explained how proud he was of her. They chatted for an hour back and forth but without arranging to meet again. Not until Sidhu could get a better sense of her situation. But maybe in a week or so, a walk perhaps in London.

Anna and Jonson discussed matters in their lounge. It was difficult to make any real sense of it. Anna apologized to Jonson for ever doubting him, which he pretended not to hear so he could milk it for all he could.

'Cool that Milly came back, though?' Jonson said.

'She's the best. And good to have around because she's so calm.'

Jonson chuckled. 'Yeah, well, she used to be a right flapper. That's success for you, I suppose.'

'Sure, but she's struggling now.'

Jonson frowned.

'No, not financially. But with her writing,' Anna added, and Jonson tutted. 'Trust me; she'll come through.'

'Yeah, I'm sure. And what about him, upstairs?'

Jonson raised his eyes to Noah's bedroom. 'He seems really smitten.'

'Well, she's like a Goddess,' Anna quipped, and Jonson looked non-plussed.

'What are you talking about? She's stunning.'

Jonson shook his head. 'Really, I hadn't noticed.'

Anna chuckled and threw a cushion at him.

'And what does it matter anyway? It's all about the inside. You need to be less shallow.'

Anna grinned. Suddenly she was wildly attracted to the man in her life. She got up off the couch and went over to lock the door.

. . .

Barry didn't like having this many spinning plates. Things beyond his orbit of control, and so he could not relax. His plans hinged on many things, including co-opting Nihal. He worried that he might see another opportunity to curry favour with team Sharma. He could easily throw Barry under his very heavy Rolls Royce and be handsomely remunerated for this information and loyalty. And, against this prospect, Barry had no insurance in place. He could not risk another concealed recording device. Too risky. This would be his biggest ever pay day, and the danger was commensurate with such a reward. And all pivoting on his instincts alone. Barry licked his dry lips. He had called in all sorts of favours to get everything set up. It was complicated and expensive. But if things went to plan, there would be plenty of money for everyone, so bring it on. He would know soon enough. He looked at his watch and thought of Nihal, the man on whom everything hinged.

Chapter Thirty-Nine

In the small hours of the morning, despite his exhaustion Sanjeev was unable to sleep, and he found himself in his office suite dealing with emails and other correspondence. People on his payroll were accustomed to Mr Sharma's odd working hours and expected incoming messages from him at any time of the day. It kept people on their toes. He read the latest email from his PR firm, Qnctd, which he was copied into. It was a compilation of all the online activity surrounding Sidhu and her blasted violin. He recalled how exciting the auction had been where he acquired it, but he could never have imagined the trouble it would cause. And as valuable as it was, he would much prefer to lose it than his daughter. He glanced at the photos on his desk, in particular, a picture of Sidhu as a little girl with her arms around him. He sensed that some of Prikash's beliefs had softened in the last week, and he felt a sense of betrayal. Right on cue, he felt Prikash's hands on his shoulders.

'I will call for some tea, and we can talk,' Prikash suggested. He agreed because they had much to discuss.

They sat quietly and chatted for an hour or so in Hindi, going back and forth and often covering old ground. They wrestled over thorny issues they had discussed so many times already, namely the cost of his business empire and his success. It had always been a worry that his family life would be compromised because continuously moving throughout the world would be most difficult for their children. Children thrive on continuity, establishing friendships and familiarity. They had also been afraid that being away from home, their cultural links and traditions might weaken also.

Their own marriage had not been formally arranged; albeit, Prikash had been introduced to Sanjeev by his aunt, who had an eye for such things and a great track record. Before they married, Sanjeev and Prikash had discussed and agreed on many things, especially if they were blessed with children. They resolved that their education would be paramount and that they would attend university and become professionally qualified. They would be bilingual and musical.

'Sanjeev, I have never seen her like this,' Prikash began, but Sanjeev sensed her manoeuvre and raised his hand.

'Prikash, please, go back to bed. Now is not the time, and I have work to do.'

Sanjeev watched her leave. He could sense his troubles mounting without knowing what Barry had in store for him. Barry, true to his word, had pushed play on his master plan immediately. Sanjeev did not have long to wait: just half an hour, in fact. It was a good thing that he was already up.

Barry had stressed the importance of striking immediately. The element of surprise is a powerful advantage. It disorientates people and hastens poor decision making. Nihal was quietly assured by Barry's confidence. Nihal logged on to a VPN that Barry had provided, and then, using the link, he accessed the web page and waited for it to load. No written text. No copy. Just the photograph of Sidhu Sharma with Noah Clarke.

Nihal consulted Barry's detailed document again with numerical points that laid out explicit and complete timings which had to be adhered to exactly. 'Extortion for dummies', Barry titled it.

3am. Copy and paste image into an email, marked 'urgent', to Simone at Qnctd requesting guidance and earliest possible response.

3.10 am. If no response within ten minutes, place phone call to Simone...

Nihal did precisely as he was instructed. Using the handset, Barry provided, he attached the image and clicked 'send'. The dirty bomb was on its way, and Nihal imagined the alarm bells it would trigger. He half expected to be called immediately by a bleary-eyed and disorientated PR executive.

At 3.10, Nihal dialed her number. It was answered immediately.

'Jesus, Nihal.' Simone blurted. 'I'm onto Sebastian now. Hold on. Stay on the line...'

Nihal smiled. Quickly, Simone was back on the line.

'Nihal, what the fuck?'

'I know. It's a nightmare.'

'When did you get this? Does Mr Sharma know?'

'Five minutes ago, and no, he doesn't, but I have to tell him.'

'No. Fuck, no. Do not tell-'

'Simone, I've had a phone call,' Nihal read from Barry's instructions. This stopped Simone in her tracks. He could feel her shiver.

'From who? Them?'

'Yes,' Nihal lied.

'What the fuck do they want?'

Nihal waited as instructed. Barry had thought of everything, and, so far, he had been right every time.

'Two million pounds....'

If such a thing could ever be audible, Nihal felt he could hear Simone almost pass out. Certainly she was winded.

'Simone, get your team out of bed. I'm going to speak with Mr Sharma. Wait to hear from me. Don't call me. I'll call you.'

Nihal ended his call and looked at his watch. It felt exhilarating to hold so much power over such people. He took a deep breath. He didn't need to consult Barry's notes for the next phase. He tousled his hair and pulled on his bathrobe. He needed to see Mr Sharma, even at this unearthly hour. It was an emergency, after all.

Chapter Forty

Nihal read Barry's meticulous notes one more time and then alerted the security guard of his intentions. The employee was new; he didn't have very much English and just wanted his quiet night to continue, so he agreed easily enough. Nihal rode the staff elevator to the fourth floor and walked the single flight of stairs to the penthouse. He paused at the door and steadied himself. He felt nauseous, and, with good reason, given the grave news he had to deliver.

'You must look anxious and angry on his behalf,' Barry had explained during their impromptu coaching session. Nihal pushed the bell and did not have to wait very long. Quickly, Mr Sharma opened the door. Wearing a robe, it was apparent that he hadn't been woken. He looked at Nihal knowingly, and, before he could even speak, he pointed to his business suite so as not to wake Prikash.

'Mr Sharma. I am very sorry, but I must speak with you urgently.'

Sanjeev closed the door. 'Speak then,' he snapped, 'what is it?'

'Thank you, sir. I am afraid I have some difficult news...'

Nihal began, following the script created by his crime mentor. Sanjeev listened intently. His cold eyes bore into his assistant. But he didn't appear surprised, as though he had sensed that something like this might have been coming. Sanjeev Sharma was accustomed to his enemies coming for him, and he long expected that Sidhu's naivety and petulance had yet to fully play out. But his quiet fury at their unseemly demands from him turned to disbelief when Nihal showed him the photo in question, and he needed to shift his position.

He stared at the photo and said nothing. Lost in his thoughts, he felt his cranial muscles constrict, and his heart rate pick up. Sidhu looked beautiful and content in the photograph. A picture of happiness. She smiled yearningly at her new 'friend'. But the image was not a happy one for Sanjeev. It terrified him. The boy was certainly handsome, but he was not a boy for his daughter. Nihal said nothing. Barry had explained that he would be in shock and would probably need a little time. Sanjeev continued to study the image. How Sidhu looked at the boy reminded him of how she used to look at him, and he felt a pang of sadness. Nihal breathed quietly, trying to keep himself calm. Finally, Sanjeev looked at Nihal; his face pinched in anger.

'Why would I trust these people?' he asked coldly. Nihal took a moment to denote the gravity of the situation, although his spirits soared because Sanjeev's question implied that he was at least considering the proposal.

'And who are they?'

'Sir, they have been careful,' Nihal continued, 'their files are encrypted, and they're using a temporary VPN that creates only a small window. Our security and Qnctd are working on trying to trace it.'

'Who are they?' Sanjeev repeated.

'Sir, it is impossible to say.'

Sanjeev had been in these situations before as he ascended the business world, but never with something so important at stake. His questions were more reflexes than genuine enquiries. Nihal shook his head apologetically. 'I wish there was something I could do, sir. I really do.'

Barry had been very precise with his instructions: 'Try not to make him angry, and never say "I don't know".'

'Because of the technology trail, sir, hopefully, they will not risk-'

'Hope?' Sanjeev roared, his anger finally bubbling over the brim, 'did you say hope?'

'Yes, sir, and I apologize; of course you will do whatever you think is right.'

'And what is that? What should I do?' Sanjeev shot back quickly. A question Barry had not planned for.

'Sir, I would not be so arrogant to think that I would ever advise you on such a matter.'

'And this picture?' Sanjeev snapped. 'This is your fault.'

Nihal said nothing.

'Where was it taken? And when?'

Nihal couldn't answer these questions either, but he didn't need to as Sanjeev became distracted.

'And how do they know?'

'Know what, sir?'

'About me? How do they know it is me?'

Nihal needed to be strong now. Barry explained that there would be awkward questions.

'We think it could be someone at her college. A staff member or a jealous student perhaps.'

'Even the boy himself?' Sanjeev suggested.

'Yes, it is possible, although unlikely because the family are living in London: if they so much as change their car, then we will ruin them,' Nihal lied easily. Barry would swell with pride.

'Who is 'we'?' Sanjeev spat, 'you keep saying 'we'.' His mind was still sharp despite his exhaustion.

'Your security, sir and Qnctd.'

Sanjeev grimaced. 'You've spoken to them?'

'Yes, sir, the moment I received the file. Should I call them in, sir? So we can speak to them?'

Sanjeev shook his head and closed his eyes slowly. Adrenalin flushed out his fatigue. He was a highly competitive man. He enjoyed a fight. Conflict was his default position in life, and he had a good win ratio. There were countless examples of him combining his cunning with his means to out-muscle his foe. The purpose of money was to acquire things, including his daughter's safety and integrity, and he had already budgeted scandalous costs for such a thing. But now, a new and more egregious haemorrhage had opened up at the hands of these loathsome opportunists, one of whom, unbeknownst to him, was standing in front of him at this very moment.

'We could call the police.'

Sanjeev's eyes widened.

'You will do no such thing, you imbecile! We will be all over the news.'

Another tick on Barry's checklist.

'You will not breathe a word of this to anyone. Do you understand?' Sanjeev seethed. Nihal nodded.

'And that includes my wife and daughter.' Sanjeev pulled at his thinning hair.

'But you can contact them?' Sanjeev presumed.

'Yes, sir, but only by email. There is no phone number.'

Sanjeev thought for a moment. He had a binary choice but a hopeless one. He bared his teeth, and, with both hands, he swiped left and right across his desk; this time, Nihal was unable to catch anything. His laptop went flying.

On all fronts, Sanjeev was being assaulted. He could not

bear the injustice of it. He couldn't believe that his daughter could be so selfish and was now being so cruelly exploited. He pressed his temples as he considered his dwindling options. All too risky, and for what? To save less money than he had spent on his in-home cinema, which he has never even used?

'The bank details?'

Nihal's heartbeat now skipped an entire beat. 'We will try to trace any payment, sir, of course. I will speak with your bank-'

But Sanjeev waved his hand in the air. They won't trace shit. The fucking banks. They're probably in on it.

'Where is the bank?'

'Macau,' Nihal added.

'And a deadline?'

Nihal shook his head. 'They said they will publish without an immediate one-time payment.'

Never pay kidnappers and never negotiate with terrorists. Everyone knows this, but of course, they are less rigorously applied in reality. Throughout his career, Sanjeev had paid many times over. Call them what you like: bribes, sweeteners? And maybe these payments have made him vulnerable, and this current situation is the result. Sanjeev snatched the printed sheet from Nihal.

'Get me my things,' Sanjeev barked as he sat behind his recently cleared desk. Nihal retrieved Mr Sharma's laptop, which appeared to have landed softly. Sanjeev opened a drawer of his desk.

'Get out,' Sanjeev barked without looking up from his screen. With pleasure. Nihal backed away a few paces before turning, and now he finally smiled.

Forty minutes later, Nihal could barely breathe as he returned to Mr Sharma's office, this time with great news, albeit expensively acquired. Nihal handed Sanjeev a printout of a short and bizarre email.

Your funds is receive. Like you, we are man of integity. We explain already; this photo and this site is now expire. You will here from us not again ever. Thanku for your bizniss. Have nice life. Peece.

Sanjeev needed to read it a few times. He even took some refuge in it because they appeared so stupid that he tended to believe them. It would be better for everyone if they enjoyed their little victory and never darkened his door again.

Barry enjoyed his sleep, but not nearly as much as he enjoyed the prospect of becoming rich, and he stayed up all night orchestrating. When he finally received notification from his contact in Hong Kong of receipt of funds, he needed to sit down. He was so elated that he wept. They cannot teach cunning at journalism college, and this was all Barry had needed. And hadn't Nihal performed magnificently. He was due his payment, and Barry would make good on this word.

Chapter Forty-One

N ihal could scarcely believe had what happened. Over
the next few days, without it seemed any sleep at all,
he kept up his guard and reported nothing untoward,
and even Mr Sharma began to believe that they had weathered
the storm. He was two million quid down, but really, so what.
His Russian deal had been ratified, and initial forecasts put
profits at £200 million. And yet this was scant consolation to
such a man who didn't like to lose. He had paid up like he pays a
service charge in an expensive restaurant, but immediately he
charged his head of security, Vaughan Saunders, with the task of
finding these despicable bastards. Bonuses were promised. And
if nothing else, it served his conscience and allowed him to sleep
a little easier.

Certainly, he didn't inform his family about his activities or
losses, and, rather oddly, nothing much was said about Sidhu's
ongoing friendship either, and with this, an odd sense of calm
descended on the household. Sidhu reverted to her old life,
albeit without her Guarneri, and a further encouraging sign was
that so few people had even seemed to notice. She was diligent
with her practice; she was attending college, staying in college

all day, and more importantly, she was returning home each day. But still Sanjeev could not relax. He tried to make certain adjustments which might help, including 'working from home', which seemed to be so popular nowadays. It went against his traditions, but it served a useful purpose, and it provided a great respite for his office staff. It allowed him some 'quality' time with his family and, as importantly, to keep an eye on Sidhu. He had given Nihal his notice, but he kept it 'open-ended' as he described it, with Nihal remaining in place until this entire matter was resolved. It was all Nihal's fault, after all.

But this tranquility was fooling no one because both issues remained very real. Prikash felt anxious too. Her husband was no fool, and he knew that things were afoot. He noted that Sidhu gave up her phone very easily and accepted also that Nihal should accompany her to college.

Ms Heinzog was quickly on hand to provide a new phone for Sidhu so that she and Noah could communicate. And Ms Heinzog, like the best Machiavels, continued to coax and orchestrate matters for her young charge. She even started to drop by the house to see Sidhu and to keep her irascible father on his best behaviour. One evening, she and Sidhu played for them both. A private audience which moved Mr Sharma to tears. Only his mother had such a hold over him as Ms Heinzog, something not lost on Prikash, who teased him about it constantly.

In contrast, Jonson and Anna knew all about the fledgling digital friendship and were supportive. Jonson basked in the reflected glory that it was all down to him. And Noah's spirits had picked up also, even playing the piano without being prompted.

'So, when are you gonna actually see her again?' Jonson asked. Noah tutted at his incorrigible dad.

'Well?' Jonson pushed.

'Dad...'

'What?'

'I've told you, I don't know.'

'How come?'

'Because. It's complicated.'

'What is?'

Noah sighed. 'Dad, you know what. You're being a dick.'

'I am not-'

'Yes, you are,' Noah said carefully, 'because of her parents.'

'Her dad, you mean?'

'You see, you do know. He doesn't want her to see anyone.'

'Fuck sake, it's like a bloody fairy tale.' Jonson huffed. 'Where does he keep her, in the tower? Is she growing her hair long?'

Noah chuckled.

'And seeing anyone, or seeing you?' Jonson asked more pointedly.

'Dad. I don't know: I've never met him, but I imagine it's both.'

Jonson scoffed. 'Then he's a knob.'

'Right, thanks dad. I'll be sure to tell him that when I see him.'

'Yeah, well, good luck, pal.' Jonson sneered. 'You tie a kid down, and you see what happens.'

Noah gestured for the answer.

'You lose 'em, that's what. Or part of 'em anyway.' Jonson reasoned.

Noah shrugged. It all felt surreal.

'Hey...' Jonson snapped his fingers. 'I've had a thought.'

Noah sighed and said nothing.

'What about if I go and see him?'

Noah's face fell.

'You? Go and see her dad?'

'Yeah, why not?' Jonson answered. 'You know, two dads. Man to man.'

Noah stared at his dad in disbelief.

'...we could go for a beer...' Jonson now caught Noah's expression. 'What?'

'Dad, are you serious? He's Indian.'

'Yeah, so?' Jonson tutted, 'what are you saying? Indians don't drink? What is Cobra beer then?'

Noah glared at his dad. 'Dad, you need to promise me that you will never go and see Sidhu's dad.'

Jonson mulled on this for a moment and then held his hands aloft as a sort of concession.

'No, you need to promise. Dad, I need to hear it.'

'Okay, fine, I promise. Fine. But I don't get it.'

'You don't get what?'

'I thought because Indians love all this family stuff-'

'Dad!' Noah shouted just as Anna entered the room.

'Mum, tell him.'

'Tell him what?' Anna asked.

'Dad's suggesting that he goes for a beer with Mr Sharma.'

Anna looked at her husband wearily.

'What d'you reckon? Jonson asked.

'Don't be ridiculous.'

Just as he had promised, Barry processed the last of his bank payments and allowed himself a little moment.

'Good job, everybody,' he said to himself quietly. If he had any scruples about extortion, then he hid them well. His rationale remained simple: Mr Sharma was merely buying what he wanted. Barry opened up some familiar websites. A real estate site was already loaded with a page of a coastal village, dotted with pastel-coloured homes and one cottage delineated by a bold white line. It had three bedrooms and views over Dartmouth. A dream property which Barry could now afford. He hovered his mouse over the contact button, but he did not click. Not yet. He thought of his mum; he couldn't wait to tell her, and instantly his throat swelled.

Gareth, too, was crying, but in pain and not ecstasy. His surgeon had mentioned that he should expect some 'pain and discomfort', but this warning had proven to be completely insufficient. It will 'hurt like a motherfucker' is what the money-grabbing bastard should have said. His chest and stomach felt as though they were on fire, and he could barely move without pain shooting throughout his entire body. On top of this, he was dealing with significant mental anguish at the recent dip in his social media platforms. @_Hot_Cop37 had lost followers, and Yvonne was called in to explain herself.

'What do you mean the story has gone quiet?' Gareth winced.

'Sometimes stories get spiked. Agencies are paid to quash them.'

Gareth groaned in general hurt. Yvonne waited awkwardly as he strained to sit up. The physios encouraged movement. Gareth now had another goal to focus on: to rekindle this story. As a serving police officer, he had a duty and a responsibility to investigate such things, and his first port of call would be the skinny violinist with the pinched face. Ms Fucking Hedgehog. Hot Cop knew she was hiding something, and no one hides anything from Officer Gareth Dibble.

Chapter Forty-Two

Late into the night, Ms Heinzog practiced in her soundproof subterranean studio. The three hours passed quickly until she was settled and completely happy with the piece. She had played Shostakovich many times before, but his first concerto for the violin was demanding. She drank some cool filtered water from her machine and rubbed her arms and neck with a warm towel from a cupboard. She pondered a moment on the forthcoming concert and thought of Sidhu and her family, who would be attending. What an unusual week it had been. She set her metronome again and picked up her instrument. Practice makes perfect, and she knew that perfection was required for the concert ahead.

Noah proposed it as casually as he could. Just a nice evening out for the whole family, but Jonson was immediately suspicious. An evening of classical music at the Royal Albert Hall?

'Shoshta who?' Jonson asked cheekily.

Noah tutted. 'Shosh-ta-kovich. He's Russian.'

'Oh well, if he's Russian, then I'm in.'

'Darling, we'd love to go,' Anna intervened. 'But can we get tickets?'

'Yeah, and how much are they?' Jonson asked.

'Don't worry; I can get tickets.'

'Oh yeah,' Jonson prodded, enjoying himself enormously.

'Yeah, I have a friend,' Noah answered a little sheepishly.

'Ah, I see.'

'No dad, no, you don't.'

'And does this 'friend' happen to be a violinist?'

Noah appealed to his mum for support.

'Jonson, be quiet.'

'I'm just saying-'

'Well don't. Don't say anything.'

Jonson smiled and complied, but not without hooting in delight.

'It's an annual thing. Their whole college gets to go, and they get tickets. So I can get us in,' Noah continued.

'Hey, can Milly come with Mitch and the girls?' Jonson added as an after-thought.

'Er... I'll need to check.'

'Yeah, good, because Milly loves all this poncy stuff. And if I've got to sit through it, it's only fair that Mitch does too.'

Anna elbowed her husband. 'You might enjoy it.'

Jonson pulled a face. 'Not sure. It's all a bit samey for me.'

Anna exhaled heavily. 'And Sidhu is going, I take it?' she asked in a kindly manner. Noah blushed, and Anna was delighted that he might want his family to attend with him. Even his dad.

'Noah, we'd love to go. Wouldn't we, Jonson?'

'Love to.'

Jonson recalled his nightmare in the concert venue, still

vivid in his mind, and he shuddered. It would be nice to visit the famous hall from where this whole thing began.

Prikash anxiously waited for Sanjeev's response. He removed his tie and was clearly still thinking about her suggestion.

'But we have our own box. With the best views in the place. She will see better with us,' Sanjeev reasoned.

'Yes, but Sanjeev, she is going with her classmates. She would rather sit with them than her boring-'

Before she could finish, Sanjeev had activated his electric toothbrush, so Prikash stopped talking. Wearing his pyjamas now, he entered their sleeping quarters.

'She doesn't want to be different.' Prikash continued on in her Sidhu-supporting vein.

'But, she is different,' Sanjeev claimed.

'How so?' Prikash asked.

'Well, according to Ms Heinzog, she is remarkable. We must remember that,' Sanjeev added proudly, and Prikash chuckled, welcoming any levity and especially from a man as implacable as her husband.

'And last year, she didn't sit in our box with me.'

'She didn't?'

'No, I sat on my own because you were away on business again.'

'And last year, she didn't have a boyfriend.'

'A friend, you mean?'

Prikash looked at Sanjeev mournfully. She noticed that he had been calmer over the last few days, although they had not explicitly discussed Sidhu and her circumstances. But his mood had lightened, and this was very welcome.

'She will arrive with us and come home afterwards - with us,' Sanjeev conceded. These were his non-negotiable terms.

'Yes, of course. This is fine and very sensible. Sidhu will be grateful.'

Sanjeev bristled at Prikash's last point. Grateful? His daughter had no idea how much she had already cost him. As he sat down on their bed, Prikash placed her hand on his shoulder as a thank you, and finally, he was able to smile.

Chapter Forty-Three

'Shoshta-who?' Mitch asked and got an elbow similar to the one Anna had aimed at Jonson.

'Hey, I'm just asking.'

'Well, don't because we're going. The girls will love it.'

'Okay, cool. At least I get to polish off the old Albert.'

Milly wondered if this might be a euphemism, but apparently not, judging by Mitch's innocent look.

'Mum, will that cool lady be playing?'

'Yes, Isla, she is.'

'I liked her. Is she a Princess?'

'No, not in the royal sense, but in the music world, then yes, I guess she is.'

'Can we meet her again?'

'No, I don't think so, darling. There will be thousands of people there. But we can hear her play.'

'Oh, okay. But I can wave at her, though?'

'Oh, yes, you can certainly do that.' I think that will be fine.'

Milly smiled at their cute exchange, and she fired Jonson a quick text.

. . .

Ms Heinzog sat alone on the stage while a few of the technical crew buzzed about the place completing their checks and making sure everything was plugged in. The Royal Albert Hall is thrilling when it is full, but it is perhaps most beautiful when it is quiet and empty. Ms Heinzog had lost count of the number of appearances she had made at the illustrious venue, yet it continued to enthral her. In front of her was an expanse of five thousand seats resplendent in red velvet. This evening, not one would be empty. She thought of all the people attending and their differing plans. Some attendees would still be in the air, no doubt, flying in from places far-flung. Baby sitters would be booked. Nearby restaurants would be getting prepared for pre and post-concert meals. Wine chilling and prawns being shelled. People would be coming by tube and road. Others in chauffeured cars like her student Sidhu. After her performance, she might deign to a meet and greet. This would serve Sidhu well, and she thought to mention it when her phone vibrated. She reached for her device and read a text message which filled her with dread. She had no intentions of ever meeting Officer Dibble again. Back in her dressing room, she would call her lawyer and suggest that he make a phone call on her behalf.

Barry sat opposite Gareth Dibble in his Dagenham flat. It was a long way to travel, but, on seeing his discomfort, he understood why the man insisted on this most convenient meeting place. Barry only took the meeting as a precaution to ensure that he had not missed anything. Presumably, Officer Dibble, in his professional capacity, had kept abreast of all such matters. Plus, it would be useful to get an update and any useful information that he could feed back to Nihal for Mr Sharma. But once the cursory pleasantries were over, it quickly became apparent that Officer Dibble had little to offer.

'So where is this violin then?' Dibble snapped angrily, which Barry attributed to his obvious pain. It showed commendable commitment that this public servant was at his metaphorical desk at all.

Barry shook his head. 'I'm afraid I have no idea. I'm not even sure if a violin was ever missing.'

Gareth tried to process this through his haze of pain relief. 'What are you talking about?'

Barry just shrugged.

'Oh, come on. What am I, a fool?'

This was a strong possibility. He was unusual and not like the other coppers Barry had encountered. And again, he thought that he might be familiar too. Barry wondered, but as much as he tried, he couldn't place him.

'Why? Is there a police investigation then?' Barry asked.

'Yes, there is.'

'An official investigation, you mean?' Barry asked bravely.

'By me. I am investigating it,' Gareth shouted.

Barry half-smiled as any threat receded even further.

'Then tell me this.' Gareth began through his pain. 'If nothing is happening, then why am I getting threatening phone calls from Eleanor Heinzog's lawyers?' Dibble asked. This was new to Barry, and he genuinely had nothing to offer. He just shrugged. This guy was merely pissing in the wind, although he was intrigued by his intentions.

'I just think there's a story here,' Gareth uttered desperately, and Barry looked at him oddly and almost chuckled. A story? Not a crime then? Was Officer Dibble considering a career change?

'And with my help, you could write it up. Get it in the papers. And even on the telly.'

Barry's turn to adjust his position now.

'What kind of story did you have in mind?'

'Oh, come on. You know. It's got everything. Rich people, a famous violinist. A Hollywood writer. A cool black guy and his sexy son...'

Barry nodded. And let's not forget the totally nuts police officer with a stupid name.

'...plus a mega-expensive violin that is still missing.'

'But we don't know that.'

Dibble's eyes looked alert now, his foggy mind flashing with ideas.

'So you think it was all a lie?'

'I don't know. No one does.'

'Apart from the owner,' Gareth snapped, 'Who is this fucking owner?'

Barry eyed him warily now. In his career, he wondered how many crimes Officer Dibble had ever solved. Maybe, none?

'I have no idea.'

'Okay, but what if I find out who the owner is?' Gareth stated. 'Will you write it then?'

Barry was pleased that he had taken this meeting now because he identified that Dibble remains a potential threat. Even as stupid as he was, he could probably identify the Sharma family, and this might complicate matters for everyone.

'Write what story, exactly?' Barry asked.

'I don't know, you tell me. You're the writer, man. Wasting police time. How about that?' Gareth snapped.

'Or maybe just a human-interest story. Someone pretending to lose a violin as a cry for help or attention. How about that?'

He now seemed to be proposing a novel rather than a piece of journalism. Barry half-smiled to placate him, mindful not to antagonize him

'May I use your toilet?'

As soon as Barry entered the smallest room in Gareth's apartment, everything fell into place. The walls were covered with framed photographs. In pride of place was a colour photograph of Gareth with a beaming Simon Cowell. There was also an array of other photos of Gareth in various television studios with TV hosts of dubious fame. Gareth had the fame virus and would do anything for it and including exposing the very private Mr Sanjeev Sharma. He had no interest in the violin or its 'story'. His only interest was his own infamy, and Barry thought of how he might assist him with this and throw him off Sanjeev's scent in the process. Barry knew exactly what to do. He smiled broadly as he zipped himself up.

Chapter Forty-Four

Sanjeev listened very carefully to what Nihal had to say about this unusual police officer and his hopes to create a story about Sidhu and her lost violin. Certainly, he was grateful to Nihal for this information and even somewhat admiring. In light of his being fired and working his undetermined notice period, it showed commendable service and loyalty. And it was kind of him that he was still considering Sidhu's welfare. Sanjeev nodded. This unfortunate development confirmed his fears and his need to protect his daughter. This hapless officer might be harmless enough, but he might be the first of many other and more able opportunists. He exhaled heavily.

'This is why the Guarneri has to go.' Sanjeev said, and he rather enjoyed seeing Nihal's confusion.

'This has always confused me, sir.'

'Really, why?'

'Because a Guarneri is rare...'

'Sidhu's violin is not rare. It is unique.' Sanjeev corrected him.

'Right, so when she doesn't have it anymore, people will assume that it is her violin that is lost.'

Sanjeev nodded. This was correct and his assessment also, but it didn't account for an unintended consequence and a very real threat.

'And if her Guarneri reappears, then what will people assume?' Sanjeev asked with a more serious air.

Nihal shrugged. 'Er... that it was not her Guarneri that was lost after all.'

Sanjeev shook his head. 'But it is unique. And there are photos of Sidhu on the train. What if this connection is made and Sidhu has her Guarneri? Sanjeev pressed, 'what will people conclude?'

Nihal pondered this. 'That it was Sidhu's violin but that it was never lost.' Nihal understood now. 'It was something she just made up,' he concluded.

'Sidhu will be humiliated.'

'Yes, but this might not happen.'

Sanjeev sighed. This was not terribly reassuring and not a risk he could afford. Nihal could see this now. He admired his sense of paternity and saw a side to him for the first time.

'So what will you do?' Nihal asked, genuinely interested.

'I don't know yet.'

Sanjeev nodded, grateful for his apparent concern as he continued to wrestle with the conundrum his daughter had set him.

The bars of the Royal Albert Hall buzzed with excited patrons quaffing their drinks and canapés on their big night out. Ahead of the auditorium being opened, a few members of the orchestra were making final tweaks to their instruments. The brass section was blowing and sucking. Percussionists were tapping and tightening, but the star of the show was nowhere to be seen.

Ms Heinzog looked at her reflection in the brightly lit mirror in her familiar dressing room. On the wall hung a photograph of Frank Sinatra taken in this very room, which always amused her. She knew Mr Sinatra well and once told him that he had finally succeeded in getting into her dressing room. She read her sheet music one last time and rubbed in a small dab of hand cream. She spied the wall clock and made some calculations. Her freshly pressed jacket hung from a rail. She pulled at her dress which had also been made for her. Ms Heinzog was ready for her people.

Sidhu felt just as nervous as her new best friend and spiritual adviser. The hall hummed with energy as five thousand people chatted and readied themselves. Her excitement for the concert aside, Sidhu felt most anxious because amongst this great throng was Mr Clarke and his family, including his eldest son. Just to be under the same roof as him was exciting. Ms Heinzog had been very specific about timings for the evening, and Sidhu texted explicit instructions to Noah. She arrived with her family as agreed and quickly joined her classmates. As she entered the beautiful auditorium, she instinctively spied the boxes on the first circle. She counted across to what she assessed was the Sharma box, and she imagined her father's beady eyes on her. She had left nothing to chance with her aisle seat, and she even thought to organize for her friend Max to sit behind her to impede her father's view. Max was a trumpet player from Ethiopia and stood tall at six feet seven inches.

Sanjeev was indeed trying to establish the whereabouts of his daughter, but it was very difficult to do so and totally impossible once the lights dimmed. A spotlight picked out the conductor, the distinguished David Robert Coleman and the orchestra was bathed in light. Coleman gently raised his baton and held it still, his command for attention: five thousand people instantly complied. Silence rang out in the hall. A conductor's great moment before he called upon the greatest musicians in the country to play.

Below the stage, Ms Heinzog waited by a small flight of stairs that led directly up to the stage and her seat. High in the gods, another spotlight operator with his headset was primed and ready with his beam for her grand entrance. A young lady, also wearing a headset, was standing by Ms Heinzog to give her a cue. Eleanor fixed her stare on a certain part of the stairs as she concentrated with her violin and bow in hand. She felt more detached than usual. Her mind fleetingly thought of young Sidhu and the clandestine meeting she had helped to facilitate. Small steps of progress, she called them. Having Sidhu, her father and Noah in the same space was certainly welcome, but this would need to recur in much smaller rooms for any real progress to be made. For now, though, Ms Heinzog could play her part by giving a brilliant performance and taking Sidhu's breath away.

The Clarke and Millhouse family watched the stage in wonder. The venue was immaculate, and the orchestra looked beautiful in their dress suits and ball gowns. Jonson squeezed Anna's hand. A lifetime spent in London, and this was his first visit to the Royal Albert Hall, his nightmare aside, obviously. Jonson stared in awe at the musicians, aware of their childhoods and the sacrifices they had each made. The opening 'number' was lost on him, however, and he hoped for some music ahead that he might recognize. Something from a television commercial, most likely. Hovis, surely?

At the appropriate time, Conductor Coleman quelled his musicians using both his hands, and then he directed the audience to a certain part of the stage. Suddenly, a wave of applause built from the stalls and emanated throughout the great hall as a spotlight picked out a diminutive figure standing all on her own. Ms Heinzog had entered the building. She took in all sides of the vast crowd and nodded her appreciation of the applause without smiling. Ms Heinzog was on stage and was already performing, and only one person watching was aware that she had a beautiful smile that she could call upon for very special occasions.

David Coleman, now the second most important person on view, finally called time on such reverence and appealed for quiet once more. Let's hear the lady play. Ms Heinzog took her seat and her face altered now, with a look of complete concentration, like a boxer waiting for the bell. She waited for the conductor to stab his baton towards her, and instantly she responded with the beginnings of one of the greatest violin concertos ever written. Jonson remained in the dark about this great work, but Noah had all the information he needed. Most importantly, he had the precise amount of time that Ms Heinzog would have the audience spellbound for before exiting the stage. Eighteen minutes exactly, time for him and Sidhu to meet where they had arranged and where Sidhu was already heading.

Chapter Forty-Five

Noah ran along a carpeted passageway and didn't stop to take in any of the photographs of past luminaries who had graced its famous stage. After Ms Heinzog's performance, the concert would continue for a further twenty minutes until the first intermission, when Sidhu had to be back in her seat. It all felt so daring and exciting that Noah could hardly breathe as he rounded the corner on a journey he had made earlier in the evening just to be sure he made no mistakes when it mattered.

In the bar, the staff were busy pouring drinks and laying out orders on various vantage places: iced buckets with wine, champagne and beer, accompanied by appropriate glasses. Sidhu's journey from the stalls was shorter, so she was already present when Noah entered the bar. He looked a little awkward in his suit, which his mum had insisted on, but she loved that he might have made an effort for her. She smiled, her heart beating every bit as loudly as the percussionist in the auditorium. Noah smiled back as they gingerly approached each other. Some of the bar staff had stopped their chores momentarily, conscious somehow of a performance unfurling before them in their empty bar.

They had not seen each other since their café meeting, but their abundant texts had progressed from friendly to flirty, and this only added to their pent-up excitement. Sidhu rushed the last few steps and fell into Noah's outstretched arms, which he wrapped about her. Any doubts that this might be a date immediately dispelled. She buried her head into his neck as he picked her up and spun her around. As brilliant as Shostakovich and the London Philharmonic Orchestra were, the two youngsters were even more compelling. The bar manager almost broke into applause and quickly instructed her staff to get back to work and not to stare at the young Romeo and Juliet, who eventually separated.

'Oh my God, it's great to see you again,' Sidhu gushed, oblivious to any onlooking eyes.

'You too. And what a place for a first date.'

'I know; I love this place so much.'

'And with your dad, too.' Noah joked. Sidhu laughed wildly.

'And how about Ms Heinzog?'

'Oh my god. Just one lady holding everyone spellbound,' Noah intoned, 'mind you, I couldn't wait for her to finish.'

Sidhu laughed again and concurred.

'So, how has your dad been?' Noah asked.

'Yeah, you know. Difficult. Angry-'

'Nice.'

'Betrayed. In denial. And yours?

'Yeah, none of them, to be honest.'

Sidhu laughed. She was even more beautiful than he recalled, and with time and circumstances so against them, he felt emboldened to act. Noah gently pulled her at the waist and leaned his head in so that he could kiss her. Instantly she responded, and this time the bar staff didn't stop working, but they all stole approving glances at the attractive young couple.

· · ·

The remainder of the concert was a blur for them both, now separated again but more excited than ever.

'How'd it go?' Jonson asked when Noah returned.

'Dad, she's unbelievable.'

Jonson nodded sagely and then leant in as though to say something profound.

'And how did you two meet again?' He asked with a smile. Noah shook his head and smiled also.

Even more instrumental in proceedings and, deliberately so, Ms Heinzog completed her role perfectly, playing exquisitely in what felt like a private concert for just two members of the audience. As promised, Sidhu had texted her in the interval to explain that they had met as planned. Ms Heinzog knew their seat numbers and sought from the house manager where they were in relation to her position on stage. Her last text to Sidhu in their rapid exchange was cryptic and very Heinzog.

"Watch out for my final two bows".

And sure enough, with everyone on their feet and cheering, Ms Heinzog took dead-aim in turn at both seats. She bowed lower than before and specifically waved. She was unerringly accurate, and Sidhu had to catch herself as the crowd cheered as if they were in on the great lady's romantic scheming.

Sidhu obeyed her father to the letter for the whole evening. She reported to the Sharma box at every interval and at the end also. Her family were spellbound by Ms Heinzog and gushed about her poise and beauty. Sanjeev considered Sidhu cautiously. He was pleased by her obedience, but still, he fretted. Prikash considered Sidhu carefully and sensed that something might have occurred. Mother's intuition. Sidhu appeared flush and not because of the sounds a violin can create. She eyed Sidhu knowingly but said nothing. At home,

Sanjeev headed to his office as was his habit, then they would talk.

The Sharma household did not manage much sleep the night after the concert. Sidhu had risked bringing her illicit phone home with her so that she and Noah could chat through the night. And the lights remained on in the penthouse as Sanjeev dealt with emails and other correspondence. Sidhu confided in her mother also, but only with her absolute promise that she would not betray her. Prikash was true to her word but only to an extent. If Sidhu liked this boy as much as she claimed, then she would need to broach her husband, and, in Prikash's opinion, the quicker she began, the better. Sanjeev was a perceptive man, and Prikash would only antagonize him if she continued to play dumb. If they argued and he entered one of his protracted sulks, it would only make her task more difficult.

Sanjeev was not surprised to hear from his wife of Sidhu's continued affection for this boy. As a pointed sign of conciliation, he did not ask if they had been communicating or whether they had dared to see each other again. This seemed like another positive sign to Prikash, but quickly her hopes were scotched.

'Prikash, why are you doing this?' Sanjeev asked ominously, and she faltered.

'What is this that you are doing?'

'What do you mean?'

'You know damn well what I mean. That this friendship is not possible.'

Prikash noted his use of the word friendship and did not know how to respond.

'It is impossible. You know this.'

Prikash nodded reluctantly.

'Sidhu has more important things to worry about.'

'Like what?' Prikash asked bravely, sensing an opening perhaps. 'More important to us maybe, but not to her.'

Sanjeev's jaw bulged as he tried to contain his fury.

'Do you remember the Korean girl?' Sanjeev seethed.

Prikash shook her head, confused.

'Just like Sidhu, a daughter of a businessman. A wealthy man. Billionaire seems to be the new term...'

'Sanjeev, what are you talking about?'

'Listen to me,' Sanjeev barked, 'she stopped a jet from taking off because the nuts in first class were not to her liking...'

Prikash tried to recall. She had a vague recollection of some such thing happening. Her father might have been the CEO of the airline?

'So, she stopped the plane.'

'Yes, I think I do remember that.'

'She became worldwide news, and she was pilloried. She was humiliated, and rightly so. Everyone laughing at the poor little rich girl...'

'But, what does this have to do with Sidhu? She would never do such a thing.'

Sanjeev shook his head dismissively. 'Having such a violin is probably an error, and this is my fault. But then pretending it is lost to gain attention. Sidhu too will be humiliated.'

Prikash listened carefully.

'I have had demands already,' Sanjeev seethed.

'Demands. From who?'

'I don't know, and I don't care. I have paid them.'

Prikash recoiled now, frightened for her daughter. 'Does Sidhu know?'

'No, and she must not. I should not have told you. But your glibness makes me so angry.'

Sanjeev went on to explain his ongoing conversations with

Qnctd and the ambitions of Officer Dibble, and his fears that this could all be a ticking bomb.

'Matters which are not helped by Sidhu's flirting with a boy she cannot be with.'

Prikash understood the connection now, and she nodded. Her fears, however, did not subside because, even if matters were to be complicated by this development, what if Sidhu insisted on seeing him? What then?

Chapter Forty-Six

Milly's trip home to London had been a great success and just the fillip she needed. It hadn't provided the inspiration for a new story as she had secretly hoped, but it was certainly a good distraction from everything else. Mitch and the girls had enjoyed themselves enormously. It was also good to see that Jonson had lost none of his verve nor his capacity for mischief, and everyone enjoyed watching his latest calamity resolve.

Milly looked at return flights while Mitch drew the shortest of straws with an impromptu trip for the girls to Madame Tussauds. The queue traumatizes Londoners, and once is always enough. Milly scrolled the British Airways website. Tuesday evening seemed like the best option, as it allowed the girls one more full day in the capital. One thing still troubled her, however, and she deliberated whether or not she should attend to it. It was probably nothing, just an inkling, and she wondered. She thought she had his card somewhere, and it might be a good idea to draw a line.

.   .   .

Barry watched Nihal carefully as he viewed his computer screen, which displayed a balance of a new bank account in Hong Kong. Barry was not seeking gratitude, but he needed assurances that Nihal remained onside. Nihal's eyes lifted from his screen and settled on Barry, who now felt a pang of alarm. On the desk, Barry placed a card reader, complete with a new bank card and next to it a piece of A4 with detailed instructions and a series of numbers.

'Everything okay?' Barry asked nervously, and Nihal nodded.

'You can draw that amount whenever you want, and it will never be traced. But as a precaution, I suggest you don't open a new account in your name.'

Nihal nodded. 'No, thank you. I might establish a company.'

Barry smiled at this. Good idea.

'Speaking of precautions, Mr Sharma's head of security, Vaughan Saunders-'

Barry quickly stopped him.

'Nihal, listen to me. If you're in the wrong field, it doesn't matter how deep you dig. All these communications have already evaporated. There's nothing to find. It's just Sharma satisfying himself that at least he's trying.'

Nihal agreed. 'I was going to say that I met with him.'

Barry gestured for an outcome. Nihal half smiled.

'He's got nothing.'

Barry was relieved and smiled also.

'Do you know,' Nihal said carefully, 'I almost feel sorry for him.'

'Yeah, I get that.'

'Not for what we've done. Because he can afford it, right?'

'And it's due. Don't forget that,' Barry added.

Nihal conceded this.

'So what then?' Barry pressed, keen to be thorough.

'Sure, he wants to retrieve his money. Who wouldn't?'

Barry shrugged.

'But he's most concerned with protecting his daughter.'

This intrigued Barry. 'Go on.'

Nihal explained Mr Sharma's considerations and why Sidhu had to give up her Guarneri.

'Hmm...' Barry mused. 'Very touching. Very human.'

The virtuous side of the billionaire. It was quite beautiful, really, and it completed the story so neatly, even if it wasn't the sort of fare that Barry usually specialized in. This was a warm tale that his mum would enjoy. Some old ladies like to knit scarves whether or not they are ever worn. Others just watch television or arrange flowers for the church, but Barry's mum liked to read. All day she reads novels, two or three a week and usually hard backs with identikit swashbuckling jackets. Sagas of wealth and corruption being vanquished by love and honour. Barry's offer on the coastal cottage had been accepted, and immediately he rued that his bid was too generous. But it didn't really matter. Finally, he could move out of his cramped flat in Watford, and his mum could join him on the Devon coast. What better place for her to sit and read her books. He could not wait to tell her his news, and now he had a story of his own to regale her with.

It was humbling for Sidhu to hear her father's explanation and his intentions for her Guarneri. She said nothing other than to apologize, which he waved away dismissively. She repeated her apology, though, and reiterated that everything had been happenstance and without anything being planned. But things had changed. There remained a distance between them, and Sidhu became tearful again. Sanjeev sighed heavily as he took his daughter into his arms for the first time since his return from

Moscow. He was surprised by her strength as she hugged him, but his actions were merely practical, and his position on potential suitors remained steadfast. He explained about the violin again. She listened carefully and understood. But it remained humiliating for her. She recalled his excitement when he had acquired the violin and how proud he was to own such a thing. And now it had to be forfeited because of her foolish antics.

Prikash entered the room now and was immediately aware of their conversation. She smiled her assurances at Sidhu. That it was for the best. 'There are other violins,' Prikash whispered to her daughter mischievously. Sanjeev considered his wife. As a couple and a family, they still had work to do. Prikash understood this and had to be patient with him. Nihal knocked on the door quietly to say that Mr Sharma's car was ready to take him to his jet. Sanjeev nodded, and Nihal left them alone. Nihal's continued loyalty impressed Mr and Mrs Sharma. Prikash would insist on his receiving the most glowing reference and possibly even a severance bonus.

Everything had already been organized ahead of Sanjeev's impromptu trip. With his light luggage already loaded into the car, Sanjeev left bound for India, and it was something of a relief for everyone. The family needed some time and space. Sidhu and Prikash talked incessantly, and their combined mood swung from hurt and anger to love and hope. There was much at stake: the solidarity of a family and its future. Prikash worried mostly for Sanjeev because she understood that he would eventually lose in this finely balanced equation. If not with Noah, then the next boy lucky enough to catch her daughter's eye and Prikash would have played an active role in his loss. Would he ever forgive her? She took herself to her private office and closed the door. The time was now, and she had to make the phone call.

Chapter Forty-Seven

It might be that the American Dream remains the most famous cliché, but in reality it has long been usurped by the lesser-known Indian Dream, and Sanjeev Sharma's life is no better an example. He was born into a middle-class family in New Delhi as the eldest of five boys. His father was a doctor and his mother a midwife, so Sanjeev was fully expected to emulate his father, and he risked his parents' considerable disappointment by choosing a different path. Fortunately, their hurt was short-lived. Sanjeev graduated with a degree in electrical and chemical engineering. He risked his parents' ire again by eschewing a Masters, and instead, he founded Sharma Chemical, quickly finding his feet and his calling in life. Immediately, it became apparent that he had a head for business and a nose for opportunity. More importantly, he possessed the ruthlessness necessary to reach the very top, something which surprised his proud parents as they watched him ascend the ranks of Indian society.

Sanjeev's father, Sunil was retired now and spent his time using his skills working on the Sharma Foundation, a charity founded by Sunil and his wife Girat but entirely funded by their son, Sanjeev. Its noble endeavour was to provide local children from deprived backgrounds with the sort of education and training that their children had benefitted from. Their son's trip home was unexpected, and Sunil suspected that something was awry. Sanjeev was not a man who did surprises. Sunil suspected that his wife might know something and was not telling him. The wily physician was correct on both counts.

Sanjeev's mother, Girat was a formidable woman. At barely five feet tall, she was easy to underestimate, but to do so would be a mistake. An indomitable matriarch, she might defer to her husband on a professional footing, but she remained the unofficial head of the family. Despite their son's generous offers, they had remained in the same house since their wedding. They had always set a high bar for their boys, all of whom still sought their approval, including their eldest. In London, Prikash waited for her call to be connected over the internet. Speaking in Hindi, she asked the housemaid if she might have a chat with Madame Girat.

Milly took Mitch's call and smiled easily.

'Two hours, Milly! Just to get into the place,' Mitch groaned. 'to see David Beckham and Daniel Radcliffe.'

Milly chuckled. 'But the girls enjoyed it, though?'

'Yeah, they had a ball, and we're getting ice cream now.'

'Okay, great, I'm just heading to The Shelton for one quick meeting, and then I will join you. So text me where.'

'But honey, about the flights-'

'Yep. All booked. Tuesday evening.'

Immediately, Milly sensed an issue.

'What's up?' she asked.

'Honey, you're gonna need to cancel.'

'Why, what's up?'

314

'Jonson's just called, and guess what?'

Mitch loved posing such things, but Milly didn't really have the time, which he sensed.

'He's got tickets to the soccer Wednesday night. The girls would love that.'

'You mean you would.'

'And in a box.' Mitch added as though this might be a clincher. 'At Ars-e-nal. They're a big club, right?'

'Are they?'

'Oh, come on, Milly, help me out here.' Mitch pleaded. The girls played soccer, and they would love it.

'Plus, Jonson has a friend who is playing-'

'Yeah, yeah, okay.' Milly conceded now. Enough.

'Great because I've already told the girls, and they're ecstatic.'

Barry felt more relaxed this time around meeting Milly, the famous writer. The familiarity of the same venue and the odd little manager who ran the place helped, but mainly because he had already prevailed, and the lady was no longer a threat. She also seemed less combative now that her friend Mr Clarke was no longer accused of anything.

'So what can I do for you?' Barry asked, in what seemed like a déjà vu for them both.

'It might be the other way round: what can I do for you?' Milly suggested, and once again, she had Barry off guard.

'You're not going to threaten me again, are you?'

Milly chuckled. 'No. Why would I do that?'

'Oh, you'd be surprised in my line of work,' Barry quipped, finding his feet now, 'so what can you do for me then?'

'Well, firstly, I might like to thank you for the fun and the adventure which brought me over from the States.'

Barry said nothing because this couldn't be what she had called the meeting for.

'I take it you know about Jonson's son, Noah and his new friendship with Mr Sharma's daughter, Sidhu.'

Barry noted her precision with the names, and he recalled now her thoroughness. She had met Sidhu, of course, at the Clarke household, but there was something in her manner, and he wondered what else she might know.

'Young love. A beautiful thing. What can I say?' Barry offered.

'Well, hopefully, nothing,' Milly answered pointedly.

'Ah, I see...' Barry understood now.

'It would be awful if a story were ever to appear.'

Barry smiled and held his hands aloft because he had no such intentions.

'You have my word. For what that's worth,' he added wryly.

Milly nodded cautiously.

'But there is a story you might like to write?' Milly suggested.

'Oh, really.'

'I'm assuming you know about the fate of the violin.'

Barry shrugged. Non-committal.

'I hear that you've been brought into the fold.' Milly added knowingly.

'Is that right? And who told you that?'

Milly didn't answer. 'You're working with Nihal, is it?'

Barry quickly processed this and then smirked. He decided this was nothing to worry about since Sidhu was chatting with Noah. But still, he needed to probe carefully.

'Go on.'

'Just that it's an interesting story,' Milly shrugged.

'Is it? And what are you after, the film rights?'

Milly chuckled dismissively. 'Well, I'm not sure if they're yours to sell. But it's not really a film, anyway.'

'No?'

'Could be a novel, though.' Milly mused. 'But I'm no novelist.'

'Never say never. What is it they say: we've all got a novel in us.'

Milly nodded. 'How about you? You're a writer. Could be your chance to go legit.'

Barry's turn to chuckle. 'This is not why you've called this meeting?'

'No. I just wanted to hear that you won't write about the young couple.'

'Like I said, you have my word.'

'And presumably, that will please Mr Sharma also?'

Barry nodded.

'We probably all owe him a sort of thank you for his generosity,' Milly added mischievously without realizing its implications, but Barry didn't panic. He was confident that he had covered all his tracks. There was nothing for anyone to find.

'Well, thank you for thinking of me.'

'My pleasure, Barry.'

Milly stood, and he joined her. They shook hands on their unofficial understanding.

'When are you leaving?'

'Er, Thursday, I believe.' Which reminded Milly, she needed to change some flights.

Chapter Forty-Eight

The disposal of a Guarneri is not straightforward. It can't be sold on eBay. There are relatively few buyers for such an instrument, so they can be alerted easily enough, but liaising with such types is not easy. There are myriad layers to negotiate, an expensive maze to navigate before getting to an individual with the sign-off. It is normally a tussle between a foundation, an offshore trust and occasionally someone who loves violins and has shedloads of cash. Factor in the lawyers, financiers, provenance people and others, and Sharma's team faced an uphill battle to get it sold under the radar. Sanjeev reasoned that he had no other choice, and he put the sale in motion the moment he saw the image of Sidhu in the café. His urgency might have reduced its price, but so be it. News of the sale at a discreet and exclusive auction house in San Francisco came through to him on his jet bound for India. His parents did not share his passion for material possessions. They hadn't said anything explicitly when he had purchased the violin, which he interpreted as their disapproval. Presumably, now though, they would be delighted with its sale and especially when Sanjeev explained that all proceeds were to go to the Sharma Foundation.

Sanjeev kissed his mother and shook his father's hand. Although he had slept reasonably well on his journey, he still appeared tired and preoccupied, and only his mother understood why. She looked at him knowingly, and he sensed something was at hand. They caught up on pleasantries, news of his brothers, nephews and nieces, and then he began to explain the reason for his visit. His parents listened intently and said little, even when Sanjeev concluded with the happy news about the Sharma Foundation's new cash injection. His father smiled approvingly. Later he would explain what remarkable things this money will achieve, better even than the sounds from a violin in the hands of Eleanor Heinzog. Girat noted that Sanjeev had made no mention of Sidhu's personal life and the complications it might pose. They ate the dinner that Girat prepared, and afterwards, she suggested that her husband might leave them alone.

'I want to speak with my firstborn in a way that only a mother can.'

Sunil did as he was told, and Sanjeev knew now that his mother must know and why Prikash had suggested his trip. Finally alone, just like Ms Heinzog had done, his mother fixed him with a piercing gaze. A look that was difficult to ignore.

'You know, don't you?' Sanjeev sighed warily, 'Prikash has called you.'

Girat smiled warmly, in contrast to her son's woe-is-me demeanour.

'Yes. Because she is a good wife and a great mother.'

Sanjeev peered at his mum curiously, who was still beaming at him. He looked confused.

'So, Sidhu has made a new friend.' Girt posed casually.

'Mother, he is not a Hindu. He is not even Indian.'

'I know, and this pains you.'

'Yes. It does. She is being disobedient.'

'Yes, I agree. And it pains me too.'

'Then why are you smiling? You look so happy.'

'Because I am. I am happy. My oldest son has returned home. And with money to create great happiness for a great number of people. A boy who I held in my arms in this very room and who is now changing thousands, maybe millions of lives.'

Sanjeev dismissed this kind but distracting flattery. For all his generosity, it was only a fraction of his wealth, and this latest gift had the ulterior motive of protecting Sidhu, not to mention himself. Girat, though, was only just getting started.

'Would I prefer that my first grandchild marries a man who is like my first son?' Girat nodded firmly. 'Yes, I would. Of course.'

'Then-'

'No Sanjeev, my son, listen to me. Firstly, no one is getting married.'

'No, but what...'

'And what I have to tell you is very important. And I am the only person in the world who you will hear it from.'

Sanjeev felt chastened in front of the diminutive woman.

'But I also very much want for Sidhu to have a happy life.'

'But mother, she will be happy with an-'

'Sanjeev, please, be quiet,' Girat snapped, and he instantly obeyed, just as he had done in this house all those years ago.

'You will not remember this because you were very little. Maybe only four. You were playing cricket in the field with some boys in our village, and an older boy kept bashing your balls all over the place...'

Sanjeev listened intently.

'And you came home in floods of tears. It was as if you had been bashed in the face by the boy.'

Sanjeev's eyes narrowed, and then he smiled. 'Mother, I remember this.'

'Really?'

'Yes, I was humiliated, and I remember that dad was smiling.'

Girat recalled this also. 'Yes, that's right. He said at the time that it was a good sign.'

'Because I hated losing.'

Girat clapped her hands. 'Yes, and do you remember what you said?'

Sanjeev tried to recall, but he shook his head.

'You told me that you would never ever lose again!' Girat exclaimed in wonder and burst out laughing. Her laugh was infectious, and Sanjeev had no choice but to join her.

'You were so young! Imagine that.' Girat shrieked, and they both enjoyed the determination of a head-strong but naive little boy.

'And look at you now, Sanjeev. My son who has achieved so much. My clever boy who wins much more than he loses.'

Sanjeev smiled. Prikash had been right in suggesting that he should go home. It had been too long, and his parents would not be with him forever. He could buy other violins, but his parent's presence was finite.

'Sanjeev, we will never know how important that cricket game was. It might not have made you into a famous cricketer like Sunil or Kapil, but it might have made you into Sanjeev Sharma.'

Sanjeev nodded. 'Maybe it did.'

'It is interesting that you can remember it.'

'Yes,' Sanjeev agreed.

'Then this bigger boy did you a great service.'

Sanjeev sighed and wondered.

'And who is he now? I don't know. But I suspect he is not playing for India or running a company such as yours.'

'Maybe yes, I agree, mother, but-'

'No, Sanjeev. No life is without loss. It is impossible.'

Sanjeev reached to hold his mother's hands.

'And how fulfilling a life is, is depending on how we cope with our losses.'

Sanjeev's mind searched for his defeats. The loss of their first child when Prikash miscarried. His failed business in Qatar. And now Sidhu?

'Sanjeev, I am very proud of you. You know this, and I love you. But no more than your brothers. You are all different. You do different things, but I love you all equally.'

'Yes, of course.'

'But, in life, it is not just coping with losses.' Girat paused now.

'What then?' Sanjeev asked.

'It is knowing which losses are necessary.'

Sanjeev flared at this, understanding where his mother was going.

'But mother-'

Girat snapped her fingers and stopped him instantly.

'Sanjeev, where do you live?'

He shook his head, confused.

'Come on, answer me. It is not a hard question.'

'In London.'

'Yes. And before then?'

'New York.'

'New York.' Girat nodded. 'And why is this?'

'What do you mean?'

'Why do you not live in New Delhi? Your business is global.

It is here in India, also. Where you were born and raised. But you choose to live elsewhere. Why?'

Sanjeev began to flounder, and Girat stopped him.

'Sanjeev, this is not a criticism and nothing to be ashamed of. I know why. You got out. Going to America. Leaving the heat and the corruption and the poverty behind.'

Sanjeev blushed.

'And in London, tell me, do you live in a poor part of the city, where other Indians are living?'

'No, mother. You have been to-'

'Yes, I have been to your beautiful home. In Regents Street.'

Regents Park, but he didn't correct her. Her point remained, and her thrust, too.

'And these decisions you have taken, presumably with Prikash.'

'Yes.' Sanjeev nodded. 'Prikash loves London.'

'I am sure. It is a great city. But it means that things will not be the same for you. It is not India.'

'No.'

'And so this is not such a surprise. That the beautiful Sidhu, whilst she is Indian, but that she might feel less Indian.'

'It is not easy rearing children in-'

'Sanjeev, it is not easy rearing children anywhere. It is the hardest job of all and the only job that never ends. No matter how many servants we can afford. Indeed, often this makes it worse when parents can afford not to be parents.'

Sanjeev smiled at his wise old mum.

'And Sanjeev, the most important thing to tell you is this. That we all have losses. Everyone. But there are some losses that we cannot bear. Losses that no one can afford. Not even you.'

Sanjeev stared into his hands as he considered her profound words.

'Better to lose a child like your first than to lose a child because of decisions we take.'

'So what then should I do?' Sanjeev asked.

'You should smile more,' Girat shot back, adding a huge smile of her own, and Sanjeev was helpless not to reciprocate.

'Sanjeev, she is not marrying anyone. Sidhu is growing up, and my hope is that she will marry and she will be blessed by the Almighty God with children of her own...'

'Yes, and this is what we want for her. But we know-'

'You know what? You know best?'

'Yes.' Sanjeev answered bravely.

'Who she has feelings for? Sanjeev, of course, a child must be instructed. Without rules and instruction, a child is lost. They will not choose to learn difficult things: music, the violin, mathematics. If a child can choose, they will choose only bubble gum and pop music.

Sanjeev chuckled at this.

'A child must be instructed, but a child must be trusted also.'

'I do trust Sidhu-'

'Good. And you are right too. But you must understand that sometimes we must lose in order to win.'

Sanjeev bit at his thumb, thinking hard on her words.

'Prikash understands this instinctively because she is a woman. She bore Sidhu, and she has none of the distractions of your business. Her life is her children and keeping them close and keeping them happy. Why else are you here now?' Girat asked him directly.

Sanjeev faltered. 'Because Prikash suggested it?'

'You could have refused. But you didn't. Because you trust your wife.'

'Yes. And because I seek your counsel. And the approval of my parents,' Sanjeev added tearfully. Girat reached for him and kissed him.

'And this is our great achievement, your father and I: that we have created this family and that you feel this way. A family that is so close for so long.'

Sanjeev hugged his mother. Only with his parents could he sit with for so long and say so little.

'Sanjeev, pride is a deadly sin for a reason. It is not as heinous as murder, but it can be more destructive. Sidhu is just like you. She wants your approval just like you seek mine. And this is your achievement too, an achievement more valuable than your house with the silly under-the-ground cinema.'

Sanjeev chuckled at this description. 'My wise old mother.' he said gratefully.

'Wise? What is wise?' Girat asked. 'I am just someone who has lived longer and made more mistakes than you.'

Sanjeev smiled because her answer so eloquently made his earlier point.

'If this boy is bad, then I will not be happy. And you will step in. You must. But do not step in because he is not like you. That will not be trusting your daughter. And I will not be happy if I have Prikash crying on the phone because your family is crumbling about her.'

Chapter Forty-Nine

To the outside world looking in, Sanjeev Sharma was an unconscionable patriarch, striding the earth and crushing anything in his path, yet only those on the inside knew the truth: that he was human and vulnerable and ultimately beholden to two women. Prikash had been brave in her planning, and, once Sanjeev had agreed to visit his parents, she had been meticulous in her timing. She counted the hours from the time his jet had taken off from the UK, accounting for the length of the flight, the time difference and the transfer time. She even factored in the familial pleasantries and a meal before Girat would be able to collar her son for her team talk. By her constant calculations, this time had now passed. By her reckoning, Girat was possibly forty-five minutes into perhaps the most important lecture her husband has heard in his life. Prikash became ever anxious and expected his phone call any moment now. She had played her hand and now felt impotent. She just prayed that Girat might have prevailed. Their future might hinge on the outcome; Prikash felt nauseous thinking about it. Then her phone rang. She jumped as she grappled for it. She spied the screen, saw that it was "Sanj", and her mouth dried.

She allowed herself one further deep breath before swiping the screen.

'Hello, Sanjeev,' she said quietly, unable to mask her anxiety.

'Hello, Prikash, my darling. How are you?' Sanjeev replied, and instantly her heart soared.

A press release was prepared by Qnctd about the sale of the Guarneri. This philanthropic good news story would sadly attract less coverage than if it had been genuinely stolen. Sanjeev read the single sheet of A4 in silence. It was not a feel-good news story for him, foregoing something he cherished, not to mention a cool twenty million pounds all-told, once professional fees and taxes had been factored in. Sanjeev considered the last ten days and their impact that he could never have imagined. The cost of protecting his family and his mother's wisdom still fresh in his mind. But his personal gains aside, the eye-watering costs meant that he had every right to scrutinize the wording of the statement, and this was not good enough. Nihal waited patiently and said nothing.

'How is your writing?' Sanjeev asked, taking Nihal by surprise.

'Fine, I think.'

'Then let's see it. You can rewrite this.'

Nihal nodded. 'Of course, any steers?'

'It needs to read more genuine. Not like a rich man chucking poor people a bone.'

Nihal blanched a little, given how big the bone was. Like an elephant femur.

'Should it mention your Foundation more?'

'Yes, good. Go to the website. It's all there.'

Unlike Barry, Nihal carried a discernible degree of guilt,

and, despite his 'moving on', he admired Sanjeev, and he wanted to help him. He turned on his heel to make an immediate start, confident of his abilities. But he had Barry to call upon also. He was bound to have ideas. He was supposedly a writer, and after all, he owed Mr Sharma also.

The atmosphere between them might have been happier, but Sanjeev understood Sidhu's embarrassment and apparent pain as she read the newly written and much-improved press release. She could never have imagined such an outcome from her impetuous action. She looked at her father, her eyes wet and her throat aching.

'Dad, I am so sorry.'

Sanjeev shook his head.

'No, Dad, I am. I am really sorry. For everything.'

By 'everything', he wondered what she meant, but he didn't ask. He shrugged gently.

'Grateful then. Can I be grateful?' Sidhu implored, 'for everything you have done for me.'

'Yes, you can, of course. But as your mother explained, there are other violins.'

Sidhu nodded, but her sense of shame continued, and they had yet to really discuss the real hurt that was more troubling for him than forfeiting his violin. Sanjeev considered his daughter. Her distress was apparent, and it felt genuine, or else she was a fine actress. In that moment, something awful occurred to him: with her looks, she might wish to become an actress.

'What else did grandma say?' Sidhu asked, steering him towards the Indian elephant in the room that was fed up with being ignored.

'She said lots of things.'

'And things you agree with or are just going along with

because it is your mum?' Sidhu asked pointedly and took her father by surprise.

'Why? Is that important to you?' Sanjeev asked.

'Important? No, dad, it is not important: it is crucial.'

Sanjeev beckoned his daughter to continue.

'For the same reason that you listen to your parents. I want your approval. I want you to be proud of me.'

Sanjeev's throat swelled, and he fought to quell his tears, but it was no use, and they fell freely. His mother had been right, and he was cross that he had ever doubted her. He embraced Sidhu warmly; she hugged him with a strength that belied her small frame.

'I love you ,dad, and I am sorry that I have hurt you.'

Sanjeev broke off from their embrace. He needed to look at her because he had something important to say, a question he now had the courage to ask.

'Sidhu, do you love this boy?'

Sidhu laughed as a reflex.

'No, dad. We have only just met.'

'But you like him?'

'Yes. I do. He is nice.'

'I'm sure he is.'

'We like each other, I think. And if in time and if it were to happen, then I hope that I am allowed to love him. Like you love mum.'

Sanjeev never knew his daughter had such a way with words. Just like her grandmother, he thought. What Sidhu had to say had a beauty and a humanity to it. A bird that wanted permission to fly. Sanjeev admired his daughter, and they embraced.

. . .

Three days later, the executive suite at the Emirates stadium seemed as good an occasion as any for Sidhu and Noah's first official date. It also seemed sensible if the date was extended to include others: less pressure, and somehow this grew to include everyone with any connection at all. The more, the merrier, Jonson reasoned. So the Carmichael and Clarke families were joined by the Sharma's, and even Ms Heinzog was persuaded to attend her first-ever football match. First pizza and now football, next stop watching the Kardashians? They all gathered to watch young Troy Bateson, who was indeed back at Arsenal Football Club and this evening would be making his debut in the first team, albeit as a substitute. Troy was the reason for the executive box, and he assured his old mate, Noah, that he would get on the pitch. Noah was royally proud of his friend, and he smiled at the notion that Troy would not be the most anxious young man in the stadium.

Noah shook Prikash's hand and carefully introduced her to his family. Anna was great, all smiles and even added a little curtsey as a nod to her wealth and the godlike status of the Sharma's in India. Jonson was trickier, obviously, even though he was under strict instructions from Anna not to 'street' it up.

'What are you talking about?' Jonson argued, pretending to be aggrieved.

'You know what I mean. Just because we're at the football. Don't say "wassup".'

Jonson huffed at this. 'Why would I say that to an Indian lady?'

Anna glared at her husband.

'What?'

'And don't say that, either.'

'Say what?'

'That she's Indian.'

Jonson tutted at his deranged wife. Like he needed to be told how to behave.

'Jeez, Anna, relax.'

'I'm just saying.'

'Well don't. I'm cool. You sound like one of those angry white people.'

'...Mrs Sharma, this is my dad, Jonson.'

Prikash smiled and offered her slim hand, which Jonson took gently and smiled his best smile.

'Very nice to meet you.' Jonson began. 'Noah has been talking about your-'

'Hey, Dad, that's cool, man. Thanks,' Noah intervened, and Jonson did as he was told.

'He gets excited.' Noah sighed.

'For the football?' Prikash smiled.

'Yeah, for that as well.'

Sidhu was not so interested in what might occur on the pitch, but she beamed at what was playing out before her. Her father was outbound again, somewhere else far-flung, and he couldn't make the match, but she knew that the time for him to meet the Clarkes would be soon.

Proceedings on the pitch did not matter either to Ms Heinzog, who was delighted to meet everyone. She chatted freely to Jonson and found him enchanting. Mitch had played some professional golf in India, so was able to find some common ground with Prikash. The whole evening seemed set up for them, with the brilliant pitch below lit up as the players warmed up, the stadium filled, and the atmosphere built.

Milly sipped her Champagne and took in the beautiful

scene before her. Her first husband Elliot had been an enormous Arsenal fan, and looking out at the throng around her, she wondered if he might even be amongst them. He had been a season ticket holder, so it was a reasonable assumption. She hoped he was, and she wished he could see her now surrounded by her perfect family and friends and with the best views of the match.

Jonson, too, was feeling romantic about the evening. He was excited to see Troy take to the pitch, a young man who he had watched playing football since he was eight. He also felt humbled that Milly and her family should be here with him and, most importantly, that Noah was so happy. He was also pleased that Mr Sharma was not present, but he reasoned that they would meet soon enough. Milly sidled up to him and cupped his waist with her arm.

'How cool is this, huh?'

'I know, it's the best. I'm so glad you're here. That you came over.'

'You're glad? The kids have had a ball. And Mitch too.'

'And you've kept me out of trouble.'

'Oh, I don't know. I didn't do anything, not really. It just played out.'

'Had my back, though,' Jonson reasoned.

'Always.' Milly squeezed his waist.

'Odd thing though, right?'

'What is?'

'All of this.' Jonson gestured to their circumstances.

'Oh, yes. Definitely odd. It's very Jonson Clarke.'

Jonson chuckled and hugged her back.

'Maybe it was all meant to be,' Milly continued.

Jonson huffed. 'Oh, not this again. Like your movies.'

Milly smiled. 'Happy endings, anyway.'

'Speaking of which, how's your writer's block?'

Milly pondered. 'Do you know what? Since I've been here, I haven't thought about it. Which is as good as a breakthrough.'

'That's it, man. Just let things flow. Stories will come, I know it.'

'Yeah, hope so.'

'Anna and I were wondering if all this might get you thinking?'

'What, the violin?'

'Yeah. Why not?'

Milly recalled her last conversation with Barry.

'Yeah maybe. But it's more a novel than a movie.'

Jonson shrugged.

'Not sure if I'm a novelist.'

'It's a good story, though.' Jonson said.

'It is; it's quirky. I love that it's Sidhu from India. And Noah from London. And all made possible by a Jamaican dad.'

Jonson took a bow at this. 'And the Italian violin and you from America.'

Milly laughed.

'And don't forget Ms Heinzog, wherever she's from.' Jonson added.

'It's a global story. But Made in England.' Milly concluded. Jonson beamed and held up his hand for Milly to slap.

'You excited for the match?' Jonson asked.

'Er... kind of.'

Jonson tutted and shook his head. An attractive couple in the same hospitality suite had caught Milly's attention. She had noticed the man earlier. He was a little older than Milly and had a certain air to him. He was assured and poised, and now she saw him with his attractive wife and young son. They made a handsome family.

'Who's playing anyway?' Milly asked, and Jonson sighed.

'Arsenal.'

'Yes, I know that, thank you. But against who?'

'Aston Villa.'

'Right, and we want Arsenal to win?'

'Yes, and we want my man Troy to make his debut.'

'Of course. He's Noah's friend?'

'Noah loves him. But he's not the only wonder-kid playing. Villa have this kid called Lewis Adele, who apparently is awesome.'

'He certainly is,' a man said in passing, overhearing their conversation. It was the man Milly had noticed earlier. He stopped now and smiled.

'I believe there are two large contingents in this suite this evening,' he began to explain, 'one for Troy Bateson wearing red and one for Lewis Adele wearing maroon. We're very much team Lewis.'

Jonson smiled and accepted the challenge. 'Okay, nice to meet you. We're team Troy.'

'Hello, my name is Tom Harper. My wife and I are here to see Lewis, and we seem to have brought an entire coach-load with us.'

'Hey, man. I'm Jonson. This is Milly. We're friends of Troy.'

'Oh, wow, how exciting for you both. May the best man win.'

Milly shook Tom's hand. She liked him instantly. There was something about him, and she felt an affinity.

'But whatever the score, let's keep it friendly.' Jonson joked.

Tom laughed his agreement.

'It's football, right. It's only a game and not life or death.' Jonson added. Tom smiled at this and agreed wholeheartedly. He was an expert in many areas of life, but none more than the joy of living and what was truly important in life.

Epilogue

Troy did get on for the second half of the match but did not score in what was a dull nil-nil draw. Perhaps the two wonder-kids cancelled themselves out.

Milly and Tom chatted throughout the match and then afterwards with Mitch and his wife, Sarah. They kept in touch by email and would become a firm friendship. In due course, Tom would share his family back story with Milly, a story so heart-rending that anyone listening could not fail to be moved. But Tom was healed now, and he and Sarah were enjoying something very special together. Tom's story about his former family had Milly spellbound, and she waited for the right moment to ask if she might dramatize it. Tom thought about this carefully before he agreed, with name changes, of course, and he liked Milly's suggestion that she might base her screenplay in America to add more distance from him. Her writing block purged, Milly wrote a beautiful script which is currently being fought over by three separate studios, including the head of Columbia, Cynthia Rosen.

Noah and Sidhu continue to be 'friends', and it appears that everything is proceeding rather beautifully. The first meeting with Sanjeev was summarily awful for everyone involved, although, to be fair to Sanjeev, he did make a monumental effort to be normal while Prikash flapped about the place. A faltering start, but to be expected with a father's understandable concerns and suspicions. Nonetheless, armed with his father's charm and soon gainfully employed writing music for an advertising agency, Noah has quickly begun to grow on the irascible and misunderstood Sanjeev Sharma.

Sidhu graduated with first-class honours, and remains under the personal tutelage of the remarkable Eleanor Heinzog, both for music and for life skills more generally.

Jonson remains at his college of further education in North London, mentoring young men. The Clarke family did finally make a trip to visit Milly and Mitch in LA, where he was on hand to inadvertently assist Milly with her new screenplay about fruit juice, of all things. Jonson remains unpredictable, incorrigible and, above all else, fun. He does still drink alcohol, but he has not been blind drunk since that fateful evening.

Barry Shenfield is perhaps an unlikely winner in this life story. He completed the purchase of his cottage in Dartmouth, Devon and moved in with his book-worm mum. Having helped Nihal with the new press release for Mr Sharma, he felt a little chastened by the man's charity, but not so much that it affected his sleep. As he expected in rural Devon, the supply of stories for him to write about was not bountiful, and with his mum's encouragement, Barry embarked on his first novel. A caper based on a lost violin on the London Underground.

Officer Gareth Dibble did leave the police force just before he was pushed. He maintained his Twitter handle and after two more painful operations, @_hotcop_37 did make it on to the third series of *Paradise Island: The Oldies*. Foregoing his police salary and the cost of looking as he does, Gareth was behind or down on his career move so far. However, there are upsides. He has been referred to as an 'influencer', and he is about to start promoting two products on his Instagram: a hair loss shampoo and fat-concealing underpants. Just as exciting is that Gareth has finally found love, online, of course. Gareth met Daphne, and his life changed. Daphne, who used to be known as Hamish, is an official influencer with over forty thousand followers on Twitter. Instantly they bonded over their love of fame and socials. They are determined to combine their followings and grow together as an 'influencer' couple.

Nihal returned to Mumbai with a fabulous reference and enough of Mr Sharma's money to establish his entire family on much better financial footings. Promptly he joined a leading Indian law firm, quickly gained a promotion and recently married the daughter of the company's wealthy founder.

Afterword

Thank you for reading *Made in England*. I am grateful to any readers who have the time and feel inclined to write and publish a review.

Reviews are a crucial device to help independent books gain visibility, so that other readers might discover my stories.

Dominichollandbooks.com - as the name suggests is a site dedicated to my writing with pre-reading and post-reading videos of individual books and an opportunity for readers to leave comments and join in discussions.

About the Author

Dominic Holland is a full time stand-up comedian and part-time author. He lives in London with his wife, Nikki. They have four boys and a dog called Tessa. He publishes a blog every Sunday at www.dominichollandbooks.com

His Book Club (more just a mailing, tbh) is where fan/s of his work can receive FREE and exclusive content. You can join here - for free, obviously.

Also by Dominic Holland

Only in America

The Ripple Effect

Eclipsed

The Fruit Bowl

Open Links (available at www.brotherstust.org)

I,Gabriel

Hobbs' Journey

Lucky No. 7

The Surgeon

Dominic Holland takes on Life Vol.1

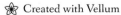

Printed in Great Britain
by Amazon

82612379R00202